I0721378

LUANN K. EDWARDS

Our Faithful Love
LuAnn K. Edwards

Dedication

To caseworkers who spend endless hours finding
the best care for the children they serve.
And to foster and adoptive parents.
Thank you!

A story of forgiveness and reconciliation.

Trust in the LORD *with all your heart and lean not on your own understanding; in all your ways submit to him, and he will make your paths straight.*
Proverbs 3:5-6

One

Mid-April
Pleasant Springs, Tennessee

I smacked my palm against the steering wheel. My first day in a new position, and I didn't want to be here. I blamed my sister, Jill Drake. She talked me into this. I loved my work helping children and families in Chattanooga, but not here in Pleasant Springs. I couldn't stand this place. And I'd vowed to never return.

My heart longed for Nashville, ninety miles northwest of this small, dull town. My hometown only offered memories. Ones I didn't care to think about.

Late Monday morning, I prepared for my first visit at Creekside Children's Home. After I parked, I took three deep breaths, plastered a smile on my face, and climbed the stairs to the front porch. Before I had a chance to ring the buzzer, a man greeted me and introduced himself as the director of the home, Todd Butler.

We chatted in the foyer, and he filled me in on Billy, an eight-year-old boy removed from his home the evening before.

"He's still upset and frightened. His mom was out of control when he called 911. He knew he needed help, but now he's scared about what will happen to him and his mom." Todd led me through his office into a medium-sized room. After he explained they often used this space for supervised family visits, he left through the kitchen to fetch Billy.

The room housed shelves filled with puzzles, books, and board games, along with craft paper and supplies. Four wooden chairs surrounded a square table in the center of the light orange painted room. I waited near the table for Billy.

Five minutes later, Todd returned with an adorable, red-eyed little boy clutching a stuffed elephant. I introduced myself as Miss Mel and assured Billy that I was there to help. Todd whispered something in Billy's ear and left him alone with me.

I took a seat on the opposite side of the table from where he stood. A terrified young boy. I wanted to give him a big hug. His large brown eyes and short, dark brown hair reminded me of an old friend when we were young. One I hoped to never see again. "Would you like to sit down?"

Billy clutched his elephant in a death grip.

"It's okay to be afraid." I made a pouty look to match his.

Poor little guy. He sounded upset. "I'm not afraid. But my mom is." Tears trickled down his cheeks. He said he thought the cops took her to jail.

"I'm sorry, Billy. Adults don't always make the right choices as grown-ups. We make mistakes. There are people helping your mom now, and I'm here to help you." I rose from my chair and pulled a book about fire trucks off the shelf. "Would you like to read a book together?"

Billy nodded and moved to the chair on my left.

I sat and slid the book toward him.

"I like fire trucks." Billy pointed at the bright red engine on the cover.

"Have you ever been inside one?"

Billy opened his eyes wide. "No. Do you have one?"

"No." I grinned. "But we might visit the fire station where you can get an up-close look at one."

"That would be awesome." Billy's smile turned upside down. "I lied to you. I am scared."

"That's okay. Sometimes I get scared too."

"But you're big. Why are you afraid?"

What could I share with an eight-year-old? "I returned to Pleasant Springs two days ago, after being gone for a long time. I don't want to see someone who hurt me many years ago."

He drew his eyebrows together. "Did they hit you?"

"They hurt me in here." I touched my chest.

"We're both afraid." Billy patted my hand. "We can help each other."

I spent an hour with Billy and promised to return the following day. Before I left, I offered to be Billy's transportation to and from his school in Shady View, eight miles north of Pleasant Springs. Todd thanked me but said they could manage his afternoon transportation.

When I returned to my car, I read a text from my sister. **Miss Risa wants you to visit.** Jill included the address. Risa McDonald was a sweet woman in her eighties who I'd known all my life from church. But our visit would need to wait. I had lunch plans with my parents and drove to their home.

"How's my beautiful daughter?" Dad opened his arms wide and hugged me.

We talked for a few minutes before Mom and I sat next to each other at the round kitchen table to enjoy homemade chicken noodle soup.

Dad sat across from me and bowed his head. "Father, I thank You for bringing us back to Pleasant Springs a few months ago and for the agency cutbacks that brought our baby girl home too. Bless and guide her, Lord. Amen."

I smirked and leaned forward. "You forgot to thank Him for the food."

He laughed, bowed his head again, and thanked God.

"You know I'm not staying here, right? I plan to move to Nashville."

Mom touched my hand. "We're praying the Lord changes your mind."

"Whatever." I rolled my eyes.

She passed a box of crackers to me. "How was your first morning at your new job?"

"Good. I guess." I dipped my spoon into the soup and told them about the little boy.

"Anyone we know?"

"Sorry, Dad. That's confidential." I took another bite of soup and complimented my mom. "This is so good."

She thanked me. "Have you seen anyone else since you've been back?"

"Jill texted and said Miss Risa wants to see me. I'll try to run by for a visit later today."

"I'm sure she'd appreciate someone to read to her." Dad wiped his mouth on a napkin. "Older people like that, especially if their eyesight has deteriorated."

"That's a good idea." After we chatted about Miss Risa for a few minutes, I stood and put my empty bowl in the dishwasher.

Mom joined me and placed her hand on my back. "Dad and I want to invite a couple of people for Sunday dinner this weekend, and we'd like you to join us." She had a glint in her eye. The look that said, "You need a man."

"And what about Jill? Did you invite her?"

She chuckled. "We see her often. But you haven't visited us since we moved back to Pleasant Springs. We wanted you to move in with us instead of Jill, so we'd get to see more of you."

I apologized for my absence during the past few months and for picking Jill over them. But I knew my mom. She had her matchmaking twinkle in her eye.

"No matchmaking. But I'm sure Luke would love to see you."

"Luke?" I cringed and in a harsh tone said, "No. I told you when I stayed in Chattanooga after college graduation, I didn't want to hear about anyone in Pleasant Springs except for Jill."

Mom pressed her fist to her mouth. "Because of Luke? What did he do?"

"I must go. Great to see you both." I hurried out of the kitchen, grabbed my jacket from the couch, and kissed my parents, who followed me to the front door with raised eyebrows.

How could I spend time in the same room with Luke, his wife, and his children? I had to get a job in

Nashville before my parents invited him and his family for dinner.

Two

Luke Gibson left his automotive shop and drove home for lunch. He expected Victor Clemmons, a social worker, to arrive at 1:30 to talk about becoming a foster parent for a young boy. Luke wanted to share his home and all the Lord had given him.

He tidied his already clean home, ate lunch, and threw a batch of cookies into the oven to make a good impression. Who could resist the smell of homemade cookies? Not that he had to win anyone over. Victor and Luke had been friends for several years. Boys needed strong father figures, and Luke had what it took, according to Victor, when he encouraged Luke to apply.

Luke's cell phone rang at 12:45 p.m. The caller identified herself as Ronni Nance from Clancy County Children's Services.

He sat while she told him that Victor had taken a leave of absence and to expect Mel instead. "Mel won't have all your preliminary information and may need to ask you questions you've already answered. I apologize for that, but I hope you'll understand."

"No problem." Luke frowned and disconnected the

call. What happened to Victor? They'd talked Saturday afternoon. And why hadn't Ronni given him Mel's last name? Luke may need to work harder to win this new guy over. Good thing the cookies turned out well.

~

Before I pulled out of my parents' driveway, Ronni Nance called. She supported families and at-risk children who were not currently in state custody. "There's been a change in plans. We need you to take Victor's 1:30 appointment. I planned to cover it but got slammed. I'll text you the address."

"Where's Victor?"

"He'll be out for a while. Sam will explain later."

Samantha Richards supervised our county office. She also functioned as the county's investigator, which was an open position. She followed up on child neglect and abuse cases.

"What kind of visit is this?"

"Foster parent application. This is a follow-up inquiry visit. You don't have the forms, or access to the software program yet, but do your best to answer their questions concerning foster care and ask them general questions in return. Victor and Sam know the man well and said he's a great candidate. At the next visit, you can update the information as needed."

"The next visit?"

"Because you're going today. Sam said she'll assign this case to you."

We disconnected our call, and I waited a few minutes for Ronni to send me the address.

Taking on this one case wasn't a big deal. I handled child placements and worked with foster parents at the agency I worked for in Chattanooga. But

Clancy County hired me to work with reuniting children in state custody with their biological families. How many other cases belonging to Victor would I need to take on until his return, besides my own tasks? The job already came with long hours and no social life. I released a lengthy breath. But with Victor out, I may not have a life at all and that stunk.

I blamed Jill for this lousy job. She meddled where she had no business to do so. She arranged an interview for me with Clancy County Children's Services—a place where I never intended to apply and didn't want to be. If only something in Nashville would come through. I'd applied to two agencies there. They had to be better than here in Pleasant Springs.

When Ronni's text arrived, I put the address into my GPS. But she forgot to include the couple's name. I texted her and asked her to send it to me. A moment later she responded: **Interested in a young boy.**

Great. But I still needed their names. I couldn't call them Mr. and Mrs. John Doe.

My GPS took me west on Mud Dauber Road, south on Main Street to State Route 481, and east past the Co-op and Maggie's Place, a bed-and-breakfast on my left. I turned right just before Turtle Creek and drove down a winding road through the woods and away from all civilization. After a bend in the road, I crossed a one-lane bridge over the creek. One hundred feet past the bridge and to the right, a long gravel driveway led to a log cabin that faced the creek.

I parked my blue, seven-year-old Ford Escape next to a black Dodge pickup along the side of the home and basked in the beauty. Tiny white flowers blossomed along the side of the cabin where I parked, and along the front, purple crocuses added vibrant color. Hanging baskets filled with blue, purple, and yellow pansies, along with a wooden porch swing, presented a welcoming appearance. The cabin would be an ideal place for a young boy. He'd love it.

I sent another text to Ronni, asked again for the couple's name, and walked to the front door with my notepad.

My cell pinged. Before I gazed down at my phone, the door opened.

I took a step back and covered my mouth.

My heart fell to the wooden porch beneath me, oozed through the cracks, and plopped to the ground.

"Luke?"

My mouth turned sour. My former best friend. As cute as when he left me eleven years earlier. For Stephanie Belmont.

~

Luke rubbed his hands through his hair. He expected a guy named Mel, but Lanie showed up instead. What was she doing in Pleasant Springs? The only woman God had asked him to love through the good and bad. He'd forgiven her years ago, but his love waned after she stayed in Chattanooga. His job as an auto mechanic wasn't good enough for her. She'd questioned him often. "Do you think you'll be happy in that line of work? You have much more you could do with your business degree. You could become the president of a major corporation one day. Your dad will find someone else to take over the shop when he retires. Your brother Eddie is smart."

Lanie wasn't interested in an auto mechanic. She'd made that clear when she stayed in Chattanooga, and he returned to Pleasant Springs.

~

I gaped at Luke. My voice quivered. "I'm here for . . ." I peeked down at Ronni's text and muttered, "Luke. Gibson?" My eyes met his.

"You found him." He moved aside and motioned me to enter his living and dining room area.

Inside, I tried to focus on my surroundings. My heart had returned to my chest but beat erratically. My thoughts jumbled and my brain turned to mush. Why was I in Luke's house? And why did he look so good? Tall, broad shoulders, dark brown hair, and big, brown eyes. He looked better than when we were best friends.

He stared at me and in a low, firm voice said, "Who's Mel? If you wanted to surprise me, you succeeded."

"The name I wish you to use." I needed to pull myself together. "Did I understand our office correctly? You're interested in fostering a young boy?"

"When did you transfer to Clancy County?" He squished his eyebrows together. "What happened to Chattanooga?"

I brought my notepad to my chest and crossed my arms over it to keep my hands from shaking. I scanned the room again. "Let's cut the small talk and get this done." I wanted to get out of there as soon as possible.

A small kitchen/dining area lay to my left, with the living room to my right. I couldn't do this. Luke would not be a good foster parent. He would hurt a child like he'd hurt me all those years ago. No way. I turned to face him. "How large is your cabin?"

"Big enough. Eight hundred square feet."

I huffed and waved my hand in dismissal. "We

have guidelines, Mr. Gibson. I'm afraid your house is too small. This won't work for any child." I darted toward the front door.

"Mr. Gibson?" He caught up to me. "They may have different guidelines, as you call them, in that big city you've been living in. But here in Clancy County, you'll find my home is big enough."

I spun on my heels and straightened my shoulders. "What about the creek? A young child might drown."

"No deeper than a bathtub." Luke sauntered to the other side of the kitchen table and peered out a window that overlooked the front porch and the creek approximately fifty feet away. "And what young boy doesn't want to fish?"

I didn't like the situation one bit. But Luke was right. A boy would love it. But because Sam turned this application over to me, I'd have to complete the home study and interact with Luke for much too long. I had to get him turned down somehow or make sure I found a position in Nashville soon. "There's a foster care inquiry form online you need to complete, and we'll need several other forms, which include a background check."

"Victor has the inquiry form, and I have a copy of the other forms he requested." He hurried to the kitchen counter, picked up his paperwork, and handed it to me. "You'll find everything you need here to get moving on this right away."

The forms he gave me included the request for a background check, medical history information, and references. "Besides these forms, you'll need to be fingerprinted, must attend an informational meeting, and complete foster parent training, which includes

CPR and First Aid. We'll also complete your home study during that time."

"I'm already certified in CPR and First Aid. I'll have a copy for you the next time we meet, and I plan to get fingerprinted later this week." He sighed and took a step closer to me. "Billy has fallen on challenging times, and I aim to help."

I gawked at him. "Billy?"

Luke glanced around the room. "Do Billy a favor and hurry this process. The boy needs a home and family."

Family? I perused a copy of the application he'd handed me with his other forms. The application only included Luke's name. What happened to Stephanie?

"Are you crazy? These things take time. Three months or more." And I wanted to find a home for Billy sooner than that.

"Then let's start the training today." He smirked and jutted out his chin. "This isn't a big city. Things move faster here than what I'm sure you've dealt with in the past. Victor said there wouldn't be any problems, and he'd rush this through."

He was in for a ride if he thought he could outsmart me. "Well, I'm not Victor now, am I?" I tossed his forms on the kitchen table and placed my hands on my hips. "For you to have requested Billy the day after his arrival to the children's home, you must know his family or Todd Butler from Creekside personally. What's your connection?"

"Billy often comes to church with friends of mine, the Wilsons. Their son, Evan, and Billy are good friends from school in Shady View. And I coached their soccer team last fall."

I snatched Luke's application from the table and checked it again. "You work as a mechanic at Pleasant Springs Automotive?"

His tone turned bitter. "I *own* Pleasant Springs Automotive. I'm a deacon at my church and a former volunteer firefighter."

"Former? Did you get injured?"

He shook his head. "Being a firefighter and the need to be on call at all hours might cause a child anxiety. If a call came through during the night, I wouldn't want to disrupt Billy by waking him and taking him to my mom's or my brother's house. I hope to offer him a stable environment."

I nodded, continued to review his application, and twisted my mouth. "Looks like you made a mistake. Says here you're single. Shouldn't you have marked divorced or widowed?"

Luke leaned closer. "I never married." He tilted back, narrowed his eyes, and sounded annoyed. "The love of my life didn't return my affection."

Three

"The love of my life didn't return my affection?" What did that mean? Stephanie didn't marry him? What was wrong with her? She let a great guy like Luke slip away? They appeared happy together after college graduation. What split them apart? I closed my eyes and rubbed my forehead. And there I was, back in the place I didn't want to be and with the person I never wanted to see again.

Luke took a cookie from a plate on the kitchen table and offered one to me.

I raised my hand. "A nice touch, but bribes don't work with me." My legs weakened. I needed to sit. Instead, I leaned my hip against a chair and reviewed his application again. "Give me a tour of your tiny home."

Luke cringed and mumbled. "Plenty big enough."

He led the way to a short hallway at the edge of the kitchen and living area. To the left was the bathroom and a laundry/storage room. To the right—his bedroom. At the end of the hallway, a door led to the backyard.

"Nice, but where's the second bedroom?"

"Upstairs." He led me back through the kitchen,

where I stopped and opened his refrigerator to inspect its contents. "This is outrageous."

"What?" He joined me.

"Expired milk, eggs . . ." I opened a crisper drawer. "Ewe. And moldy cheese." I stuck up my nose. "This will never do."

"The fridge will be perfect the next time you visit." He closed the refrigerator door and walked to a steep set of stairs that led to an upstairs attic bedroom.

"You must be kidding. You expect Billy to climb up and down that ladder to get to his room?"

"They're stairs, albeit small ones, but with much larger steps than a ladder." He groaned and muttered something under his breath. "Lanie, why are you being difficult?"

"Mel. Got it?" I had to get out of there before I crumpled to the floor.

"If I call you Mel, will you let up on me?"

Movement above and to my right caught my eye. I screamed and grabbed my chest. "You could have warned me that you have a cat."

He chuckled. "Sorry about that. She likes to perch on top of the kitchen cabinets and keep her eye on everything and everyone."

With irritation in my voice, I said, "But you hated cats."

His face and tone softened. "I didn't hate them, but I enjoyed teasing you and making you think I didn't like them." He smiled and cocked his head. "Your cats grew on me."

He'd had that same effect of growing on me over the years when we were close friends. "What's her name?"

He wrinkled his nose. "Name? I call her Cat most of the time."

"Original." I raised my eyes to the gray and white feline still perched on top of the cabinets, staring at me. "Hello, Cat." I glanced at Luke and stiffened. "There may be something in Billy's records that shows an allergy to cats."

"Then I'll find someone else to take her. Maybe you? You were a great cat mom."

"I've seen enough." I darted to the front door.

"Don't you want to see the upstairs bedroom?"

"No reason to if it won't qualify anyway." I opened the door and stepped out onto the porch.

Luke followed and let the screen door slam shut. "But Victor said the upstairs bedroom wouldn't be a problem."

"I'll check with Samantha, my boss." I made my way to my car and climbed inside. Somehow, I would document my report in such a way that Sam would see a definite problem with Luke becoming any child's foster parent.

~

Luke held onto Lanie's car door handle to prevent her from closing the door. "I'm sure Sam will find my cabin to be a perfect home for Billy. Have you seen the shack he lives in with his mom?"

Lanie peered at him with her big blue eyes and batted her long lashes the way she had when they spent time together. Times he'd missed over the years.

"Not yet. I've been on the job for what?" She peeked at her watch. "An entire six hours, and one of those was for lunch." She scowled and gripped her steering wheel.

"Go check it out. Mine is a mansion."

"When did you see it? Were you stalking his mother or him?"

He grimaced and backed away from her door. "I took the Wilson boy and Billy home from soccer practices a few times." He slammed her door shut and watched her drive away.

When he returned to his cabin, he sat on the sofa and stared out the front window. What had hardened his former best friend? Still stubborn but seemed tougher. Rigid. Had someone in Chattanooga hurt her like she'd hurt him?

All he wanted was to help a boy or two. To be a godly father figure to a child in need of a male role model and to make a difference in their life.

His cat jumped down from the kitchen cabinets, strutted toward him, and rubbed his legs. Luke bent and stroked her head. "I call you Cat sometimes. I didn't lie." He lifted her to his eye level. "I couldn't tell her that I named you Mims. She'd know I used her initials and would think I missed her. Melanie Irene Meadows."

Mims squirmed. He placed her on the sofa and strode to the kitchen counter for his truck keys. On his way back to his shop, he pondered the relationship he and Lanie had once shared.

Eleven years? A long time to have no contact with someone you'd held dear to your heart from elementary school through college. Not only had she stayed in Chattanooga, but she never stopped by to see him when she returned home to visit her sister. The few times he'd seen Jill, she rarely mentioned Lanie. He'd wondered if she had left the country. She'd never called, texted, or communicated after graduation. Why hadn't she stayed in Chattanooga and found another job there?

Luke would be friendly and do his best to get along with her, for Billy's sake. But he couldn't allow her back into his heart. Not when she'd broken his. And his dad's.

~

I drove back to work to update the office database on my time with Billy and Luke. When I entered our open office space, Sam stood, hobbled to the coffeepot along the wall behind her desk and poured a cup of coffee.

I joined her at the coffee station. "Ronni said Victor will be out for a while?"

"Yes. For a few weeks or more." Her desk phone rang. She shuffled back to her chair, shooed me away, and picked up the receiver. "This is Sam. How may I help you?"

A few weeks or more? That didn't sound good. I had a list of cases already. How many more would I need to add? I logged into my computer.

Sam ended her phone conversation and called me over to her desk. "Victor notified me yesterday he'll be out on medical leave. You'll need to pick up the slack."

"All of it? All his cases, I mean?"

"Is that a problem, Ms. Meadows?"

"No, ma'am." I combed my fingers through my bangs. This would be worse than I thought.

"Good. Have a seat." She pointed to the chair across from her desk. "You made an impression on your visits today."

My heart raced. Had Luke called in and

complained about me?

She looked at her computer screen. "I like to follow up on new employees and get immediate feedback. I spoke to Todd Butler and Luke Gibson."

"And?" I pulled my shoulders back and hoped I appeared confident.

"Todd said Billy cried after you left."

I frowned and brought my hand to my chest. "Did I upset him?"

She shook her head. "He cried because you left and didn't take him home with you."

"I'm sorry if I gave him any indication that I would take him home." But the thought of fostering or adopting had weighed heavy on my mind. Marriage wasn't in my future, but parenting could be.

"Remember, he's never been in this situation before, and he doesn't know what to expect." She rested her elbow on her desk and rubbed her forehead. "Unfortunately, he'll learn soon enough unless his mom gets an excellent lawyer. She may spend several years in jail."

"That's too bad. Billy seems like a sweet boy." And he needed a better home than Luke could provide.

I picked at a fingernail.

"Luke Gibson wavered when I asked him about your visit."

No big surprise there. "Oh?" Didn't he know I could make this challenging for him?

"He said your thoroughness and notice to detail far outdid Victor's. But he's concerned you may try to instill big city procedures in a small town and make things harder than necessary."

How should I respond? Did she agree with me

following the rules or Victor's haphazard approach, according to Luke?

Sam leaned toward me. "I told him we follow state guidelines, and your procedures should align with Tennessee. Are there any distinctions between what the State requires and the private agency you worked for in Chattanooga?"

"None that I know of."

She nodded and relaxed back in her chair. "You've been gone from Pleasant Springs a long time and may not realize Luke is a model citizen in this community. We will follow state guidelines but also hurry his approval through as fast as we can." She tapped her fingertips on her desk. "I know him. He'll make a wonderful foster parent."

"Yes, ma'am."

I returned to my desk to update my findings on my visit with Luke, which I hoped would raise enough red flags that Sam would change her mind. I had little to go on, but a little exaggeration wouldn't hurt, would it?

If Sam insisted after she read my report, I would hurry Luke's application along. The quicker I found a solid reason to turn him down, the sooner I wouldn't have to see him again. With me having to complete his home study and follow-up visits afterward, if Victor hasn't returned, even four visits would be more than I could stomach. I would do what I needed to keep my job until something in Nashville came through, but no way would I make things easy on Luke Gibson.

He couldn't break my heart and then expect me to give him what he wanted after he'd destroyed my dreams.

Four

Luke's afternoon dragged along. He sat in his office and stared through the full-length windows out into the garage bay. Bills needed to be paid, but he struggled to focus on them. He rested his elbows on his desk, closed his eyes, and massaged his temples. "Why now, Lord?"

He lifted his head at the shuffle of feet.

Eddie stood in front of his desk and stared. "Hey, bro. Is there a problem?"

His brother was his top mechanic and became his best friend when Lanie lost that title.

Luke shook his head and in a defeated tone said, "Nope. Everything's great."

"Then what's wrong with your face?" Eddie sat in the chair across from Luke's desk.

"Are you saying I'm not my joyful, charming self?"

"You look like you ate something bad. Like you need to vomit."

Luke set the paperwork aside. "I had a surprise when I met with the social worker today." He sighed and rubbed the back of his neck. "I expected Victor

Clemmons, but I got Lanie Meadows."

Eddie scooted to the front of his chair. "Why is Lanie back after all these years?"

"I don't know."

Eddie stood, moved to the back of Luke's chair, and patted him on the shoulder. "Looks like God is ready to work all things together for good." He ambled to the doorway and turned back. "Praying for you, bro."

~

With everything caught up in the office, I slipped out and drove to Miss Risa's house. She lived on the north side of Pleasant Springs, off Mud Dauber Road, near my parents. When I arrived, I parked in the driveway along her white picket fence.

Miss Risa greeted me from her front porch on my way down the sidewalk. "My, my. Look at you." She eyed me from head to toe. "You're as pretty as I remember."

"You haven't had your eyes checked for a while, have you?" I slumped my shoulders. Jill got Mom's good looks. I got Dad's—only they weren't all that good. Big ears. My light golden-brown hair was my best quality, but I kept it cut short. I hated to mess with it and didn't care for makeup either. Why bother?

"Now, now. Been too long since I've seen you. I hope you'll stop by often." She insisted we talk on the front porch. "Have a seat, dear."

With temps in the mid-fifties and overcast skies, a front porch didn't seem the best place for a visit.

I zipped my jacket and sat in a rocker across from a porch swing. "Are you still active at the church?"

"Yes dear. I love our little church community. Though I can't say that about my mail carrier. He's abusive."

"Abusive? What happened?"

She took a seat on the swing. "Oh my. Where are my manners?" She leaned toward me. "Would you like a cup of hot peppermint tea?"

I thanked her but declined. "I have another appointment soon."

"Well dear, he quit bringing my mail."

"Excuse me?" Was she for real? She'd always been a little quirky, but her mail carrier? "How is that abusive?"

"Isn't it obvious, dear?" She wrinkled her already wrinkly face. "Age discrimination. He doesn't like me because I'm old. He said I need to pick up my mail at the post office."

I played along and rubbed my chin. "This is a serious matter. I'll check with the postmaster, and he'll sort this out." I stood and descended the steps.

"You're going to skedaddle already?" She rose from the swing and frowned. "Can't you stay awhile?"

I turned toward Miss Risa. "I'll get back to you after I speak to the postmaster."

"Before you go, dear, I have a word for you."

I waited for Miss Risa's word. "Yes?"

"Things aren't always as they seem." She leaned against the porch railing, smiled, and waved. "Have a good day. When you can chat longer, stop by and see me."

I made my way to my car. "Things aren't always as they seem? With her mail or with the mail carrier?" I shook my head. She was an odd one. Sweet, but different.

Later that afternoon, on my way to Jill's house, I

received a call from Todd Butler. He offered to have someone take Billy to school the next morning if I picked him up from school to spend time with him. I agreed and looked forward to quality time spent with someone who needed an advocate and a friend. I'd interacted with many wonderful children over the years, but in that one visit, Billy tugged at my heart more than most.

After I parked my car in front of Jill's home, I made my way inside. An excited beagle greeted me with lots of wet kisses. I knelt and scratched her behind her ears. "Hi, Babs. Are you ready to go outside?"

My sister owned a comfortable ranch home south of town in an older neighborhood. The yard needed a little tender loving care, and flowers would help. But she kept the inside tidy. The front door opened to the living room on the left and a hallway to the right leading to three bedrooms and the guest bathroom. Access to the kitchen/dining area could be gained from the living room or the hallway.

One of the bedrooms held Jill's yarn projects—knitted and crocheted hats, scarves, and mittens for the children's home where Billy lived. Jill and her best friend, Becca Peterson, had taken the project on for the past several months.

Becca moved to Florida when she remarried the month before. But a move back to Pleasant Springs looked promising. Ben, her new husband, would preach at Jill's church the following Sunday and become their new pastor if they voted him in.

I appreciated my small bedroom across the hall from Jill's, but I craved independence. As soon as possible, I needed that job in Nashville.

I meandered through the kitchen and dining room and let Babs out the back door. After I changed into casual clothes, I went outside and sat on Jill's wicker bench across from her barbeque grill and watched Babs chase squirrels. Hummingbirds fluttered around the two feeders that hung from the covered patio. Jill loved all birds, but these little guys were her favorite.

Several minutes passed, and Babs followed me back inside. I fed her and started supper. By the time Jill arrived home, chicken tacos awaited her.

"This is great." She thanked me with a hug. "I'll expect this every evening."

I chuckled. "You'd better try them first. You might change your mind."

Jill took a seat across from me at her round kitchen table and asked me to say the blessing. I squirmed and bowed my head. My prayer life ended when Luke returned to Pleasant Springs. If he didn't marry Stephanie, why didn't he contact me? I was supposed to be his best friend forever.

Jill cleared her throat. "Are you okay? Would you like me to pray?"

I glanced at her and fidgeted. "Sorry. My mind wandered." I bowed my head and said a quick prayer of thanksgiving.

"Tell me all about your first day on the job? How did things go?"

"Okay." I grinned at the thought of sweet Billy. "I'm working with a young boy who needs a foster home placement. A sweetheart."

"That's nice." Jill took a bite of her taco. "Yum. This is delicious. Can't wait to see what you make tomorrow."

"Tomorrow's your turn. I have a date with my young sweetheart. Taking him to supper."

Jill sipped her sweet tea. "Did you see Miss Risa?"

I shared about our visit.

"Did you run into anyone else you know?"

"I can't discuss people I meet with by name." I looked down at my plate. "But I knew one of them." I stood, refilled my water glass, and hoped she wouldn't ask me any more questions.

"Were they excited to see you after all these years?"

I snickered. "He wasn't all that excited." I sat and played with my napkin. "He was rude and . . ." I'd said too much. If I'd continued, she might have figured out who I'd seen.

"I'm sorry that didn't go well." Jill picked up her empty plate and carried it to the sink. "You were busy with unpacking yesterday and didn't attend church, but I look forward to you going with me this Sunday."

She made a big assumption. "I never said I would."

Jill jerked her head toward me. "But you will, won't you? Or are you going to Mom and Dad's church?"

I walked to the sink and stood next to her. "I doubt I'll go to either."

"But Becca will be there. Her husband preaches this Sunday." She opened her mouth and widened her eyes. "Where do you plan to go?"

I rinsed my plate and placed it in the dishwasher. "No place. I don't attend church."

Jill gawked at me. "Since when?"

"You don't need to look at me like I've grown two horns on top of my head." I threw my shoulders back.

"Since college." I turned away from her stare and darted to my room. I didn't need her sermon that was sure to follow.

Five

Tuesday after lunch, I debated if I should talk with Sam regarding Luke's application. So far, she had said nothing about the notes I sent her. Notes I expected her to question to discover why Luke wasn't a good fit as a foster parent. I made my way to her desk.

"Do you have time to discuss the report I filed on Luke Gibson?"

She raised her head and creased her brow. "Have you updated it yet?"

"Updated? No."

"I commented in the database." She shook her head. "I'm not sure what you found at Mr. Gibson's home, but I recommend you take another look and hurry this one along, like I asked you to do yesterday." She tapped her finger on her desk. "You're looking for trouble where you won't find any. Luke is A-plus material."

I swallowed hard. Did I need to do a little more exaggerating?

She grasped a folder from the corner of her desk. "Here's a list of Victor's cases. They're your responsibility until he returns. Follow up with each placement and be sure to update their records."

I zipped back to my desk. Her comments in the database mirrored what she'd said: "Hurry this along."

Why was this so important to her? Hurry it along, even if Luke would make a terrible foster parent?

And Victor's case load? Sure, someone had to pick up the slack while he was gone. But why me? Couldn't Ronni help too? I would do my best for each child and foster family, but I didn't have to like it. I snatched my purse from my desk drawer.

Ronni stopped me on my way out the door to tell me the court had scheduled Billy's state custody hearing for the following afternoon at 3:00.

I thanked her and left to pick Billy up from school.

When I got there, Billy met me in the office, dropped his backpack onto a chair, and greeted me with a hug. "I thought I'd never see you again. You were gone a long time."

I bent down in front of him. "I'm here for you. But I have other things I need to do and other people to visit too. You may sometimes have to wait for me, but I'll be close by."

"Okay."

"I'm working to find you a wonderful home to live in while your mom isn't available."

"Why can't I live with you?"

I grinned. He knew how to pull my heartstrings. "My job is to find homes for boys and girls who need one."

Billy peered at his shoes.

"Besides. I don't have a place to live either. I'm staying with my sister for now."

"We both need a new home." He yanked his

backpack off the chair. "Can we see my mom?"

"Not today." I rose and ruffled his hair. "But how about the park and supper?"

"That sounds fun." He raised his fist and waited for my bump.

I laughed at his eagerness. "But we have to get you back to Creekside before it's too late to do your homework."

He stuck up his nose. "I don't have homework today."

"We'll check when I drop you off."

I strapped him into a booster seat in the back seat of my car.

We left Shady View and drove back to Pleasant Springs. I took Billy to Turtle Creek Park and parked near the playground.

"Would you rather play first or visit the pond and feed the ducks?" I reached into my back seat and grabbed a bag of breadcrumbs that lay next to his booster seat.

"Playground first." He cried out in frustration. "This stupid door won't open."

"Hold on. I'll get you out." I hurried to his door and gripped his hand. "I keep the doors locked to make sure you're safe."

He jumped out onto the pavement. "But I wanted out."

I squatted in front of him again. "Yes, you did. But you need to wait for me next time. Okay?"

He nodded with a cute pout.

"Now, let's go play."

After time on the slide, swings, and climbing tower, we strolled to the pond and fed the ducks. Billy seemed to enjoy himself until he backed into duck droppings and whined.

"You're okay." I had him wipe his shoes off in the grass. "Let's get something to eat."

He quieted and smiled. "Can I have that circle spaghetti from a can?"

"How about pizza instead?"

He agreed, and I drove to the Pizza Shack. He told me he didn't like vegetables, so we ordered a pepperoni pizza. Hand tossed crust, lots of cheese, and tasty. I realized how much I'd missed this place. They made the best pizza.

When we finished, I paid the bill, took Billy by the hand, and we stepped outside at 5:45 p.m.

"Grizzly." Billy pulled away from me, threw himself onto a huge deep brown dog, and buried his face into the dog's thick coat. "I've missed you so much."

A black pickup pulled into the parking lot. "Great. Luke."

I bent forward and tugged at Billy's shirt. "Let's go. We need to leave now." Was he crying? I crouched next to him. "What's the matter?" I patted Billy's back. "Whose dog is this?"

"Belonged to Mr. Jed. He died two years ago." Luke hunkered next to me. "The townspeople take care of the dog now." He rubbed the massive dog behind his ears.

Billy raised his head and in an irritated tone said, "Not Jed. His name was Granddad." Tears filled his eyes. "But he died? That's why I don't see him bring food no more." He rubbed his hand over his eyes.

Food? I needed to get him away from Luke to ask

Billy about his granddad and the food in private. I whispered in his ear. "Let's go. We have other errands to run before I take you back to Creekside."

Luke and I stood.

"I can't leave him. He needs me." Billy lingered with his arms around Grizzly.

"Billy . . ."

My head snapped toward Luke. "Too early for you to interfere." I clenched my teeth. "Let me do my job."

"But I want to reassure him."

"Now is not the time."

He straightened and puffed out his chest. "When is the time?"

I cut him a look. "I don't know, but it's not now."

"Do I need to place another call to your supervisor?" Luke narrowed his eyes.

"Another call?" I avoided his eyes and took a deep breath before I looked his way again. "She said she called you."

"She did." He lifted his chin and gloated. "I called her back."

I straightened my shoulders and glanced at Billy, who'd raised his eyebrows. "Let's go." The nerve of that man. Trying to intimidate me. I wouldn't let that happen.

Billy leapt to his feet and pulled on Luke's shirt. "Hey." He stared at Luke. "You're my coach."

Luke beamed. "That's right."

"How did Granddad die?"

"I don't know." Luke peeked at me. "You go with Miss Lanie now, and I'll stay with Grizzly for a few minutes to make sure he's okay."

Billy scanned the area. "Who's Miss Lanie?"

"I am." I squeezed Billy's shoulder. "Mr. Luke has a tough time remembering I'm Mel. But you can call me Miss Lanie too."

Luke rubbed his hand along his chin. "I've got a great idea." He winked at Billy. "I'll take Grizzly to my house. I'm sure Miss Lanie will let you visit us sometime soon if you'd like that."

Billy raised his fist to Luke. "Yay."

Luke responded with a bump.

I lowered my voice. "Are you crazy? That dog will cost you a fortune in food. He looks a lot like the Newfoundland my first supervisor in Chattanooga owned, but Jerome's dog was black. He weighed 150 pounds and drooled a lot."

Luke eyed Grizzly again. "He may be a mix. Part Labrador or something."

"Either way, he seems content lying here in front of the restaurant. I doubt he wants to go home with you."

"You're upset you didn't think of it first."

I raised both palms and backed away. "He'd flatten Jill's small dog into a pancake."

"Can we visit Coach Luke and Grizzly and play together?" Billy clutched my hand.

Luke chuckled and patted Billy on his back. "Sounds good to me." He eyed me and smirked.

Low down conniver. Reminded me of the time he bought an Xbox with his allowance money because I wanted one. He told me I had to come to his house to play because if he gave it to me, I'd never leave my home. I called him a conniver then, but he was cute because of it. Now? I covered my mouth with my free hand to muffle a snicker. Who was I kidding? He was still cute after all these years.

I squeezed Billy's hand and led him to my car.

"I like him." He twisted toward Grizzly and Luke.

"Grizzly seems like a friendly dog. I like him too."

He gazed at me with his big brown eyes. "I *love* Grizzly. But I meant Coach Luke."

I opened the back passenger side door. "Hop in and buckle up." After I helped him, I trudged to the driver's side and climbed in.

I liked Luke, too, but not enough to back down.

~

Luke watched Billy and Lanie hop into her car. She sounded panicked when he mentioned her supervisor. She deserved it for being too hard on him. But he needed her approval to become a foster parent. He didn't need to make waves.

Her supervisor told him that he was stuck with Lanie. Sam didn't use those exact words, but that's how he took the news when he asked if he could have a different caseworker. What she said was, "You learn to work with Melanie now, or wait for Victor to return, which may take anywhere from three weeks to three months. But we hope to place Billy with a family before then." He didn't like the sound of that. He needed to stick it out with Lanie.

But were complaints to her supervisor the way for him to win? What happened to his belief that kindness outweighed getting what you want in life?

Luke strode to the market down the street to purchase a bag of dog food. When he arrived at the market, he bought an eight-pound bag of food and headed back to the Pizza Shack. Time to figure out how he'd get that huge mutt into his truck. He had to have

Grizzly at his cabin whenever Lanie brought Billy by for a visit. But when he made it back to his pickup, he couldn't find the dog.

Six

On our way to Creekside, Billy told me what he remembered about his granddad, Grizzly, and the food. He hadn't seen the older gentleman or his dog since he was in kindergarten two years earlier. His mom never told him that Granddad had passed away. She led Billy to believe Mr. Jed had deserted them like so many other people in her lifetime.

Why would a mom lie to her son about a beloved family member?

If Billy had a grandfather, there might be other relatives too. Children's Services hoped to place children with family members if possible before looking to foster care. I needed to confirm that Mr. Jed's obituary didn't list any other family besides Billy's mom.

I smirked and wiggled in my seat. If I found a family member, Luke wouldn't be in such a hurry to get approved to foster Billy. He'd wait for Victor to return before he followed through with this idea of his, and I wouldn't have to spend time with him.

Billy yelled at the top of his lungs. "Did you hear what I said?"

"No. Sorry. What?"

He sounded frustrated. "I said we still get the food on Tuesdays, but not from Granddad."

I turned into a church's parking lot on the north side of Pleasant Springs and twisted in my seat. "You've been getting food at your house every Tuesday?"

He nodded. "And today is Tuesday. I need to get home and put the food away for Mom or she'll get mad at me."

"Can you show me how to get to your house if I drive back to Shady View?"

He shrugged.

"Let's try." I turned north onto Main Street and left onto Chicken Coop Road. We drove for three miles and turned right at Miller's Hog Farm onto Rattlesnake Road. I pulled off the road just past the Shady View welcome sign. "Does any of this look familiar?"

He peered out each window. "Is there a place nearby where they sell food near the road?"

"Let's drive a little farther and see what we can find." I pulled back out onto the road and drove for another half mile.

"That's it." He pointed to the road on the left. "Turn here. There's a trailer with a broken door on my side of the road. My home is after that on your side, past a white church with dead people."

"Do you mean a cemetery?"

Two houses farther, I pulled into the dirt driveway and parked. Billy unhooked himself and yanked at the door handle. I jumped out, darted to his door to help him before he exploded again, and followed him to the back of the house where an outhouse stood.

"He leaves the food on the back porch."

Someone had placed four bags of food at the backdoor along with a Styrofoam cooler packed full of ice, milk, cheese, butter, and eggs. Everything came from the Corner Market in Shady View.

"Here's the key. We keep it under that rock." He pointed to a rock near the bottom porch step.

We carried the groceries inside the three-room shack. The house smelled of rotted garbage. I'd visited worse, but not by much. Four cockroaches scurried across the kitchen floor. Luke was right. His cabin looked like a mansion compared to Billy's house.

I tried the sink faucet. "No water?"

"Sure. Out back. We have a pump, and I do the pumping. That's how I got my muscles." He flexed his upper arms.

I chuckled. "You get a good workout, don't you?"

Billy pulled a jar of peanut butter and other items from the first plastic bag. "Can I take these to Creekside with me?" He grouped together his favorites.

"I'm sure they have plenty of good food for you to eat." I peeked inside each remaining bag. "Let's put everything back into the bags, and we'll return the food to the market on our way back."

He pouted. "But it's mine. All of it is mine."

I did my best to explain to him that he didn't need it, but someone else might. He repacked the bags.

"Can I get my Spider-Man pajamas?"

"Sure."

He ran into the one bedroom he shared with his mom and returned with a ratty old pair of pajamas that were ready for the trash. I would have taken them from him, but his smile engulfed his face. He loved his pajamas.

I bent forward. "May I borrow those and wash them for you before you take them to Creekside?"

He plugged his nose. "Can you get them to smell better?"

"I'll try." I took them from his outstretched arms, and he wrapped me in a hug. "Thank you, Miss Lanie." He pulled back and smiled. "I love you."

That wasn't the first time I'd heard those three words from one of my kids, but it touched my heart in a deep and personal way. I wanted to be a mom. But without a man.

~

After two hours of searching for the dog, Luke returned to the PS Market, parked out front, and found Grizzly curled up behind the store.

"There you are, boy. How long have you been here?"

An employee stood nearby. "I arrived at 6:00 p.m., and he was here then."

Luke tapped his foot and frowned. "You followed me here when I bought the dog food, didn't you?" How much time had Luke wasted? "Stay. I'll get the truck and bring it around back."

He drove his pickup to the back of the store and snagged a handful of dog kibble. He climbed out of his truck and almost stepped on Grizzly's front right paw. The dog followed Luke to the back of the truck and sat while Luke opened the tailgate. "Hop in." He patted the truck bed in hopes Grizzly would jump up into it.

"Okay, boy." He held the kibble to the dog's nose and placed it on the truck bed. With excitement in his voice, he said, "Come on, boy. Let's go for a ride."

Luke rubbed his stiff neck and hunkered in front of Grizzly. "We need to go home. Billy wants to play with you when he comes for a visit."

Grizzly got up and moseyed to the passenger side door.

"Not in my new truck, buddy."

The dog plopped onto the ground.

"You win." Luke opened the door to the cab. Grizzly bounded inside and wagged his tail.

"Boy, I hope I won't live to regret this decision." Luke groaned and rubbed the knot in his belly. He'd forgotten to take his cat, Mims, or Grizzly's drooling into consideration when he made his promise to Billy.

~

After we visited Billy's house, I drove to the Corner Market to meet with the store manager, but he'd already left for the day. When I took Billy to Creekside, I met his house mom, Teresa. I told her and Billy that I'd take the food home with me, keep the cold items in the refrigerator, and return the food to the store the following morning.

Babs greeted me when I got to Jill's. Funny dog. She sat and wagged her tail until I acknowledged her. I patted her head and spoke to her before she ran off, picked up her rope toy in her mouth, and brought it to me to play tug-of-war. I soon tired of the game, zipped into the kitchen, and greeted Jill, who'd prepared spaghetti for supper. She held a bowl filled with salad and a bottle of dressing.

"I hope you weren't expecting me. Billy and I went out for pizza."

"I remembered, but would you like a little salad?"

"Sure. Some veggies would be good for me."

We finished setting the table, sat, and Jill prayed. "How was your day?"

"I met Grizzly." I poured ranch dressing onto my salad. "What can you tell me about his owner, Mr. Jed?"

"Sweet, older gentleman. Been gone for two years." She reached for a piece of garlic toast. "The townspeople care for Grizzly. He's become the town's mascot."

I shook my head. "Luke decided the dog needs a permanent home and plans to take him in."

"Luke? You've seen Luke?" Her eyes sparkled, and she brought her hand to her chest.

"Forget I said anything." I stared at my salad. "How was your day?"

"Not so fast. Where did you see him?"

I rose and strolled to the refrigerator for shredded cheese to add to my salad. "I'm going to throw in a load of laundry and turn in early tonight."

Jill wrinkled her nose when I returned to the table and took a seat. "I'm glad you saw him. Was it a cordial encounter?"

"Why wouldn't it be?" Luke was a prospective foster parent. I couldn't say much.

"Are you going to get together soon?" Jill grinned and lifted her brows.

I crossed my arms. "What do you expect to happen after all these years? Let it go. Our friendship ended eleven years ago."

Jill scrunched her nose. "I've never understood that. Enlighten me."

I picked up my plate and utensils. "Nope." I carried them to the sink, scraped my leftover salad into the garbage disposal, and loaded everything into the dishwasher. My stomach couldn't handle any more food. I dashed to my room, gathered my laundry, grabbed Billy's pajamas, and threw everything into the washer, which was behind bifold doors in the kitchen. Would his pajamas survive? In case they didn't, I planned to order Billy a new pair of Spider-Man pajamas online.

Jill tapped her foot behind me while I added detergent to the load. When I turned to look at her, she grimaced. "You threw away years of friendship with a man who idolized you. I don't understand, and I doubt he does either."

"Idolized?" I scoffed. "He cared nothing about me."

Seven

Luke couldn't get Grizzly inside the cabin. But if the dog stayed outside, would he wander off? He seemed content on the front porch, lying in a heap.

Luke checked the bag of dog food he'd bought and realized the eight-pound bag wouldn't last a week at five cups per day. He planned to make a trip to Clancy Farmers Co-op soon for a fifty-pound bag and added a reminder in his phone to make a vet appointment.

He entered his cabin, found an old bowl, and filled it with dog food. When he stepped out onto the porch, he again tried to lure the dog inside to eat. "Come on, boy." But Grizzly wouldn't budge.

Luke went inside and closed the screen door but left the front door open. He prepared his supper of bacon and eggs. Within minutes, Grizzly whined at the door.

"Guess you like bacon, right, buddy?" He opened the door, and the dog moseyed inside. Luke broke up a slice of bacon, mixed it in with the kibble, and placed the bowl on the floor. Hissing sounded above him, and he glanced at Mims, who'd perched on top of the kitchen cabinet. "You behave and come down here to meet your new brother."

Grizzly looked up and barked.

Mims jumped onto the refrigerator and then the counter, laid down, and swiped a paw at the dog whose nose was an inch away.

Grizzly yelped and barked louder.

The cat jumped over the dog's head and tore up the stairs to the attic bedroom.

Luke turned off the burner and took a seat at the kitchen table. He rubbed his aching temples. "What was I thinking? I didn't need a dog in my life."

The next morning, Luke awoke to a barking dog who wanted to go outside. To his relief, Grizzly returned to the front door and came inside for breakfast. Frying more bacon and adding it to the dry kibble helped.

Luke left for town and prayed his house, Mims, and Grizzly would be okay while he worked. He expected Lanie that afternoon for another home visit and wanted everything to be perfect.

~

Wednesday morning, I drove to Creekside Children's home to pick up Billy and take him to school in Shady View. Billy's house dad, Steve, met me at the door. "Teresa is helping Billy get ready, but they'll be a few more minutes. Have you toured the full home?"

I told him that I'd only seen Todd's office and the visitation room. Steve took me on a quick tour. To the right of the foyer was a study room with two computers, where the children did most of their homework. To the left was Todd's office. The foyer opened into the living area with two bedrooms to the right, a master bedroom for Steve and Teresa and one used by a teenaged boy, James.

The kitchen and dining area lay to the left, and a hallway behind the kitchen led to Billy's room. We walked through the kitchen to the front of the house where the family visitation room and another bedroom were located. The home felt pleasant and cozy. A beautiful place for children and teens to live until a foster home became available.

Billy and I said goodbye to Steve and Teresa and headed to Shady View Elementary School.

"They both seem nice. Do you like them?"

"I like my mom better."

"Of course, you do. And soon you'll have a place to live until your mom can take care of you again." I dropped Billy off and drove to the Corner Market to return the groceries and talk with the store manager.

I liked him. Friendly, polite, fortyish, and good looking. But what did I care about that? He confirmed he brought the groceries each week for Billy. When I told him the food was in my car and I wanted to return it, he suggested I donate the groceries to Creekside, because that's where Billy lived. I thanked him and smiled. "May I ask you a few questions about the food deliveries?"

"Sure." He led me to his office in the back of the store and offered me a chair. "What would you like to know?"

"I understand Mr. Jed delivered the food each week until two years ago, when he died. Why do you continue to bring food to the house?"

"Jed named me as the executor of his will because he and my grandfather were close friends. They both drove school buses after they retired. Jed wanted to be sure someone took care of his great-grandson."

Great news. If Billy was Jed's great-grandson, Billy may have a grandparent too. A much better place for him to live than with Luke.

"How many children did Jed have?"

"One daughter. And she had one daughter as well—Pamela—Billy's mother."

"Where might I find Jed's daughter?" I rubbed my palms together. Would this be my lucky day?

"She's been away for a long time. Jed tried to find her a few years ago."

Not what I wanted to hear. "What's her name?"

"I'm sorry. I don't remember. He didn't leave her anything in his will."

I sighed. A dead end. "That's all of my questions."

He grinned. "Keep me posted when Billy returns home, and I'll make the deliveries again." He led the way to the store's front entrance.

"One more question. Who got custody of Grizzly?"

He chuckled. "I did, but the dog took off to Pleasant Springs often to visit Jed's favorite places, and I gave up."

I thanked him for his time, returned to my car, and checked my messages.

Ronni scheduled me for another visit with Luke at 1:00. I peeked at my watch—9:15 a.m. I had plenty of time before my meeting.

On my drive back to Pleasant Springs, I decided I needed to further research Jed's daughter. Someone somewhere must have information concerning her whereabouts.

When I arrived at the office at 9:30, I researched Jed Dickson's obituary. Crazy. No mention of his daughter, Pamela, or Billy. I expected the information to at least say something about a granddaughter and a great-grandson, even if they didn't print names. I read everything I could find on the Internet too.

My stomach soured. I needed to find Billy's grandmother. I grabbed my purse and stood to leave. The library had local history books I could check.

"Hold up, Mel." Sam shuffled my way. "Where are you off to?"

"Following up on information about Billy Oliver's relatives."

She frowned. "His only relative is in jail, and she wouldn't approve of a family member if you found one."

"What about Pamela's mother? Where is she?"

Sam shook her head. "From what I've found, she's been gone many years and lived a lot like her daughter." She pulled her glasses down her nose and peered at me over the rims. "Meet with Luke, verify that he plans to attend the virtual informational meeting tomorrow night, and once that's completed, we can move ahead with his training and home study."

"And he'll attend the weekly virtual and in-person training sessions for prospective foster parents over the next six weeks, like everyone else?"

Sam raised her voice. "He'll meet with the trainer both virtually and in Chattanooga over the next *three* weeks. You'll take care of his home study."

"But that's a lot of information for him to digest in three weeks."

Her body stiffened. "That's the way this is going to play out. You will work with him to make sure he understands each lesson and completes the assignments.

Do you understand?"

I nodded. But I'd never had to work one-on-one with a prospective foster parent's training before. Why was this so important to her?

"Luke and Billy are your priorities for the next three weeks. Be sure to get Billy over to Luke's house often and spend time together to see how they get along. Note it in your reports." She stared over my head.

"Okay." What other choice did I have? I needed my job. For now. I took a step toward the door.

Ronni ambled toward me. "The judge's schedule changed. Billy's state custody court hearing moved to 10:30 this morning." She handed me a piece of paper. "Here's the address and the information you'll need."

I thanked her and headed out to my car. Before I pulled out of the parking lot, I received a text from Jill. **Miss Risa wants you to stop by again. Give her your number while you're there.**

I'd forgotten to visit the postmaster like I told her I'd do. I drove to the post office, waited for the postmaster for fifteen minutes, and he gave me ten seconds of his time. He said they had delivered Miss Risa's mail since Monday. Just a little mix-up.

My next stop was the county courthouse, where I met with the judge regarding Billy's case. Afterward, I opened my contact for the Meade Agency in Nashville. Sam held too tight of a rein on me and working with Luke didn't sit well either. I clicked on the number, bit my lip, and waited through five rings before it went to voicemail. I left a message for the human resource director, disconnected the call, and pulled out of the parking lot. No way could I work with Luke. I needed that job in Nashville.

When I arrived at Miss Risa's home, she again met me out front and threw her arms around me. "You're a lifesaver, dear." She thanked me three times for getting her mail delivered. I tried to explain I had done nothing, but she wouldn't listen.

I gave her a business card with my cell number and asked her to contact me when she wanted to chat. "How may I help you today, Miss Risa?"

"Could you spare ten minutes to sit on the porch and read to me? My eyes are tired today."

I pursed my lips and held back a giggle. "Sure. Where's the book?" Dad was right. I should have expected this.

She pointed to the porch swing, told me she'd be back in a jiffy, and slipped inside her house. With temps in the mid-seventies, sitting outside on the swing sounded ideal. Miss Risa returned with her Bible and handed it to me before she sat in the chair across from me.

My heart raced. When was the last time I'd read my Bible or prayed except for the quick prayer before my meal with Jill? "What would you like me to read?"

"My bookmark is where I left off yesterday."

"Second Corinthians Chapter Two." I read the first eight verses, paused, and reread verses seven and eight. "Now instead, you ought to forgive and comfort him, so that he will not be overwhelmed by excessive sorrow. I urge you, therefore, to reaffirm your love for him." My thoughts turned to Luke, but I didn't know why.

I understood forgive but not comfort him because of sorrow. And reaffirm your love? I snapped the Bible shut. Heat climbed up my neck and face, and I stood. "I need to go now." I swallowed hard. "But I'll stop by and read again sometime soon." I descended the steps, stopped, and spun. "Do you know anything about Jed Dickson's family?"

"Why do you ask?"

"Doing research. Were you acquainted with him?"

"A little."

"And his family?"

"I'll think it over and tell you when you come back to read to me again."

"Friday?"

"Sounds good, and remember what I told you last time, dear?"

In unison, we said, "Things aren't always as they seem."

Eight

Luke arrived home later than he'd hoped. He had thirty minutes to eat and get ready for Lanie's visit. He climbed out of his pickup and dashed into the cabin. Good thing he didn't have close neighbors, or they would have called the police for excessive dog barking and whining inside the house. Grizzly sounded like someone tortured him. Luke yelled, "What's going on in here?"

Grizzly cowered. He crawled under the kitchen table and knocked over a chair.

Luke scanned his living room. Dog hair covered the sofa. A shredded throw pillow lay scattered on the floor. He glared at Grizzly. "You've had a busy morning."

No time for lunch. Luke tidied the kitchen, threw away the pillow scraps, brushed dog hair from the couch, and called for Mims. He massaged his temples and lifted his head. She sat perched on top of the kitchen cabinets, ready to pounce on an easy target. He hoped that didn't include Lanie or him.

At the sound of a car door slamming shut, he opened the screen door and stepped onto the porch with

Grizzly close behind. After they greeted Lanie, Grizzly wandered off.

"How's he working out for you?"

"Great. I see the makings of a wonderful companion."

"Good to hear." She climbed the porch stairs.

Luke opened the screen door, and they walked inside. Mims leapt from the cabinets to the floor.

Lanie jumped, screamed, and grabbed her chest. She spun toward Luke. "I can't believe Cat scared me again."

"Sorry. I don't know what's gotten into her." He touched Lanie's shoulder. "Are you okay?"

"Fine." She pulled away from his touch and placed her notepad and a manila folder on the kitchen table. "May I use your bathroom?"

Luke hesitated. He hadn't checked the bathroom yet. "Sure."

She made her way down the short hallway and laughed. "Now, this is what I expected from a cat. Not the flying trapeze act I witnessed."

When Luke hurried to the bathroom door, he found half a roll of toilet paper unraveled on the floor. "May not have been the cat. Grizzly had a tough morning here in the house." Luke told Lanie about the dog hair and throw pillow while he gathered the wasted paper and threw it in the trashcan. "I'll check on the dog and bring him back inside."

Lanie sat at the kitchen table when Luke and Grizzly returned to the cabin.

Luke took a seat across from her and handed her a copy of his CPR and First Aid certifications.

She placed them into a folder. "After making a

search for Billy's relatives, I've come up empty. Jed was his great-grandfather. I thought there might be a grandparent available but had no success with that."

"Does that mean you're ready to move forward on my home study?"

"Unless we find a relative." She smirked.

"What's my next step?"

"Attend the two-hour virtual informational meeting tomorrow night at 6:00."

He wrinkled his nose. "Tomorrow night?" He'd need to cancel his Bible study.

"I thought Victor already told you."

He shook his head. "But I can do that."

"I'll send you the link. Then a trainer will complete your training in Chattanooga, both virtually and in-person, which includes four training modules and a medication administration session with a nurse. And I'll cover your home study over the next three weeks here at your house. You'll meet with the trainer one last time for a review meeting before we can approve your home study and place Billy in your home."

"I'm glad we're ready to move forward."

"I'll spend time with Billy and mention that you want to have him visit you and Grizzly. We'll get him more familiar with you before I tell him that you're interested in having him live with you." She stood and in a professional tone said, "Are you free on Saturday afternoon?"

"Sure. How does a hike at South Cumberland State Park or Fall Creek Falls sound?"

Lanie stuttered. "I meant here for a brief visit or to meet at Turtle Creek Park."

Luke rose from his chair. "Okay. But I remember

how much you enjoyed the waterfalls. Might be fun to show them to Billy."

~

Forget waterfalls. Luke's idea sounded like a date. He and I had been best friends since third grade, but we never dated. We grew up in the same neighborhood and were more like siblings. I chuckled. If we were like siblings, why did it hurt when he proposed to Stephanie? He'd become much more to me than a best friend or brother, but I never had the nerve to tell him. He would have made fun of me.

On my way back to the office, my phone rang. I pulled into the parking lot at the Pizza Shack and answered the call.

The caller introduced herself as the human resource assistant from the Meade Agency in Nashville. They'd postponed all interviews but would keep my resume on file and get back with me if they were interested in meeting me in the future. I disconnected the call, smacked my steering wheel, and stared at the clouds.

"You don't plan to help me, do You?" Why should He? I hadn't spent time with Him since Luke left me alone in Chattanooga.

I drove to the office and spent an hour there before I left to visit Billy. When I arrived at Creekside, I found him in the study room where he worked on homework. I slid into a chair next to him. "Do you enjoy math as much as I do?"

He frowned and dropped his pencil onto the table. "Too hard for me."

I rubbed his back. "Do you need a quick break?"

He shushed me. "They make us be quiet in here."

I winked at him and took his hand in mine. "Let's

take a short walk."

We stood and strolled through the foyer and kitchen to the visitation room, where I bent forward and looked him in the eye. "Would you enjoy a field trip on Saturday afternoon?"

He pinched his bottom lip.

"You can bring your elephant if you'd like."

He widened his eyes. "Just me and you?"

I nodded. "Someplace special."

"Okay, as long as I'm with you." He smiled.

I loved this boy. He'd captured my heart.

~

Thursday's virtual informational meeting ended at 8:00 p.m. Luke leaned back in his kitchen chair, perused his notes, and exhaled a lengthy breath. Foster care sounded more intense than he'd expected.

Children in foster care suffered not only from neglect, but abuse and trauma. He'd need annual training to learn how to best help and care for Billy and other children that he might welcome into his home. Their personal loss and lack of trust toward adults might also cause serious attachment issues. He had to grasp hold of the realization that caring for a child may never result in their love or even appreciation in return.

Would the benefits to Billy and other children in the future outweigh the commitment involved from Luke? He knew the answer. He wanted to settle down, be a dad, and pour his and God's love into a child's life more than anything else.

Nine

During their lunch break on Friday, Luke squirmed under his brother's scrutiny. "Don't you have work to do?"

Eddie chuckled. "Not during my lunch hour. But I'll leave you alone if you answer my question."

Luke stood and wandered to the window that overlooked the parking lot. "There's nothing between Lanie and me. Never will be again."

"Which means you refuse to forgive her?"

Luke spun to face Eddie. "I've forgiven her, but once this home study concludes and Victor comes back, I'll be happy to get her out of my life."

Eddie rose and ambled to Luke. "The Lord told you to rid her of your life?"

"This doesn't concern you. Leave me alone."

"You've pined over that woman for eleven years. Now she's back and you want nothing to do with her?" He pointed his index finger at Luke's chest. "Sounds to me that you haven't forgiven her, Mister Hot Shot Bible Study Teacher."

Luke scowled. "I know what you're trying to do, but it won't work. I will not get mad at you, especially when you're right. Her being back hasn't been easy for me." He struggled to find the right words. "You understand better than anyone."

"Are you sticking to your story that you want nothing to do with her?"

Luke strode back to his desk and sat with his back to Eddie. "Yep. We're done."

"Does that mean you won't mind if I ask her out?"

Luke twirled his chair around to look Eddie in the eye. "You? Ask Lanie out? Mister Too Shy? You haven't asked a woman out in how many years?"

"She was always nice to me." He leaned forward. "Maybe I'll have a chance."

Luke grunted. "Go for it, man. You have my blessing."

Eddie left, and Luke returned to the window and crossed his arms. Lanie would never go out with Eddie. He wrinkled his brow. Would she?

~

Jill and I met for lunch at Mama Lou's Café, where she told me more about Becca Peterson's visit.

I didn't know Becca well, but I liked her and looked forward to seeing her again. But not enough to go to church with Jill. "Ask her if she can meet us for lunch tomorrow."

"She and her husband are meeting with the church board then."

"What about supper? Or coffee? Or lunch after church?"

"Seriously? You won't go to church, but you'll meet us for lunch?"

I scooted off the bench and picked up my bill. "Never mind. I'll catch up with Becca after she moves to town."

"But what if the church doesn't vote them in?"

"Where's your faith, Sis?"

Jill shifted in her seat and pursed her lips. "I'll see you at home. This discussion isn't over."

I paid for my meal at the counter and drove to Miss Risa's as promised. She'd want me to read her Bible again, but to get information on Mr. Jed's daughter, it was worth it. Sam may have told me to give the relative search a rest, but she hadn't forbidden me.

Miss Risa waved when I got out of my car. "I've been waiting for you." She clutched her Bible to her chest.

When I got to the top of her porch steps, she pointed to the rocker, and I sat. "Do you have any information for me about Mr. Jed?"

"Oh, my. Let's read awhile first." She held out the Bible.

I flipped it open to her bookmark in Matthew. "Chapter Six or Seven?"

"Chapter Six, please."

A long chapter with thirty-four verses. I hoped she wouldn't expect me to read all of them, but none of the section headings said anything about forgiveness for which I was grateful.

I read the first eight verses and came to the Lord's Prayer. In verse twelve, that word forgive caused me to pause. And verses fourteen and fifteen made my chest tighten. "For if you forgive other people when they sin against you, your heavenly Father will also forgive you. But if you do not forgive others their sins, your Father will not forgive your sins."

I closed Miss Risa's Bible. "That's enough for

today." I stood, hugged her neck, and climbed down the stairs.

"Don't you want to learn what I found out about Jed's family?"

I smirked. "If I have to finish the chapter, then no."

She followed me down the steps. "Why do the words upset you, dear?"

"You know why."

She embraced me and squeezed. "Come back when you can stay longer, and we'll talk more." She pulled away but kept her gaze fixed on me. "As far as Jed's family, I remembered his daughter's name starts with a 'W,' but I haven't been able to recall the rest. But her last name isn't Dickson like his. I'll contact you if I remember anything helpful."

"Was her last name Oliver?"

"Doesn't sound familiar."

I thanked her and turned to leave.

"I'll see you at church Sunday morning."

My pulse quickened. "I doubt I'll make it."

She moved to my right and looped her elbow around mine. "I'm sure the Lord would like to see you there."

"I doubt he cares all that much."

"Child. He cares a great deal." One side of her mouth curved up. "If you come to church, I'll give you a free visit."

I pinched the bridge of my nose. "What's a free visit?"

"I won't ask you to read the Bible the next time you come to see me."

"Church or the Bible? I'll think about it." I frowned.

She released my arm, and I darted to my car. When I backed out of her driveway, she called out to me, and I rolled down my window.

"Remember, dear. Things aren't always as they seem."

Would she ever tell me what she meant by that comment? She realized things about me that no one could have told her. How did she know I couldn't forgive someone? Now I had two reasons to get out of this town. Luke and Miss Risa.

I drove back to the office to prepare for my follow-up sessions with Luke's training the following week. An hour later, I went to Creekside to visit Billy after school and to give him a gift.

Such a sweetheart. When I'd told him two days before that we'd visit Grizzly on our field trip, Billy did a little dance. I expected he'd get excited again when he saw what I had for him.

When I arrived, he and James sat on stools at the kitchen counter sharing a snack of apples with caramel sauce.

James slid off his stool, said, "Hey," and swaggered to his room.

Billy offered me a bite of his apple, but I declined and thanked him for his willingness to share.

"What's in the bag?" He squirmed and tried to peek inside.

"Sit still and I'll show you." I pulled out his old but clean pajamas.

He pulled the pajamas into his arms and hugged them. "It took you a long time. I missed them."

I pretended to pout and apologized. "Now, close your eyes. There's something else in the bag."

He closed his eyes and grinned.

I pulled out the new Spider-Man pajamas I'd ordered online. Billy squealed and yanked them out of my hands.

"You cheated. You opened your eyes." I laughed and enjoyed his excitement.

"Can I wear them to bed tonight?"

I nodded and reminded him that I'd pick him up after lunch the following day to visit Grizzly and Mr. Luke. He hugged me and kissed my cheek. Smitten described me well.

~

Luke tugged and pulled at Grizzly's leash to get him into the truck on Saturday morning for his 9:00 a.m. vet appointment with Doc Winston. After ten minutes, Luke succeeded, and they were on their way. They arrived late, but Jill greeted them with a smile and a treat for Grizzly, who didn't want to come inside. She convinced him the treat would be worth his effort.

"What's a civil engineer doing here?" Luke stopped at the check-in counter while Grizzly plopped onto the floor.

Jill stepped behind the counter and jiggled her computer mouse. "I work for Doc part-time. His full-time assistant plans to retire soon and requested Saturdays off. I offered to help him out on Saturday mornings until his niece moves to town and takes over full-time."

"Do I need to complete any paperwork?"

"Grizzly is in the database. We'll update your information now." She sat and asked him a few questions to bring everything up to date.

Luke leaned over the counter. "Can you tell me

anything else about him? How old he is? Vaccinations needed?"

Jill stared at the computer monitor. "He's a Newfoundland. Age shows seven years." She paused. "Life expectancy for this breed is eight to ten years. Doc did vaccinations last August. His estimated weight was 125 pounds."

"Estimated?"

Doc Winston stepped out into the waiting area and shook Luke's hand. "I look after his vet needs when I see him around town. I guess you might say I make house calls for Grizzly. Lou at the café sees he gets his heartworm meds each month." He rubbed the dog's head. "Let's put him on the scale and check his actual weight."

Luke followed Doc to the scale and Grizzly climbed on. "He's heavier than I thought. One hundred forty-seven pounds."

"Not surprising with all the scraps he gets in town. Do you plan to keep him at your place?"

"If he'll stay."

"That would be good for him." Doc looked at Jill. "Do you need any other information from Luke for Grizzly's records?"

She peeked at the screen. "I need a new emergency contact. I'll remove—"

Doc cleared his throat.

"Oops, confidential information. I forgot." She placed her hand over her mouth.

Doc smiled and shook his head. "What am I going to do with you?"

Jill's eyes brightened, and Doc slipped away.

Luke moved closer to the counter, lowered his

voice, and asked Jill if the person listed was a relative of Jed's.

Jill made a zipping motion across her mouth. "You can go into Exam Room One."

Who would Mr. Jed have listed? Billy's mother? Another relative? A friend? Yes, one of Mr. Jed's friends. No need to be concerned or mention anything to Lanie.

Grizzly's exam went well. The dog was in good health, but Doc recommended he get more exercise.

When Luke checked out, he asked Jill if Lanie had mentioned his application for foster parenting or that they were working together.

"Foster care? That's great. You'll make a great dad."

He thanked her and rubbed his chin. If only he could convince Lanie of that.

"How's that going? I mean, spending time with Lanie?"

"Some days are better than others." He glanced down. "She's upset with me, and I don't get it."

"And you're not upset with her?"

He rubbed his hand along the back of his neck. "If she's upset with me, she's been that way since graduation. Which makes no sense to me. She stayed in Chattanooga. Not me."

Jill shrugged. "She won't talk to me regarding whatever happened between the two of you, and she doesn't want to stay here either. She's applied at agencies in Nashville. If you want to know why she feels she needs to get away from here, you'll need to ask her."

"Not my business." He turned to leave and yanked

on Grizzly's leash.

"Do you still have a singles Bible study at your place?"

He twisted and peered over his shoulder. "Thursday's at 7:00 p.m." He gave her a thumbs up. "Join us." He slipped out the door, dragging Grizzly behind him.

Ten

When I arrived at Creekside at 1:00 on Saturday afternoon, Billy waited for me in the foyer with his house dad, Steve. He asked to speak with me in private and followed us out to my car. After Billy buckled up in the back seat, I stepped back to speak with Steve.

"He's had a tough morning. Anger issues. Because he responds to you better than anyone, Todd asked if you could talk with him and get him to share his feelings. Might make him feel better to get them out in the open."

"I'll see what I can do." I climbed into my car and said to Billy, "Do you have your elephant?"

He kicked his foot against the door. "No. I'm not a baby."

I turned in my seat. "Of course not. Did someone tell you that you are?"

Billy gritted his teeth. "I'm a big boy."

I smiled. "Yes, you are." I turned back to the front and pulled out onto the road. "What did you eat for lunch?"

"A hotdog and cold chunks of potatoes."

"Cold potatoes?"

"With mayo or something white mixed in."

"Potato salad?"

"That's what I said. Tasted yucky. I wanted chips."

"Did you eat it all?"

"The hotdog with ketchup." He whined. "I'm hungry. Do you think Coach Luke will have food?"

I chuckled. "I'm sure he will. At least he'll have dog food for Grizzly."

In a concerned tone, he said, "I won't have to eat dog food, will I?"

"We're not going there to eat. You're going to play with Grizzly and visit Mr. Luke."

"So he can be my pretend dad for a while until my mom comes home?"

I peeked into my rearview mirror. "Who told you that?"

"James at Creekside. He said if you take me to meet someone, I might live with them if I'm good enough and they like me."

I pulled off to the side of the road and turned toward Billy. "Mr. Luke already likes you." I tilted my head and sighed. "He hopes you'll come to live with him for a while."

A single tear fell on his cheek.

I reached back and patted his leg. "He thinks you're a wonderful young man. He takes care of Grizzly and wants to take care of you too."

Billy squeezed his eyes closed and hit the armrest on his booster seat. "No. I want to live with you."

When he eyed me again, I said, "I would love to have you live with me, but as I told you before, I don't have a house."

"Then let me stay at Creekside until you buy a

house."

I couldn't tell him that I hoped to move to Nashville soon or that I couldn't foster a child while I was their caseworker. "But I thought you'd love to be with your granddad's dog every day. Won't that be fun?"

He wrinkled his forehead. "I guess."

I did my best to speak with excitement in my voice. "Are you ready to visit Mr. Luke now?"

We pulled out onto Main Street and headed southeast to Luke's cabin. How many more times would I need to pretend happiness regarding visits to Mr. Luke?

~

Luke tidied everything and threw in a batch of chocolate chip cookies. Lanie might not eat one, but Billy would. He expected them to arrive soon. Grizzly slept on a rug in the kitchen's corner, and Mims rested on the back of the couch. Luke breathed a prayer that the two animals would behave.

He gazed out the window at the sound of tires crunching along the driveway. The timer beeped before he got out the front door to greet his guests, and he pulled the cookies from the oven.

Lanie arrived at the door without Billy. "We're here." She raised her voice and turned toward Billy, who dallied on his way to the porch steps. "I smell something delicious. Fresh baked yummy cookies." She crossed her arms but teasingly said, "You'd better hurry or Mr. Luke and I won't save you any."

Luke stepped onto the porch. "Someone tired and in need of a nap today?"

Billy grumbled and pouted. "I'm. Not. A. Baby."

He picked up his pace and stomped up the stairs.

Luke hunkered in front of Billy. "I agree. You are a fine young man. But I'm old and need a nap sometimes."

"Where's Grizzly?"

"Inside and taking *his* nap." Luke opened the door and motioned Billy and Lanie inside.

Billy glanced around. "This is awesome." He spotted Grizzly, ran to him, knelt, and laid his head on Grizzly's enormous body. And that fast, he jumped up. "Can I have a cookie?"

Luke pulled out a chair at the kitchen table. "Would you like milk too?"

"Yes, please."

"You forgot something." Lanie stared at Billy. "You need to wash your hands first."

"But I washed them this morning."

She led him to the bathroom, made sure he used soap, and she returned to the kitchen. "He knows he's not here to only visit Grizzly. An older boy at Creekside told him this was an audition."

"How did he take that news?"

Billy returned to the kitchen table, picked up his cookie, and dunked it into his milk.

"That looks good." Lanie lifted her eyebrows. "May I have milk with my cookie too?"

Luke tried to hide his smile but failed. He remembered when the two of them would eat cookies her mom baked, and Lanie always dunked hers before she took a bite. She'd say they tasted better that way.

"I know. Some people never grow up." She grinned.

~

My heart rate increased. Luke's blush did me in. What was wrong with me? He didn't care about me, and I didn't care about him. Too much pain there.

Things aren't always as they seem.

Miss Risa? Was that her voice? Her comment had something to do with Luke.

Luke nodded toward the door. "Let's go outside. Time for Grizzly's exercise."

Billy sprinted to the front door. "Come on, Grizzly."

The dog stood and moseyed toward Billy with drool dripping from his mouth.

"Yuck. What's wrong with him?" Billy frowned and backed away. "Is he sick?"

Luke rubbed Grizzly's head. "He's fine. Some dogs drool a lot."

Grizzly followed Billy outside, with Luke and I close behind. When Billy was out of earshot, I answered Luke's question about how Billy took the news that his visit was more than spending time with Grizzly. We descended the porch stairs and watched Billy in the side yard.

"With all these trees surrounding your yard, do you see much wildlife here?"

"Lots of deer. Racoons, squirrels, skunks, and birds."

"Have you ever seen a bear?"

Luke brushed his shoe across the grass. "They're not a problem."

"Luke Gibson. Why didn't you answer my question? You've seen them, haven't you?"

He squared his shoulders. "The boy will be fine here with me."

"But look at all those trees. Bears and bobcats galore might hide in there. What if Billy plays outside by himself? What if he sees a bear?"

"No bears. I've seen one bobcat."

"But—"

Luke placed both hands on my upper arms and peered into my eyes. "Billy will be fine here. I'll take loving care of him. You know I will."

I stepped back and out of his grip. "I'll need to report this in your file. Sam will make the final decision on qualifying you to be a foster parent."

Billy squealed and laughed while he ran in circles around Grizzly. The dog sat. His eyes followed Billy each time he ran past.

"Your dog is great with him. Gentle and affectionate."

"He's intelligent too."

"Oh?"

"He knows it's not time for him to eat until he smells bacon."

"The life of a dog." I snickered. "Sounds like you're spoiling him. Do you plan to spoil Billy?"

"That's up to you and Sam."

Eleven

Late Saturday afternoon, I arrived home and found Jill in the kitchen cleaning a hummingbird feeder.

She hummed a tune I didn't recognize, rinsed her feeder, and in a cheery voice said, "I understand you've seen a lot of Luke this week."

I narrowed my eyes and twisted my mouth. "And where did you hear that?"

She told me about Luke and Grizzly's appointment with Doc.

"No big deal."

"Has it been good to see him again?" She placed the clean feeder on the counter.

"No big deal."

"Are you renewing your friendship?"

"Are you hard of hearing?" I turned, trudged down the hallway toward my room, and raised my voice. "No. Big. Deal."

She darted after me and stuck her foot in the doorway to keep me from closing the door. "I'm meeting Becca and Ben for dinner in thirty minutes. Would you like to join us?"

"No. You need to enjoy your friends while they're here."

"They wanted me to ask you."

I grimaced. I'll bet they did. Wanted to get me back into a good relationship with the Lord. "You have an enjoyable time. I'll visit with Becca when she moves to town."

"*If* the church approves and votes Ben in." She rested her head on the door frame. "If they don't, it might be years before you see her again." Jill lowered her eyes to the floor.

"Please remove your foot. I'd like to change my clothes." My cell phone rang. "And I have a call to answer."

Jill pulled the door closed, and I answered my phone.

"This is. Uh. Eddie. Want to get a pizza? With me?"

"Eddie Gibson?"

"Yeah."

"That's a name from the past." I pulled the phone away from my ear and stared at it. Why would Eddie invite me out for pizza?

A faint hello emerged from my phone, and I brought the phone back to my ear. Had Luke put his brother up to call me? "Sure. What time?"

"Really?"

"I'll meet you there. The Pizza Shack, right?"

"Yeah. How about 6:00 p.m.?"

We disconnected, and I went looking for Jill and found her primping in her bathroom. "I have dinner plans. Hope you have a fun time with Becca."

"Luke?"

"Leave it alone."

"Sorry." She frowned. "Eddie?"

I jerked my head back and stiffened. "How did you know?"

"I saw him at the grocery store this afternoon, and he asked me for your number." She applied blush and watched me through her mirror. "Have you decided to go to church with me in the morning?"

"Nope." I snickered. "Not happening."

"I'm praying you change your mind." She turned, marched into her room, snatched her purse off the bed, and said goodbye. The door to the garage moaned and closed soon after.

Church? She needed to back off and give me a break.

I changed my clothes and prepared to leave at 5:50. Eddie and I had gone on one date—the senior prom, although he was a junior. Luke wanted me to ask Eddie because Luke knew Eddie would never ask me or anyone else. But Eddie wanted to. All of Luke's coaching before our date vanished when Eddie and I were together. His shyness prevented him from saying more than two words to me all night. He'd come a long way to call me and ask me out for pizza.

But what did he want? Was this about Luke or a real date?

~

Luke shook his head and pulled on his polo shirt. If Eddie hadn't told him that Lanie said yes, he wouldn't have asked Natalie Simmons out for pizza. Now he'd feel like a spy. Luke had a hunch Natalie would agree to go out with him, because she attended his Thursday night singles Bible study. But this wasn't fair to her.

And it was hard to believe Lanie would date Eddie. Their last date failed early in the evening. Luke had to leave Natalie often to give Eddie pep talks. Natalie told Luke then she'd never go out with him again. And now, both couples were going out. Luke needed to take her to another place, or she'd know he was up to no good.

Luke left his cabin at 6:00 and drove to town to pick up Natalie at her parents' home, where she had dropped off her three children. She'd divorced two years earlier and reentered the dating scene in February.

When they pulled out of her parents' driveway, he said, "How does Pete's in Poplar Ridge sound?"

"What happened to pizza? For the past thirty-five minutes, all I could think about was pepperoni and pineapple on top of lots of mozzarella cheese." Her shoulders drooped.

"Okay. If you're sure that's what you want." He drove to the Pizza Shack.

~

By the time I arrived at the Pizza Shack in my navy-blue slacks and white blouse, I'd convinced myself that Eddie wanted to talk with me about Luke and Billy. He wanted to make sure his brother got what he wanted. But I'd dismissed the idea that Luke put him up to this. If that were the case, Eddie would have asked Luke for my number instead of asking Jill.

I entered the restaurant and scanned the tables. Many were full. Was that Eddie to my left near the back, in a booth by the kitchen? He'd filled out since high school—in a good way. I strolled toward him but stopped when I spotted a bouquet on the table. I sighed. This was a date.

He glanced up, and I continued to his booth. "Hey,

Lanie." He opened his mouth like he wanted to say something, but instead, he pointed to the bench seat across the table. "Thank you for meeting me."

He'd already spoken seven words.

"You can have those flowers." A sheepish grin grew on his face. "Do you like roses?"

I nodded. "But these are carnations. Beautiful carnations." I brought them to my nose and sniffed.

"Oh. Sorry."

"I love them. They smell wonderful."

"You look nice."

I brought my hand to my chest. "That's sweet. Thank you." Eddie may still have been a little awkward and shy, but he amazed me. He'd matured since high school and had only gotten cuter over the years. My neck and face warmed at his gaze. "What kind of pizza do you want to order?"

He pulled a menu from the rack on the table. "I want a ham and cheese sub instead of pizza."

"Sounds great. I'd like to try the Italian sub. Been a long time since I've had one of those."

The server came to our table, and we ordered our meals and drinks. Within minutes, she brought a cola for Eddie and a sweet tea for me.

"Tell me about your job? Is Luke your boss?"

He grinned. "And I'm his top mechanic."

"Great." I took a sip of my drink and asked a few more questions, but he gave short responses or nodded. I needed to carry the conversation which wasn't easy for me either.

"What do you like to do in your free time?"

"I race cars on a track in my house."

"You and Luke had one growing up, didn't you?"

"I never outgrew it." He chuckled. "My buddies come over. We hang out and race."

"What else?"

"Play with my puppy. Take him for walks."

"What kind of dog do you have?"

"A beagle."

"Jill has a beagle too."

We chatted about dogs and the dog park for a few minutes while we waited for our food. When the server brought our meals, Eddie offered a brief prayer but said nothing more.

What could I say to get him to loosen up and talk to me? My thoughts turned to Billy.

"What do you think about Spider-Man?"

~

Luke opened the door to the Pizza Shack for Natalie. She led the way to a table on the left and stopped. She spun, faced Luke, and whispered with frustration in her voice. "Who's that with Eddie?"

Luke followed her gaze. "Lanie Meadows." His heart raced. She'd caught him. He took Natalie by the elbow and led her back to the door. "We can still go to Pete's for barbeque."

"Did you know she and Eddie would be here tonight?"

Luke rubbed the back of his neck. "That's why I suggested Pete's."

She blinked several times and tucked her hair behind her ear. "Are you feeling nostalgic? Did you want to relive our senior prom?"

"I don't want us to join them at their table, if that's what you mean?"

She led him to a booth near the entrance along the

right side of the restaurant and pointed. "Sit there where you can't see them, and I'll sit across from you." She slipped onto her bench and scowled. "What do you want to know?" She grabbed a menu and flipped it open in front of her face. "I should ask you to take me home now, but like I said earlier, I've been craving pizza since you called."

In an apologetic tone, Luke said, "Nat, I'm sorry."

"Only my friends call me Nat. So don't." She placed her menu on the table and huffed.

Luke leaned back in his seat. "Eddie doesn't date much or at all. I wanted to watch and give him pointers later."

"Really? That may be a small part of it because I don't think you'd lie to me. But you wanted to spy on Lanie to see if she seemed interested in Eddie, didn't you?"

"Why would I do that?"

"You baffled the entire graduating class when the two of you didn't marry."

He looked down at his opened menu. "We were always good friends. Best friends. Nothing more."

"And look at you." She reached for his hand on top of his menu. "You're still in love with her." She yanked her hand away and leaned back on the bench. "You always were."

He squinted at Natalie. "Is that what everyone believed?"

"They still do." She shoved her menu to the side and pursed her lips. "But I never imagined she'd come back home."

Twelve

Eddie and I did okay with small talk during dinner. Afterward, he offered to walk me out to my car. We scooted out of our booth, and I grasped my purse and bouquet. When we neared the door, I took a step back and landed on Eddie's foot. Luke sat in a booth with a woman I recognized but couldn't place. They both looked our way and waved.

Eddie ambled to their booth and greeted them. "What're y'all doing here?"

The woman's smile seemed forced. "Craving pizza."

When I joined Eddie at their table, Luke greeted me. What *was* he doing here? And who was the attractive woman with him?

With an edge to her voice, the woman with Luke said, "I heard you were back in town." She glanced at Eddie. "This reminds me of senior prom. Lanie with you and Luke with me."

Natalie? She'd blossomed. Perfect complexion, shoulder length, silky dark hair and seated across from Luke. "Good to see you again, Natalie." I turned to Eddie, gestured toward the door, and said goodbye to the couple on their date.

Eddie followed me outside and caught up to me. "You okay?"

I avoided his eyes and kept plodding forward. "Why wouldn't I be?"

"Luke and Natalie." Eddie touched my elbow.

I stopped in the middle of the parking lot and gawked at him. "Do you think I care?"

He stuck his hands into his pockets. "I like you. But you're Luke's girl."

I shrugged. "Luke and I were only friends. Best friends. Nothing more."

"He thought you were more." Eddie touched my elbow again and motioned to an SUV that entered the parking lot. We moved closer to where I'd parked my car. "I don't know how he hurt you. But you hurt him." He took a step back. "I think it's fixable."

My voice rose an octave. "I hurt him? Are you kidding me?"

"You need to ask Luke."

"Because I stayed in Chattanooga?"

"Part of it."

"But nothing would have been the same had I come home after college graduation. Staying in Chattanooga was the best thing for both of us." I pointed to my car. When we reached my Escape, I leaned against the door.

"Because he was just an auto mechanic?"

I cringed. Where did that come from? "What? That's ridiculous."

"He thinks his job embarrassed you. That you believe he threw his life away."

I brought my hand to my chest. "No. That's not true." I bit my lip. "I . . . ."

"You what?"

I opened my car door. "Nothing. I need to go." I turned back to Eddie. "If it embarrassed me to be with Luke, why would I agree to meet you tonight? You're a mechanic too." I watched another car pull into the lot and park. "I'm not like that."

"Prove it. Go out with me again. Let Luke see you're not too good to date a mechanic."

I touched his arm. I wasn't embarrassed to date him. Or Luke. But that's never going to happen. "Of course, I'll go out with you again. When? Where?"

"Church tomorrow and lunch after."

I wrinkled my nose. "Church?"

He nodded.

"You don't attend where Jill does, do you?"

"No. Joy Fellowship."

I stared across the street at Mama Lou's Café and clenched my teeth. "Did you know he'd be here?"

"Luke? Nope."

I peered at Eddie. "I'll go to church under one condition. Billy comes with me."

"The boy Luke's wanting to foster?"

"Yes. What time should I meet you?"

"Church begins at 10:30." He ran his hand through his hair and lowered his gaze. "Because you're Luke's girl, let's hang out together. I need you to help me get over my shyness with women." He mumbled. "I'd like to be a husband and dad, too, one day."

"So, tomorrow's not a date. We're just buds."

"I like that." He grinned. "Buds."

I drove home confused regarding what Eddie shared with me. How could I have possibly hurt Luke? Because it embarrassed me to be with him? If he thought we were more than friends, why didn't he ever tell me? And that might explain why Eddie thinks I'm Luke's girl.

I plodded inside at 7:30 p.m. and found Jill in the living room with Becca.

Becca greeted me with a hug. "I'm happy to see you." She pulled back. "Jill told me how wonderful it is to have you back home."

In a monotonous tone, I said, "A week today, and it's been a long one."

"And she's already had a date." Jill shoved Babs off her lap and rose from the couch.

I shook my head. "Just friends."

"How did it go?" Jill's eyes twinkled. "Are you going to see him again?"

I looked at Becca. "Where's your husband?"

"He's meeting with Pastor Oldham. My former pastor wants to make sure we win over the congregation tomorrow. He wants to retire as soon as possible."

"Sorry to cut this short." I crossed my arms. "But I'm going to turn in."

"So soon?" Becca frowned. "Please stay and join us."

I wanted to be alone, but I didn't want to be rude. "Okay. For a few minutes."

Jill and Becca sat on the sofa, and I took a seat on the recliner across from them.

"Well?" Jill brought her hands together. "Tell us about your date."

"Eddie and I are going to lunch tomorrow as friends after church."

Jill's eyes lit up. "Church?"

"I'm sorry. His church. Not yours."

"That's great. People say good things about Joy Fellowship. You'll like it."

I eyed Becca and furrowed my brow. "Are you upset that I won't be there tomorrow to hear Pastor Ben?"

Becca smiled. "Not at all."

We chatted for a few more minutes before I stood and said goodnight.

Jill also stood. "You appeared to be troubled when you got here. Are you feeling okay?"

"I'm fine."

"Did everything go well tonight?"

My eyes darted from Jill to Becca. "I don't know. There are things that don't add up. Eddie told me things that make little sense. And Luke has too." I brushed my foot along the carpet.

Becca moved closer and softened her voice. "Would you mind if we prayed for you?"

Sarcasm escaped my lips. "Jill probably prays for me often."

Jill reached for my hand and squeezed. "The three of us will pray together."

I gazed into their eyes, eyes filled with concern and acceptance. No doubt they'd already discussed my lack of church attendance. "Sure."

I took Becca's hand, she held Jill's, and they took turns praying for me. For clarity and understanding. For wisdom and guidance. And for me to trust the Lord again and forgive those who'd hurt me.

After a group hug, I thanked them and walked to my room. I should have grabbed my Bible, but my mystery novel won out. Tomorrow I'd go to church.

Wasn't that enough?

~

Luke dropped Natalie off at her parents' house after he'd apologized three more times. What a jerk he'd been. But she seemed to understand.

She said Lanie had a look of pain in her eyes when she noticed them together. He tapped his finger on the steering wheel. Why would she? She didn't care about him like that. Never did.

Luke's phone rang on his drive home, but he didn't answer it. When he arrived at his cabin, he checked his voicemail.

A call from Eddie. "Hey. Lanie's going to meet me at church tomorrow. I'll let you decide if you want to join us or not. She's bringing Billy. I guess that means she hopes you'll join us. And we're going to lunch after church. Want to come?"

Bringing Billy? To go to lunch together?

He went into his cabin, took Grizzly outside, and dialed Eddie. "How did your date go?"

"Great. She's totally into me."

Luke's stomach tensed. "She is?"

"No, man." Eddie chuckled. "She's your girl. I wouldn't try to steal her away from you."

"Why do you think she's *my* girl? Did she say something?"

"Not really. I talked about you more than she did."

"There's nothing between us."

"Then why does she want to bring Billy to church with her? To be sure to see you and let you spend more time with him?"

"She's doing the professional thing. Assumed I'd be there anyway, so bring Billy along."

"Sure. If that's what you want to believe."

"Look man. I appreciate you wanting to look out for me, but Lanie and I are history."

"If you say so." Eddie chuckled again. "I guess this is date number two for Lanie and me." He ended the call.

Luke paced across his living room. How could he and Lanie work things out and start over? She hurt him too much when she'd stayed in Chattanooga and didn't acknowledge or come home for his dad's funeral. A man she said she cared for like her own father. Hard to love a woman who says one thing but does another.

Thirteen

Sunday morning, I awoke at 7:30 and got ready for church. I ate a bowl of cereal while I finished my novel.

"Good morning." Jill met me in the hallway, as chipper as usual, on the way to my room. "Is that what you're wearing?"

I focused on my dress pants and flowery short-sleeve top. "What's wrong with it?"

"Nothing if you're going with me to Pleasant Springs Community, but you're overdressed for Joy Fellowship. They're pretty casual."

"Like jeans and a T-shirt casual?"

"Or jeans and the top you're wearing."

"If you're sure, I'll change."

"And what about your hair and makeup? I have things you can borrow if you need them."

Annoyed, I said, "Do you want me to wear a ribbon or flowers in my hair?"

She frowned. "No, but you may borrow my curling iron."

I slipped into the hall bathroom. "My hair does look flat, doesn't it? But fixing my hair and wearing more makeup won't help. Why bother?"

She nudged my hip with hers. "Stop dissing yourself. You're beautiful inside and out. Besides, I'm an artistic genius."

"You're a left-brained civil engineer. You don't have an artistic bone in your body."

She huffed and backed away. "Are you saying my makeup is all wrong for me?"

"You're stunning. With or without makeup." I eyed my reflection in the mirror. "But all the makeup in the world won't fix this." I pointed to my face.

Jill wrapped her arm around my shoulder. "Women would die for your thick, shiny hair and deep blue eyes."

"And my big ears?"

"They're not that big, and I can hide them under your hair."

In a perturbed tone, I said, "I go out into the world like this every day. I know how to look professional."

"But wouldn't you rather turn heads?"

I grinned at the spark in her eyes. "Bring me your curling iron." I opened my vanity drawer and pulled out foundation, powder, mascara, and blush. "This is all I have. Anything else I need I'll have to borrow from you."

She giggled. "I'll be right back."

Jill gave me new eyeliner and eyeshadow. I applied the rest of the gunk to my face while she oversaw everything I did.

"You look great." She picked up the heated curling iron and curled my hair. The curls added height and bounce. "What do you think?"

"I like it a lot, but it's too much work. I can't do

this every morning."

"Set your alarm a little earlier." She added a little hairspray, grabbed her curling iron, and took it to her room.

I changed into jeans and headed out to my car at 10:00, in time to pick up Billy and take him to church.

~

Luke shaved and applied his cologne. He pulled out his best jeans and a blue button-down shirt— Lanie's favorite color. He smiled and remembered a lot about her favorites, including forget-me-not flowers. He chuckled at the memory of him leaving for a week of summer camp when he was twelve and Lanie's handpicked bouquet.

"Don't forget me," she'd said.

He ran the comb through his hair, glad she hadn't seen her favorite blue flowers along the creek or those along the far side of his cabin yet. He hoped when she did see them that she'd think they were wildflowers and not ones he'd planted.

Luke pulled out his phone and searched for the meaning of forget-me-nots. Faithful love and loyalty. Might be a good idea to pull those weeds as soon as possible.

He said goodbye to Grizzly and Mims and headed to his truck. When he arrived at the church, he found Eddie seated on the far left of the worship center near the back. "Is she here?"

"She took Billy to Kids Zone. Getting him checked in."

Eddie scooted to his right, and Luke took a seat at the end of the row. "Lanie can sit here." Eddie patted the chair between them. "Wait until you see her."

Luke widened his eyes. "What do you mean?"

"She looks good."

Luke always thought of Lanie as pretty. He loved her wholesomeness, but when she appeared on his left, he agreed with Eddie. A true beauty.

She greeted Luke and squeezed in between him and Eddie. "I met the Wilsons and their son, Evan, when I dropped Billy off. I liked them a lot." She glanced around. "Anyone I should know here that I haven't seen in years?" She turned to Luke. "Do we need to save a place for Natalie?"

He shook his head. "She attends Jill's church."

Eddie inched closer to Lanie. "You need to keep up now that you're back. Read Maggie's blog each Wednesday and you'll know what's happening in town."

"Maggie?" She pinched my bottom lip. "The bed-and-breakfast owner?"

A man on stage pounded his drums. Guitars blared. Singers took their places in front of microphones. The congregation rose, as did Luke, Lanie, and Eddie.

Luke raised his voice. "Maggie Stone. She was a few years ahead of us in school. You were a hot topic in last week's post."

~

What did Luke mean by his comment? I remembered Maggie, but why would I be a hot topic on her blog? My pulse quickened. I wanted to leave. But as the morning progressed, something attracted me. The friendliness of the people. Joy surrounded me as people lifted their hands and sang to the Lord. I liked Joy Fellowship. Until the pastor preached.

Of all the topics in the Bible, he preached on

forgiveness. I didn't dare squirm or fidget. I didn't want to appear uncomfortable. But deep inside, I knew I needed to forgive Luke. I had to work with him to approve his home study. *Help me, Lord.* I bounced my knee and brought my fingers to my lips. Had I just prayed?

Luke leaned toward me. "Are you okay? You seem restless."

I whispered, "A little nervous about reading Maggie's blog post."

"Don't be. I tease when I shouldn't." He placed his hand on top of mine.

I stared at his hand, and he jerked it away. I focused on the preacher while he wrapped up his sermon. He prayed and dismissed us. Amazing. I made it through my first church service in eleven years.

Eddie walked me out of the worship center. "What did you think?"

I nodded. "I liked it."

Luke caught up to me and asked if he could tag along to the children's area to pick up Billy.

"Sure." I peered at Eddie. "You're coming too, right?"

"I'll head home," he said. "You three go to lunch without me."

"What? Wasn't this a date?" I pouted. "Are you dumping me already?"

He moved closer and whispered. "I would never dump a hot babe like you."

Heat rose on my neck and face. I cleared my throat and coughed.

Luke shoved Eddie's shoulder. "What did you say to her? She just turned three shades of red."

Eddie's shoulders slumped, and he stuttered. "I . . ..
I . . .."

I touched his upper arm. "Everything's fine. I don't
hear those kinds of comments often. You caught me by
surprise." I pulled my lips inward to keep from
laughing at his adorable baby face. "You must come
with us. As Luke's brother, you'll be a part of Billy's
life too. He needs to get to know you."

Luke agreed, and we made our way to the
children's area. We found Billy and his friend Evan
playing together.

Billy ran over to me and gave me a hug. "I like this
place. Can I come next week?"

I rubbed the top of his head. "We'll see, but now
it's time for lunch."

The four of us walked outside to the parking lot
and piled into my car. Luke got in the back with Billy
and Eddie rode in front with me.

"Where should we go?"

Luke suggested Pete's barbeque in Poplar Ridge.

I assumed he wanted extra time to spend with Billy
because the trip would take twenty minutes. He asked
Billy about Kid's Zone and what he'd learned. Billy
laughed about a joke someone told and sang a song.

We arrived at the restaurant and waited a few
minutes for a table. Across the room sat Jill, Becca, and
I presumed Pastor Ben, but they hadn't spotted me. Had
the church voted for Ben to be their new pastor?

The host seated us in a booth in another section of
the restaurant, away from Jill and her friends.

Billy sat against the wall and Luke took a seat next
to him.

I sat across from Billy, scanned the menu, and

asked him what he wanted to eat.

"Macaroni and cheese."

"Great." I gazed at Eddie next to me. "Please order this hot babe a chopped pork sandwich and sweet tea." I batted my eyes at him. "My sister is here with her friends. I want to say hi. Would you let me out?" He moved out of my way, and I slid off the bench.

Billy sounded concerned. "Can I come?"

"You stay with the men and get to know them better."

"Okay." He looked down at his lap.

Eddie's face colored to a deep maroon. I hadn't gone far before he said, "Did you see that? She flirted with me."

Fourteen

After a brief visit with Jill, Becca, and Ben, I returned to the three good-looking gentlemen at my booth. They jabbered on about the Nashville Predators and encouraged Billy to play hockey.

I slid in next to Eddie. "Teach him how to skate but forget hockey."

"But I like hockey, and I want to play." Billy pouted. "Coach Luke said I'd be a good player."

I squinted at Luke and crossed my arms. "I'll add this to my final report."

He glared back and mimicked my gestures. "I'm sure you will."

Eddie chuckled. "Our food is here." He passed my tea to me while the server passed him a plateful of ribs. Luke ordered ribs too. The tangy aroma of the smoked meat covered in a sticky glaze of barbeque sauce teased my senses. Why hadn't I ordered ribs?

While we ate, the boys chatted about various sport topics, and I focused on what took place at Jill's church. They voted Ben in as pastor, but he hadn't accepted yet. If he did, Becca would move into Jill's extra bedroom. She'd search for a house while Ben stayed in Orlando to submit his resignation and to put their house on the market.

That news didn't sit well with me. I liked Becca, but if she were living with us, that would be two against one in matters regarding church. They would preach to me daily. Weren't Miss Risa's mini sermons enough?

Luke waved his hand in front of my face. "Are you with us?"

"Sorry. Thinking." I took a bite of my sandwich and a sip of tea. "This barbeque pork is as good as I remember."

Billy stabbed a piece of macaroni with his fork and held it out for me. "Here, try this. It's good too."

I wrinkled my nose and thanked him. "You eat it. I'll try it another time." I glanced at Luke's baby back ribs. "Those look tasty too."

"Would you like a bite?"

I shook my head and took another bite of my sandwich.

"I would." Billy jiggled in his seat.

Luke broke off a rib and placed it on Billy's plate.

He took a large bite and smiled. "Can we come back here again? I want to order ribs next time."

Luke picked up Billy's napkin and wiped a smudge of barbeque sauce from his lips. "I'm sure we'll be back."

We finished our meal and drove back to the church. I climbed out of my car and sashayed to Eddie, who'd exited the passenger side. "Thanks for the date." I winked.

"Anytime."

Luke got out and strode to my side. "The trainer contacted me yesterday. My first virtual session is tomorrow morning at 9:00."

"Samantha asked me to review each session with you and answer questions you may have. Covering two modules a week is daunting."

"What time tomorrow do you want to meet?"

"I could come by your place after dinner tomorrow around 6:30, or we could meet on Tuesday."

"Tomorrow's fine, but I can meet you at 3:30, if that's better for you."

"That works. But I hate to mess up your workday again. You're busy running a successful business, and you'll be busy all morning with the training session."

I peeked at Eddie, who stood behind Luke, and he gave me a thumbs up. Luke needed to realize I didn't think less of him for being a mechanic. A great profession, and he ran the business well from the look of things when I drove by the other day.

He insisted we meet at 3:30 the following day.

"I'd better go. Billy's making faces in the car." I dashed to my car door and waved at the guys. "I enjoyed lunch. One hot babe and three handsome gentlemen. What's not to enjoy?"

~

Luke watched Lanie drive away and sneered at Eddie. "She'll never be the same after your babe comment." He narrowed his eyes. "Why do you suppose she cared about the auto shop and my work there? Seemed odd to me."

Eddie shrugged. "Maybe she never thought you being a mechanic was an issue. She's gone out with me twice and knows I'm a mechanic. Could you have been wrong about her reasons for not returning to Pleasant Springs after college?"

"I doubt that. But over time, she may have changed her mind, and no longer feels the way she did." He strolled with Eddie to their vehicles. "I can't come up with any other reason for her to stay in Chattanooga."

"There's a simple way to learn the truth."

"And what's that?"

Eddie climbed into his car. "Ask her." He grinned. "Until you do, you'll drive yourself crazy."

Luke reflected on his afternoon with Lanie while he drove home. Was she flirty with Eddie to make Luke jealous, or was there something between them? Eddie would tell him if their relationship turned serious, wouldn't he?

No, Eddie wouldn't steal her away. But Luke told him he was no longer interested in Lanie.

Why had he placed all the blame on her? But if she didn't stay in Chattanooga because his profession embarrassed her, she must have known what he'd planned to ask her, and she didn't want what he wanted.

~

Monday morning, after I checked in at the office, I called Miss Risa to see if she was available for a visit. She asked me to stop by Baker's Dozen on my way and pick up her order of pastries for her 10:30 Bible study.

"Are you sure? I can come this afternoon if that's better for you."

"No, dear. This morning is perfect. Gives us plenty of time to visit."

Sam caught me before I left the office. "Is everything set for Luke's training and your follow-up with him?"

"He's completing the first training module this morning and we'll meet this afternoon for a review session."

"Good. Does that mean you've dropped the relative search like I told you to do, and you'll complete Luke's home study by the end of his training?"

"Yes, ma'am."

When she shuffled back to her desk, I rushed to my car. I'd need a lot more than a "W" to find Billy's grandmother. And after telling Sam that I had dropped the search, I needed to keep my word.

When I pulled into the bakery's lot, I peered across the street at PS Automotive. I knew two men there who'd enjoy a delicious treat. Inside Baker's Dozen, the smell of chocolate drifted past my nose. Brownies or cookies? Didn't matter to me. But what would Luke and Eddie enjoy? I decided on a brownie for each of us.

After I picked up Miss Risa's order and paid for mine, I zipped across the street to drop off two brownies. I nodded at a mechanic in the bay.

Eddie and Luke both sat in the office behind floor-to-ceiling glass windows with the door open. Eddie wore navy-blue coveralls and Luke sported jeans and a navy-blue polo shirt. "Hello?" I waved the bags in front of my face. "Would either of you like a treat?"

Luke jumped up and turned pale. "What are you doing here?" He closed his eyes and ran his hand over his face.

Why was he agitated? I glanced at Eddie.

He grimaced and dropped his chin to his chest.

"I see I'm not welcome here." I tossed the two small bags on Luke's desk and spun back toward the door.

A chair squeaked behind me. Luke followed me into the garage bay and touched my arm. "We weren't expecting you."

I flinched at his touch and faced him. "If that's the way you greet all of your unexpected customers, Mr. Gibson, it's a wonder that you have any business at all." I darted to the door that led outside and crossed the street, puzzled that he allowed me to leave and didn't try harder to explain.

My phone pinged with a text from Luke: I'll see you at my place at 3:30.

I gaped at my phone. No decent explanation? No apology? He didn't even thank me for the brownies. I drove to Miss Risa's and grew more irritated the closer I got to her home.

But when she met me on the porch wearing her cheery disposition, my tension eased. Her love and acceptance warmed my heart.

I handed her the box of sweets. "The bakery said there are six pastries inside. Does that sound right?"

"Yes." She opened the box and showed me her stash. "Which one would you like to share with me?"

The cream cheese Danish enticed me, but I declined and told her I had a brownie in the car for later.

She took the box inside and returned soon after. "Your call surprised me. Is everything okay?"

"Yes. I've enjoyed our visits and wanted to stop by for a chat." I frowned. "But after what just happened, I need a friend to talk to, and you seem to understand me better than anyone else."

She took my hands in hers and squeezed. "Let's sit." She pointed to the swing for me, and she sat in the rocker. "What's on your mind, dear?"

"Do you know Luke Gibson?"

"I remember he came to church with you and your family often, and I've had him work on my car a few times."

"I saw him before I drove out here and he acted odd, like he hated to see me. We've been working on something together, and I've tried to have a good relationship with him, but today he seemed aggravated. Like I was the last person he wanted to see."

"Will you be seeing him again soon?"

"This afternoon."

"Is there a reason you must *try* to get along?"

I lowered my eyes to her porch. "Our past." I gazed at Miss Risa and saw kindness and understanding. "We were best friends. We did everything together. But we never dated. When we had a date with someone, we always told each other. We didn't keep secrets. This continued through college."

I rose from the swing, moved to the edge of her porch, and stared out over her yard at a large maple tree. "When our graduation ceremony ended, I wanted to say goodbye to a friend, and Luke needed to meet with someone at the University Center. He asked me to wait for him in front of the library. He had something he needed to tell me before we drove to the restaurant where our families had gathered for dinner." I brought my finger to my lips and watched a cardinal take flight.

"After I waited for several minutes, I went to search for him. He sat at a table outside of the University Center with Stephanie Belmont, my freshman roommate." I hesitated. When I continued, my voice quivered. "I watched while he opened a ring box. She squealed, hugged his neck, and kissed him."

"Please come and sit down, dear." Miss Risa stood.

"I'll get tissues and be right back."

"I won't need tissues."

"Well, I might."

She padded inside, and I lowered myself onto the swing.

Miss Risa returned and handed me the box of tissues. "Go ahead, dear. Tell me what happened next."

"I hurried to where we were to meet, sat on the steps, and braced myself for the news he wanted to tell me before he announced it to his family. He'd proposed to Stephanie, and she'd accepted." I leaned toward Miss Risa. "Devastated at the realization our friendship was over, I couldn't come back home to Pleasant Springs."

"Why? You could have remained friends."

"Stephanie could be mean with jealousy. Once they were married, I wouldn't have gotten within 100 yards of Luke." I snatched a tissue and rubbed it along my nose. "But what upset me was that I didn't know he'd dated her. He never told me. And what made things worse was two weeks before graduation, I realized that I . . ." My heart ached too much to continue.

"What did he say when he found you at the library?"

"I didn't give him a chance to tell me anything. I told him I planned to accept a job offer in Chattanooga." A soft breeze blew across the porch. "He acted stunned by that news but didn't try to convince me to return to Pleasant Springs. I assumed he, too, thought that was for the best because of Stephanie's jealousy."

"Did he share the news at dinner?"

"Perhaps he did. I called my mom, thanked her and dad for coming to my graduation, and told her I didn't feel well and would call her the next day. I went to my apartment and never spoke to Luke again until seven days ago."

"Oh, my." Miss Risa joined me on the swing. "Let's pray and ask the Lord to reveal the truth. I'm sensing the same thing I've told you each time you've visited."

"Things aren't always as they seem?"

She took my hands in hers. Her prayer amazed me. A personal conversation with her Savior. Her words poured over me like a fountain of peace. When she finished, I believed the truth would come soon.

"You need to talk with Luke. To my knowledge, he never married."

"Stephanie must have changed her mind."

"Or he never proposed to her."

I stiffened. "But I saw—"

"You *think* you saw." She bowed her head for a moment and then looked me in the eye. "What if he showed Stephanie the ring he'd bought for someone else?"

Her stare sparked something within me, and I grabbed her arm. "Do you mean me?"

"Is that possible?"

My voice turned to a somber whisper. "But as far as he was concerned, we were only friends."

"But you loved him, didn't you? Could it be that he loved you too?"

I clutched my chest with one hand and covered my mouth with the other. "That means I, not Stephanie, let a great guy get away. For no reason except . . . stupidity."

Fifteen

I'd messed up. Or had I? Miss Risa couldn't know what Luke had planned that day. She didn't know him well. No. He'd proposed to Stephanie. She accepted but changed her mind. That had to be the truth.

But why was Luke rude when I took in the brownies? And Eddie? He acted embarrassed. About what? I didn't look forward to my afternoon visit with Luke. Returning to Pleasant Springs had brought nothing but trouble.

I needed Nashville to come through soon.

~

Luke tidied his cabin. Lanie would arrive soon, and he still didn't know how to explain his earlier actions. He didn't think she'd heard his conversation with Eddie, but he wasn't certain.

When Eddie asked why being a foster parent meant so much to Luke, he never expected Lanie to show up. If he'd ended the conversation with how he wanted to settle down and be a dad but thought it impossible with few available women in town, that would've been fine. Even if she'd heard him talk about his two broken relationships in the past eight years and the woman who'd turned down his proposal and married another guy.

Embarrassing situations but not as bad as if she'd heard how much he'd struggled with having her back in his life. Feelings he thought he'd buried years ago. She wouldn't be good for him. She'd hurt him again. *Lord, help me keep my mind and heart on You.*

He glanced outside. Lanie walked toward the cabin. He stepped out and met her on the porch.

She climbed the stairs, mumbled her greeting, and plodded into his cabin.

He followed her inside and let the screen door swing shut.

After she placed a notebook on the kitchen table, she sat back in a chair and crossed her arms. "Let's get this done."

Luke sat across the table from her. "I'm sorry about how I acted earlier. Eddie and I were in a personal conversation, and I was afraid you'd heard part of it."

She peered at him. "No. I only experienced your rudeness."

Luke moved to a seat next to her. "Again, I'm sorry."

She rubbed her temples. "This may take us over an hour to review, and it's important that I visit Billy this afternoon."

"Is he okay?"

She nodded and closed her eyes. "His teacher called and said he's struggling in class, and she asked me to help."

Luke moved back to his original seat and picked up

the notes he'd jotted down earlier during his training. "I could come with you and tutor him too. If it's not poetry, I'd be glad to help." He hated poetry.

She opened her eyes and in a stern tone said, "I wouldn't want you to spend any more time with me than necessary. You made it clear earlier you don't want me around." She flipped open her notebook. "Today's topic was Navigating the Child Welfare System. Let's review what you learned and see if you have questions on the homework assignment."

Luke's chest tightened. His aggravation with her elevated. "Lanie. I said I was sorry."

"Yes, you did." She scowled. "What questions do you have after today's training?"

His eyes remained on hers, and he reached across the table and touched her hand.

She yanked her hand away, stood, and forced a smile. "Mr. Gibson. Your questions, please."

Luke asked a few questions and Lanie answered them while she paced across his living room. When they finished their review, she grabbed her notebook.

"While you look over the homework, I'll inspect your home and make a few notes on my home-study checklist."

She lifted her chin and scribbled on her notepad. How could he pay attention to the assignment with her scrutinizing every inch of his cabin? She acted like a K9 sniffing for clues.

He glued his eyes to the required reading. Lanie distracted him several minutes later when she marched to the sofa and sat next to Mims, who slept curled in a ball. "Hi, Cat. You sure are a beautiful kitty." Lanie petted the cat's head.

Luke continued to read, and he wrote out a few more notes. He wanted to keep his eyes on Lanie, but if he did, she'd scold him again. The next time he peeked at her, Mims had sprawled out on Lanie's lap. Looked like the two of them had become best friends. An honor he once held with Lanie.

After they reviewed the assignment at the table, Lanie gathered her materials and stood. "When is your next training?"

"Wednesday morning at 9:00 in Chattanooga. I'll meet with the trainer." Luke suggested Lanie return on Wednesday afternoon to review the lesson.

She smirked and pulled out a sheet of paper from her notebook. "Here are items that need to be updated to pass your home study."

Luke scanned the paper. "Bathroom mirror, banister, locked cabinet in laundry room." He gazed at her. "Anything else?"

"Let me check your refrigerator again." She opened the door, examined a few items, and closed the door. "Looks much better today."

He thanked her when she returned to the table.

"You'll need a booster seat for your truck."

Luke jumped up. "No problem. I'll get these taken care of right away." He rubbed the back of his neck. "When may I see Billy again?"

She'd made it to the door and stopped with her back to Luke. "He'd love to visit the fire station. Could you arrange that for Wednesday afternoon too?"

"Before we meet for our review?"

She turned to face him. "I'll pick him up from school and meet you at the station. Afterward, I'll drop him off at Creekside and come here. We'll finish later than today, but he'll love to see the fire trucks."

Luke sounded hopeful. "I'll fix dinner. We can eat after our review and then finish the assignment."

"No. If you need to eat that early, we'll make our start time later." She opened the door and clomped down the stairs.

Luke stared after her. *Lord, should I try to break down the wall that stands between us or keep it there to protect me?*

~

Luke confirmed I was the topic of their conversation earlier that morning. What did he say that he didn't want me to hear? Must have been terrible. To review three more training modules with him sounded like more torture than I could bear.

But I knew what would help. A hug from my dad. He knew how to make me feel better. I pulled into my parents' driveway and climbed out of my car. The garage door opened, and Mom and Dad made their way toward me. They had dinner plans with friends in Chattanooga and needed to leave. What a letdown. I didn't even get my hug.

I drove to Jill's house, parked, opened my door, and slammed it shut again with me still inside. I'd forgotten to visit Billy. When I arrived at Creekside and found him in the visitation room, most of my troubles disappeared as soon as he greeted and embraced me.

"Have you been playing or doing homework?"

"Building a tower with Legos." He clasped my hand. "See?" He bumped into the table where a tall skinny tower stood, and it tumbled down onto the table and the floor. "Aww, man. Now I need to build it all over again." He slumped into a chair.

"I'll help you after we finish your math."

"Math stinks. Let's rebuild my tower first."

I pursed my lips. "Math first. Play after."

He stuck out his lower lip, placed his arms on the table, and laid his head on top of them.

"If you don't want to cooperate, I won't be able to stay and help you, and that would disappoint me, because I love Legos. My sister doesn't have any at her house."

He lifted his head and muttered. "Okay. Let's do math first." He brightened and wiggled in his chair. "Then build an even bigger tower."

After thirty minutes of homework, we built a bigger, stronger tower, and I said goodbye.

When I arrived home, Jill had homemade pizzas ready for us. "Where's Babs?"

"Chasing squirrels out back."

We sat next to one another at the table, and she asked about my day.

I shook my head. "Losing my position in Chattanooga was easy compared to what I've dealt with since coming home."

Jill scrunched her nose. "What happened?"

"Luke."

She touched my hand, which reminded me of him earlier in the day. Jill did it to comfort me. Why had Luke done it?

I told her about my visit to the bakery and automotive shop and how Luke and Eddie acted while I was there.

"Did he try to explain when you saw him this afternoon?"

I told her that he was afraid I'd heard their private

conversation. "Which means I was the topic."

"And you assume he told Eddie what a horrible person you became after college? And he must have been crazy to have ever called you a friend?"

"Something like that."

"But what if he told Eddie how much he'd missed you and how he wanted to take you into his arms and smother you in kisses?"

I stood and pushed in my chair. "Did Becca leave her romance books for you to read?"

Jill grinned. "No. But things aren't always as bad as we make them out to be."

I told her about Miss Risa's similar comment. "Why do I focus on the worst? He told me what he said was personal. I automatically thought that meant bad. May have been good, I guess."

Jill rose from her chair and hugged me. "Think good thoughts. You'll be happier." She released me and backed away. "Do you hope to rekindle your friendship with Luke?"

"Not possible, but I'd like that." I carried my plate to the sink. "I'll clean this up. Finish your romance novel and let me know how it turns out."

She chuckled. "What else, but happily ever after?"

LUANN K. EDWARDS

Sixteen

Miss Risa's house had become a regular stop for me—one of my favorite places in town. I visited her again on Wednesday morning. She had a way of opening my heart to explore new ideas. Ideas that didn't always resonate with me but left me wanting to know more. On this morning, she asked me to read to her again.

"Begin with Colossians Chapter Three." She handed me her Bible.

I opened to where she'd placed her bookmark. "Rules for holy living?" I cringed. "Are you going to preach to me today?"

"No, dear. I'd like you to read through verse fourteen."

I read aloud and came to verse twelve. "Therefore, as God's chosen people, holy and dearly loved, clothe yourselves with compassion, kindness, humility, gentleness and patience." I peeked ahead to verse thirteen—that dreaded theme again. "Bear with each other and forgive one another if any of you has a grievance against someone. Forgive as the Lord forgave you." I finished as if I hadn't noticed the forgiveness references. "And over all these virtues put on love, which binds them all together in perfect unity."

I closed Miss Risa's Bible, folded my hands on top of it, and stared at my lap. "I attended church on Sunday."

"That's nice, dear."

"I'm trying to be good."

"Good?" She stood and sat next to me on her porch swing. "You know the Scriptures. You can't earn your way to God. God's gift of grace is free to receive."

"But I walked away. I haven't been living for Him."

"Do you remember 1 John 1:9?" She shared a warm smile. "If we confess our sins, he is faithful and just and will forgive us our sins and purify us from all unrighteousness."

"Yes," I said, "and Romans 10:9. 'If you declare with your mouth, "Jesus is Lord," and believe in your heart that God raised him from the dead, you will be saved.'"

"What's holding you back from surrendering your life to Christ?" She patted my arm.

"Unforgiveness. I need to forgive Luke, but he keeps hurting me. Do I forgive and forgive again? Over and over?"

She grinned. "You know the answer to that."

I released a heavy sigh. "Yes. I do."

"Would you like to pray about this?"

I shook my head. "I'm not ready. But thank you." I hugged her and stood. "I focused on my challenges on Monday and forgot to ask you something when I visited. Did you enjoy having Becca back at church?"

"Indeed, I did. I hope they come to stay."

I descended the porch steps and turned to her. "If you are right about things not always being what they seem, it's possible something good will come out of seeing Luke again these past two weeks."

She nodded and waved. "I'll continue to pray for you."

I darted to my car, backed out onto the road, and said aloud, "Thank you, Miss Risa. I'm going to need lots of prayer."

~

Luke left his automotive shop and drove to the Pleasant Springs Fire Station at the corner of Main and West High Street to meet Lanie and Billy at 3:30. Something had bothered him for several days, and he needed to come clean with Lanie. When he stopped at the stop sign on Main, he shook his hands and rolled his neck to relieve stiffness. He had to tell her that Jill had access to Mr. Jed's emergency contact information. Luke hoped it wouldn't reveal a guardian for Billy but knew it might. He couldn't continue to hide the truth from Lanie. He rubbed his hands down his pantlegs and turned right.

He arrived at the fire station a few minutes early and waited inside. As a former volunteer firefighter, he would enjoy showing Billy and Lanie all the fire equipment.

Lanie and Billy strolled through the open station door hand in hand. Luke had to admit that she and the boy had developed a special bond in a short amount of time. Luke remembered her fun and compassionate disposition from years before, her caring manner and generous heart. She'd make a great mom. He blinked several times and averted his eyes to a bulletin board.

Billy waved and greeted Luke.

Luke looked him in the eye and ruffled Billy's hair. "I'm glad you're here. Are you ready for the tour?"

Billy released Lanie's hand and bounced up and down on his toes. "I want to see everything."

"Thank you for arranging this. I'm sure Billy will love his visit." Lanie furrowed her brows, backed away, and placed her hand on Billy's shoulder. "I'll be back in approximately what?" She peered at Luke. "Forty-five minutes?"

Billy pouted and grabbed her hand again. "I thought you were staying."

Luke narrowed his eyes at her. "So did I."

She sighed. "Errands to run. Going to be a late night."

Luke moved closer to Lanie and whispered. "I can throw a couple of burgers on the grill for a quick supper tonight while we work. Is that okay?" He wanted non-reviewing time to talk with her concerning Jed's possible relative.

She frowned and in an annoyed tone said, "Why?" She closed her eyes and bowed her head. "I suppose. If we don't take too long."

"Great. And you'll stay? For the tour?"

Billy wrapped his arms around her waist. "Please stay."

Lanie crouched in front of him. "I have things I need to do. Mr. Luke will take good care of you while I'm gone. I'll see you soon." She stood, placed Billy's hand into Luke's, and zipped out the door.

Billy tried to pull away, but Luke kept a firm grip. "Doesn't Miss Lanie like you?"

"What do you mean?"

"She seemed upset when we got here."

Luke gazed outside. "I'm not sure." He led Billy toward two trucks. "What do you want to see first? The fire truck or fire engine?"

He pointed to the fire truck. "This looks shiny and new."

Luke took Billy around the truck and showed him the equipment they use. "We have our protective gear, first aid items, and our search and rescue equipment, including special cameras to help us locate victims in a burning building." He strode to the front of the truck and opened one of the passenger doors. "Climb inside." He helped Billy in and climbed in next to him. "Some firefighters ride in here, others ride in the fire engine, and the rest meet at the scene of the fire."

"This is cool. Where's the siren? Can I turn it on?"

Luke chuckled. "Not a good idea. We don't want to make anyone think there's an emergency when there's not." He slid out of the cab and helped Billy down. "Let's check out the engine."

Billy focused on the fire engine with wide eyes. "What does this do?"

"This one arrives at the scene of a fire first with firefighters who put out the fire. This truck holds water, pumps, and hoses."

"Awesome."

"We have two tanker trucks, too, that we use when fighting a fire away from town. They hold more water than the fire engine and are kept at a different location."

Luke showed Billy around the bunk rooms, kitchen, showers, and laundry area. He included a tour of the property outside and introduced Billy to the two full-time firefighters on duty. "That's about it. What did you like the most?"

"I want to hear the siren. Are you sure we can't turn it on?"

"Sorry, buddy. Can't do." Luke and Billy returned to the front where the trucks were parked and talked about school, sports, and Grizzly.

"When can I come and see Grizzly again?"

"Whenever Miss Lanie can bring you."

"Tomorrow?"

Luke glanced up. "Ask her."

~

Luke and Billy must have hit it off well after I left. Before they saw me, they smiled at one another. When Billy spotted me, he ran to me and laughed. "This place is so cool. Come look."

He told me about the fire truck and how that differed from the fire engine. "And Coach Luke took me to the back and showed me a bunch of cool stuff there too."

Luke took Billy by the hand. "Let's show her inside the truck where the firefighters ride."

I followed. Luke would make a wonderful father figure for Billy. Kind, hard-working—a real man. And a godly one at that. I'd been too hard on him. Our difficulties happened years ago. Miss Risa was right. Time to forgive.

He opened the door to the truck, and I stepped up and poked my head inside.

"I agree with Billy. This is cool." I climbed down and hugged him. "I need to get you to Creekside. You don't want to miss dinner."

"But I want to see Grizzly."

I eyed Luke. "Will Saturday work for you?"

We agreed on Saturday afternoon. I told Luke I'd meet him at his place for our review session as soon as I dropped Billy off, which was only a mile away on East High Street.

Fifteen minutes later, I drove south on Main toward Luke's cabin. When I got out of town, I drove past blue flowers growing along the road, which reminded me of Luke in our younger days.

I pulled into his driveway and up to his cabin. He sat on the front porch steps. He'd changed from his navy-blue polo shirt to a mint green tee.

He looked good. I sighed. Too good.

Seventeen

Luke hollered from his porch steps when Lanie exited her car. "You need any help?"

"I'm good." She strolled toward him with her notebook. "Ready to get started?"

He opened the screen door for her and followed her inside. Grizzly raised his head from his sleeping position in the kitchen's corner and wagged his tail.

"Hey, boy. I'll come over to see you in a few minutes, okay?"

Grizzly laid his head down but kept his eyes on Lanie.

"He's dying for your attention." Luke chuckled. "You've got time to say hi."

"You're a sweet boy." Lanie knelt in front of Grizzly and rubbed his head and neck.

Luke sat at the kitchen table and waited.

She rose from the floor and took a seat across from him. "Today's lesson was 'Exploring the Impact of Trauma.' You covered a lot today on the brain, levels of stress, trauma, abuse, neglect, grief, and loss."

"Rather intense."

She nodded. "Billy has had a few angry moments

with me, but overall, he's dealt with this well. We're in a honeymoon period for now."

"Are you saying you think outbursts will follow?"

"According to his teacher, his anger has surfaced at school. We've taken him from all he's known and thrown him into a whole new world. We see it as a better place for him, but he misses and loves his mom."

"Do all children go through this?"

"Most have a time of either anger or withdrawal. The quiet ones internalize their emotions, and we need to watch for depression and self-harm."

He rested his elbow on the table and spread his hand over his forehead. "Is it your intention to scare me away from foster parenting?" He lifted his head.

"Not at all. This is part of the training for all foster parents. We need to keep you informed of the potential challenges you may face. This isn't as easy as what people think."

Luke's mind wandered while Lanie continued with her review. Was he equipped with what it took to be a good foster parent?

He focused again on Lanie. The lesson included a lot of information to read before his next session and videos to watch too. Luke tried to stop her halfway through, but she wanted to finish. By the time she wrapped it up, it was 7:00 p.m.

His stomach growled. "Ready for a burger?"

"I should go."

"Please stay. There's something I want to talk to you about over dinner."

"If it's regarding what happened on Monday morning, I'm fine. You don't need to explain further." She closed her notebook and folded her hands on top.

"I'm sorry I came across as rude. I never meant to hurt you."

"We're good."

He twisted his watch band around his wrist. "Great, but there's something else I need to tell you."

She hesitated. "Okay?"

"I'll get those burgers ready." But would she still be good after he told her about Jed's emergency contact person?

~

What did he need to tell me? I stood and scanned the living room and kitchen. "Where's Cat?"

Luke creased his brow. "I don't know. Maybe she's found a quiet hiding place somewhere and enjoying alone time."

I called for the kitty while Luke formed two hamburger patties and sprinkled seasonings on them.

"Would you set the table? I'll run these outside and fire up the grill."

"Sure." I found plates and napkins and placed them on the table a moment before Luke returned inside. "Ketchup? Mustard? What do you put on your burgers these days?"

"The same thing I've put on them for the past twenty years." Luke placed his empty burger plate in the sink with his back to me.

"Cheddar cheese, mayo, and Dijon mustard."

He spun and peered at me. "You remembered?"

"Of course." I tilted my head. Something seemed to click between us. A sparkle in his eyes. Was it possible to become good friends again? "Do you remember what I put on mine?"

He glanced away and strode to the refrigerator.

"Sure. Swiss cheese and yellow mustard." He opened the fridge. "Sorry. I don't have either."

"No problem. I'll try it your way." I stood beside him. "You check on the burgers, and I'll get out the condiments."

I placed the cheese, Dijon mustard, and mayo on the table and found two kinds of potato chips in the pantry. Regular and barbecue. After I placed the barbecue chip bag on the table, I opened the regular chips and pulled one out.

Luke came through the door and laughed. "I bet you can't stop with one."

"You know me too well." I popped it into my mouth and savored the saltiness and the crunch.

He grabbed the bag from the table and raised it over my head. "No more until we pray."

I turned my back to him and closed my eyes. I'm not a crier. But we'd played this little game for years.

"Lanie, are you okay? Did I insult you? I meant it to be funny." He placed his hand on my shoulder.

The first time since I returned home that I didn't mind his touch. "I'm fine." I turned to face him. "Are the burgers ready?"

He opened his eyes wide. "I'll be right back." He zipped out the door and returned with two beautiful patties.

I placed a hamburger bun on each of our plates and poured us each a glass of sweet tea. "Hurry and pray. I want another chip."

He grasped my hand, said a quick prayer, and asked me again if I was okay.

"The chips brought back memories." Good ones.

"We have a lot of those, don't we?" He released

my hand with a squeeze.

But none I chose to recall in front of him. "What did you want to talk about?"

He twisted his mouth and moved his head from side to side. "What should we do with Billy Saturday afternoon?"

"You come up with something." I peeked at my plate. "I'll drop him off and let the two of you spend time together."

"He'll want you here. He's easier with you around."

"But he'll be living with you. Not me. You need to bond with him." I leaned closer to Luke. "Are you having second thoughts?"

"Not at all. I see the special relationship you've built with him and hope you'll be around to help if I need advice."

"What makes you think I won't be around? I told you I'll check on you both from time to time, at least until Victor returns."

He brushed something from his shirt and rubbed the back of his neck. "That's right. I remember."

When we finished eating, I cleared the table and loaded the dishwasher while Luke took Grizzly outside.

Cat meowed and rubbed against my legs.

"There you are." I dried my hands and picked up the cuddly creature. Her purr delighted me.

Luke opened the door and Cat leapt from my arms and flew across the room.

"What just happened?" I stared at Luke with my mouth open. "Is she afraid of Grizzly?"

"Nope. She's not all that fond of me. Never has been." He shook his head. "But she seems to love you."

"Of course, she does. She knows a cat lover when she sees one." I grinned, washed my hands, and finished cleaning the kitchen.

Luke took a seat at the table and frowned.

"What's wrong? Are you upset that Cat likes me better than you?"

"I need to tell you something." He pointed to the chair across from him.

His face held a pained expression. I sat. My stomach fluttered while I waited to hear the terrible news.

"Something that I should have told you four days ago."

My heart rate increased. A confession? "Okay."

"I kept information from you concerning Billy." He folded his hands on the table and gazed at them. "He may have a relative that you may want to find."

I dipped my head to look into his eyes. "Did Billy say something?"

"Mr. Jed had to list an emergency contact on Grizzly's vet record. When I took him to Doc Winston's on Saturday, Jill updated Grizzly's record with my information."

"My sister has information about Mr. Jed's family?"

"She has information on his emergency contact. She couldn't tell me anything. Maybe it's Billy's mom, another relative, or a friend."

"Why didn't you tell me this Saturday afternoon?"

"I should have. I'm sorry." He reached across the table to touch my hand. "I was wrong to not alert you sooner."

I bolted from my chair and yanked my notebook

off the end of the kitchen counter.

"Lanie, please. Try to understand."

I whirled toward him. "No. You try to understand. You've put me in a tough spot. Our preference is to place a child with a relative. Even though it's only been four days, for me to follow up on this information now causes me to disregard my supervisor's orders to drop the relative search." I plodded toward the door and turned back to face Luke. "The only thing I can do now is to pretend I don't know a relative may exist."

Luke stood and in a soft tone said, "I'm sorry for putting you in this position."

"Do you mean you're sorry for keeping another secret from me? I see you haven't changed over the years." I stormed out the door, down the porch steps, and darted to my car.

Luke followed me out and shouted, "What do you mean?"

I slammed my car door to drown out his voice, backed up, and peeled out of his driveway, spewing gravel as I drove. I wasn't upset that there might be a relative. Sam clarified that if I found one, Billy's mom would never approve the placement, or she would have told us of a relative earlier. But it troubled me to think Luke kept another secret from me.

I couldn't trust him.

Eighteen

Thursday morning, while I set the table with bowls, milk, and cereal, I mumbled under my breath. "I've tried to be nice. Tried to be civil. But he's impossible to work with."

"Luke?"

"Who else?" I placed two forks on the table next to our bowls.

Jill widened her eyes and picked up the forks. "Spoons might work better."

I groaned. "He kept information from me that may have helped Billy. Information on Mr. Jed's emergency contact for Grizzly."

Jill placed spoons on the table. "Doc Winston said that's confidential information. I can't tell you anything more."

"I understand. Wouldn't do me any good now anyway." I had no choice but to let this go. I hurried through my breakfast, thankful for my spoon, and left for the office.

Soon after I arrived, Sam approached my desk and narrowed her eyes. "I have a courtesy visit for you to make. A teenager. She checked into Creekside thirty minutes ago. I told Todd that I'd send you right over."

"Courtesy visit? Where's she from?"

"Hamilton County. They need a place to keep her until another foster home comes available. They asked us to check our records for a placement, and they're checking with other counties too."

"What's her name?"

"They're sending me her profile."

I stood and grabbed my purse. "I'm on my way."

"Take thorough notes this time. I expect a complete report."

I zipped out the door to the parking lot to get away from Samantha. What did she mean by "this time"? I always kept detailed notes and reports.

At Creekside, Todd ushered me into his office and we both sat. "You're here to meet Kylee, right?"

My pulse quickened. "Is she the teen from Hamilton County?"

He nodded and opened a file folder. "James left yesterday, and we had plenty of room to take her in. I'm scheduling volunteers to spend the night for as long as she and Billy are here together. Something we don't have to do when there are only boys or girls."

"What's her last name?"

"Morris. She won't be an easy one. I can tell you that much."

Her name took me back five years, and I touched my chest. "I know her."

Todd rested back in his chair. "You've worked with her before?"

"She was my last case while I was still with the county. I haven't seen her in five years."

"She's a thirteen-year-old troubled teen." He

closed the folder and handed it to me.

When I opened the folder, a picture of a somber young girl with long disheveled blonde hair glared back at me. I scanned her records and gasped. "Seven foster homes in five years?" I covered my mouth with my hand and shook my head. "At eight, she was one of the sweetest children I'd placed." I continued to read the report. She'd run away, stolen money, broken other children's toys, constant cussing, truancy. The list continued. I glanced at Todd. "Where is she?"

"In the living room. But Billy might be in there too. I'll put you and Kylee in the study room." He rose from his chair. "Wait here."

I rested my elbow on the arm of the chair and rubbed my forehead. "What happened to my dear, sweet Kylee?"

Todd returned and stood inside his office door. "Steve tried to calm her. They're in the study room, but it seems you're the last person she wants to see."

"Another caseworker or me personally?"

He wrinkled his nose and stared out into the hallway. "You. Sounded—"

"Me?" I pointed to myself and jumped up. "We got along great." I marched past him into the foyer and hurried to the study room. I paused at the closed door while Kylee spoke harsh words about me.

Todd joined me and pulled out his phone. "I'll call Sam and ask her to send Ronni over."

I squeezed my eyes shut. "No." I leaned back against the wall to steady myself. "I've got to find out what's caused her to hate me." I placed my hand over his phone. "I don't think Sam likes me. Asking for Ronni could make things worse." I placed my palms on my cheeks. "Let me try to fix this with Kylee. Please."

He lowered his voice. "Okay. But I'll stay with you." He opened the door and entered before me.

My eyes met the eyes of an angry and desperate child. Would my recent review of traumatized children from the day before help me through the next several minutes—or hours—with Kylee?

~

Luke brushed loads of fur from Grizzly's coat Thursday afternoon before his Bible study guests arrived. He couldn't stop thinking about Lanie. He'd hurt her again. Something he didn't want to do. They'd been best friends for years and more than best friends to him. He wasn't worried any longer about losing the opportunity to be Billy's foster dad. If God wanted that for him, God would make it happen. But if he lost the opportunity to repair his relationship with Lanie, that would be a substantial loss. She meant a lot to him. She always would.

He patted Grizzly on the head and stood. But he needed to find out what she meant when she said his secret kept her away. He'd kept no secrets. She stayed away for her own reasons. No way could she blame that on him. But he had a reason to blame her. A good one.

~

I arrived home at 5:30 p.m. after I'd spent over an hour with a troubled teen who blamed me for her situation. I took a seat at the kitchen table with my head down, resting on my arms.

Jill entered the house through the door to the garage. "What's wrong? Did you have another rough day?"

I remained with my head down and muttered.

"Yes."

"Let's go out to eat. My treat." She placed her hand on my upper back. "You pick."

I moaned and lifted my head. "I don't want to go out."

"Let me know if you change your mind." She hurried through the kitchen and into the hallway. "If we stay home, I'll fix us each a peanut butter and jelly sandwich."

That sounded as awful as my day. "I scrambled down the hall and knocked on her closed bedroom door."

"La Casa. I'm in the mood for Mexican."

Jill opened her door. "Sounds good. Are you ready to go?"

She gave me a few minutes to freshen up, and we were on our way.

At the restaurant, we sat in the back at a quiet table for two and ordered grilled chicken fajita burritos covered in melted white queso. The delicious aroma of grilled onions and bell peppers drifted past my nose before the server placed my plate in front of me.

I grinned when I took my first bite. "This helps a little."

"Do you want to talk about it?"

"I don't want to even think about it. The most awful day since I became a social worker."

"Luke?"

"No."

Jill chuckled. "I'm glad to hear that."

"That I had a terrible day?"

"No. That Luke wasn't a part of your awful day."

We finished our meal and left the restaurant. Jill

headed south on Main Street toward her home, and I pulled out my phone to check my email and spend a few minutes catching up on social media.

I looked up at the sound of gravel underneath her tires and shuddered. "Why are we at Luke's cabin?"

Nineteen

Jill parked along the side of Luke's cabin near three other vehicles.

I clenched my teeth. "Why are we here?"

"I thought because you've gone back to church, you wouldn't mind attending a Bible study with me. I've wanted to attend this singles group awhile now. This will be a terrific opportunity for us to spend quality time together and meet new people."

"But with Luke?" I crossed my arms and narrowed my eyes. "We spend too much time together as it is. I'm upset with him, and he wants answers from me that will only make things more difficult."

"Be reasonable. He won't question you here during the Bible study. With all of us present, he'll be polite and kind, like he usually is."

"Great. I'll be the only grumpy person at the Bible study."

Jill opened her door and inched her way out. "Let's go."

I opened mine but didn't move. "I can't do this."

Jill eased her way to the passenger side of her car. "We will soon enter a nonjudgmental zone. This will be good for you."

I climbed out and slammed the door. "After a terrible day at work, you should have more compassion for your kid sister."

She chuckled and darted for the cabin. Jill was halfway up the steps when I called out to her.

"I can't." I strolled past the steps and trudged to my right, where I stopped to listen to the creek as the water trickled by and splashed against the rocks. The peaceful sound comforted my weary heart.

Jill clomped down the steps and laid her hand on my upper back. "The creek is beautiful. Calm."

"I could use calm and peace in my life."

"And I know where you can find both." She took my hand. "Inside at the Bible study that is supposed to start in five minutes."

I yanked my hand away and meandered along the creek and past the cabin. "Look at the delicate white flowers growing along the edge of the water."

Jill wandered farther down the creek and called out to me. "Look at *these* flowers."

I caught up to her and stared with my mouth open. "Forget-me-nots?"

"Brings back memories, right?"

"Are they wildflowers or did Luke plant them?"

"Either way, I'll bet he thinks of you every time he sees them."

"That was a long time ago."

The screen door squeaked, and we turned toward the cabin.

Eddie stood on the porch. "Y'all coming inside, or are you here on a field trip?"

"We're on our way." Jill pushed me toward the

door and stopped. "Look. There's more here along this side of Luke's cabin."

"I don't understand."

"He must have planted those." She grabbed my arm and tugged me forward. "Let's hurry inside. They know we're here. We can't back out now."

We climbed the steps and followed Eddie inside. I didn't see Luke. Did he know I was here? Natalie sat expressionless on one end of the sofa and a guy and gal shared the loveseat that faced the fireplace. Eddie introduced us to Jeff and Cassie and offered us the other two spots on the sofa. Jill took her seat along the opposite side, which left me the middle cushion. Next to Natalie. But I wasn't ready to sit.

I turned to Eddie. "Where's Grizzly and Cat?"

"Grizzly is in Luke's room, and I think Mims is upstairs."

I twisted my neck toward Jill. She opened her eyes wide.

"Mims?" I focused again on Eddie. "Luke told me the cat's name was Cat."

Eddie whispered. "Yeah. Don't tell him I told you. Her name is Mims."

Forget-me-nots and Mims. What was I to make of that? Made no sense. Luke missed me?

The bedroom door opened, and Luke slid through with his head turned back as if he were checking something inside. He clicked the door closed, backed up a couple of steps, and spun forward. When his eyes met mine, he took two steps back and raised his eyebrows. "Lanie. Great to see you."

He seemed to have recovered well from his surprise at seeing me without rudeness this time.

I thanked him and pointed to Jill. "She didn't give me a choice."

"Have a seat." He motioned to the sofa.

He and Eddie sat on two chairs in front of the window that overlooked the creek, and I took my place on the middle sofa cushion between Jill and Natalie. When they finished their chat about Natalie's day at Poplar Ridge High School, where she taught, Luke cleared his throat.

"We're a small group today. The others can't make it. But we're happy to have Jill and Lanie join us." He opened his Bible and tapped the pages with his finger. "We usually begin with fellowship and catch up on each other's week." He smiled. "Any news from anyone?"

Everyone remained quiet. Did Jill and I make everyone too uncomfortable to speak? Or perhaps I only made everyone uneasy. I'd sure caused problems for Kylee.

Jill nudged my elbow. I peeked at her and squinted. She leaned closer. "Tell them about your day. Someone can advise you or we can all pray for you."

I turned away from her. Under no circumstances would I share something that personal with a group of people like this. I'd look like a total failure.

Jill squirmed in her seat. "Lanie has a prayer request. Is now okay to mention that? She had a tough day today."

I glared at her and gritted my teeth. "Butt out."

Natalie patted my leg. "That's what we're here for. We study and pray."

I gazed straight ahead over Eddie's shoulder. I didn't want to look to my left at Luke. "I'm fine."

Luke sounded concerned. "Is Billy, okay?"

I nodded without looking his way.

"This is a safe place. If you have a request, we want to pray with you." Luke seemed sincere.

I pressed my lips together. I was afraid I might lose it. Angry with myself and emotional. What was wrong with me?

Jill rubbed my arm, and I released a heavy sigh.

"A young teenaged girl came into our care at the children's home today. My boss asked me to visit the girl." I rubbed my hands together in my lap. "When I met with her, I found out she hates me. I'd placed her in her first foster home five years ago when I worked for Hamilton County."

Natalie touched my arm. "She's upset with you for taking her away from her parents?"

I shook my head. "She was my last placement before I changed jobs to work for a private agency. She blames me for placing her in her first home, promising to be there for her whenever she needed me, and then deserting her."

Jill wrapped her arm around my shoulder. "She still blames you?"

When I glanced at Luke, he settled back in his chair and smirked.

In a sharp tone, I said, "What?"

"You want us to pray for what, exactly? That you won't hurt someone else like Billy when you move to Nashville?"

I leapt from my chair. "Nashville?" I turned toward Jill, but she didn't make eye contact with me.

Luke stood and met me face-to-face in the middle of the room. "Or pray that she forgets you abandoned her? You make a habit of that behavior."

"Who abandoned whom?" My hand shook. If no one else had been present, I would have slapped him. But people watched. I recoiled and dashed to the door.

His voice boomed behind me. "Or do you want us to pray regarding your unavailability when she needed you? I've experienced that feeling too."

I twisted the doorknob. It didn't matter if Jill followed me or not. I'd walk home.

"Where were you when I needed you to support me at my dad's funeral?"

I turned and took three steps toward him. My mouth dropped open. That couldn't be. I would have known. A chill ran through me. No words came. I backed away toward the door, grappled for the handle, and let myself out.

~

Luke scanned the room. Jill followed Lanie outside without a word to anyone.

Eddie stammered. "Are you for real?"

Luke returned to his chair, placed his hands over his face, and groaned. "I can't believe I did that. What kind of Christian am I?"

Eddie smacked Luke on the back of his head. "Aren't you going after her, bro?"

"I can't. Not tonight." He focused on Jeff and Cassie. "I'm sorry you had to witness that." He looked at Natalie. "You too. I'll talk to Lanie when she brings Billy for a visit on Saturday. I'll make it right."

Eddie huffed. "And how are you going to manage that? She opened her heart for help. What did you do?"

"I know. You don't have to make me feel worse. I'm a jerk with Lanie."

Jeff stood while Cassie fumbled with her purse. "We're going to leave. We'll pray for the Lord to give you wisdom when you talk to her again. Sounds like you've got baggage you need to deal with."

Luke agreed. "I'd appreciate your prayers, and I'm sure she would too."

They made their way to the door and said goodbye.

Natalie rose from the sofa and placed her hand on Luke's arm. "Don't be too hard on yourself. Jeff and Cassie will be back, and so will I. Not sure about Jill and Lanie, but you can work all that out if you want to." She bent forward, hugged his neck, and stepped outside.

Luke lumbered to the sofa and plopped onto a cushion. He tossed a throw pillow across the room. "I'm not sure Lanie will show up on Saturday. I messed up."

"Yes. You did." Eddie picked up the pillow. "And I hope I didn't make things worse."

Luke peered at him.

"I saw Lanie and Jill outside along the creek, while they admired your little blue flowers. So, when Lanie mentioned Cat, I told her your cat's real name." He grinned. "If you explain those things to Lanie, and the tough time you've had without her in your life, she might accept your apology."

Luke placed his head in his hands and moaned.

Twenty

Jill caught up with me in Luke's driveway. "I didn't realize how volatile things were between the two of you. I've never seen Luke so, so—"

"Unchristian?" I plopped into her car and crossed my arms.

After she climbed in and backed her car around, I said, "I was more of a Christian than he was, wasn't I?"

"This isn't a contest on who's the better Christian. We all have our bad days." She turned left on State Route 481. "The two of you have a lot of stuff to work through."

"I will not work out anything with him. He can jump off a cliff."

Sarcasm laced Jill's voice. "That's Christ-like of you."

My chin trembled. "Is it true? Luke's dad passed away?"

Jill nodded and pulled off the road into the co-op's parking lot.

"Why didn't you tell me? That's something that would have brought me home."

"I tried. I emailed you and left a voicemail, but you

didn't respond to either of them."

"How long ago?"

"Three years."

"Whenever you sent me anything with Luke on the subject line, I deleted it without opening. Or if you mentioned him in a voicemail, I didn't listen to the rest of the message." I stared out the passenger side window. "I understand his anger. His dad loved me like I was his own daughter. And I loved him."

"Don't be so hard on yourself. But I would like to know what happened between you and Luke that would cause you to delete anything that pertained to him."

"I'll tell you when we get home. But first, would you take me to Mrs. Gibson's house? I need to see her and apologize for not acknowledging her husband's death."

~

Luke sat at the kitchen table after everyone left the Bible study and peered at his cell while it rang. Now was not a good time to talk to his mom. She'd know something was wrong and lecture him on how he allowed this rift between him and Lanie to go on far too long.

"May as well answer the call." He greeted his mom in his cheeriest voice.

In a perky tone, she said, "You'll never guess who came to see me a moment ago."

His heart raced. "Lanie?"

She sounded defeated. "How did you know?"

"Did she tell you what a jerk of a son you raised?"

"Of course not." She paused. "Are you okay?"

"Why was she there?"

"She'd just heard about your dad's passing and

extended her condolences."

"And you believed her?" He chuckled. "She's known about this for three years. Why did she try to convince you that she found out tonight?"

"I believed her. She acted upset and as if she'd received the news a short time ago."

"Acted. All an act."

"Son, you have this all wrong. Lanie couldn't act if her life depended on it."

"Why do you say that?"

"Remember when the two of you were freshmen in high school? She wanted to audition for a part in the school play *Annie*. What a disaster."

"I was there. She messed up big time." Like he'd done with her earlier. "But a lot can change in almost twenty years."

"She wasn't acting. She wept in my arms and apologized at least three times for not being here."

"Okay, Mom. I've got to go." He thanked her for calling and disconnected the call. His mom believed the best about people, especially with Lanie. But he wasn't like his mom.

~

When we arrived home after my visit with Luke's mom, I dropped onto the couch, grabbed a throw pillow for my head, and stretched out on my back.

Jill knelt next to my head. "Are you ready to talk about this? To tell me what happened between you and Luke?"

I faced her, pulled my knees to my chest, and spilled out the story as I'd told Miss Risa. "He proposed to Stephanie."

Jill stood and paced across her living room and

repeated my story while she mumbled to herself. She flopped onto the floor next to my head and sat cross-legged. "Luke dated Stephanie but didn't tell you. You got upset by this because you felt he kept a secret from you. Right?"

"Yes."

"How often did they date?"

"I told you. Before the proposal, I didn't know they dated."

"If they dated, that means you and Luke spent little time together that last semester of school, right?"

"We were together all the time."

She lowered her voice to a whisper. "So, when would he have had time to spend with Stephanie?"

I shrugged and whimpered. "He must have hung out with her between classes. Or perhaps when I went with you to Knoxville to visit Mom and Dad."

"They would have had little time to develop their relationship between classes and the one or two visits we made to Knoxville."

I jumped up and raised my hand. "I know. During my field work away from campus." I shook my head and sagged onto the sofa cushion. "That doesn't make sense either. He worked an internship too."

"Then why do you think he dated Stephanie?"

"Because he proposed to her." I scowled. "This isn't rocket science."

Jill raised her voice. "Sis." She paused and frowned. "You messed up."

I opened my mouth to speak but nothing came out.

"What if the ring wasn't for Stephanie? What if he showed it to her on his way to give it to you?"

I closed my eyes. "That's what Miss Risa

suggested too."

"She's a smart woman." Jill placed her hand on my knee. "What would you have said if Luke had proposed to you that day?"

"I don't know." I squeezed my eyes shut.

"Yes, you do. You loved him. You still do."

I stood and winced. "No. You're wrong." I considered that possibility. "And even if you're right, he doesn't love me, and he never did. Except for you, no one cared whether I stayed in Chattanooga or came home after graduation." I stormed down the hallway to my room.

Jill called after me. "What are you talking about?"

I stopped inside my bedroom door and faced Jill, who'd followed me down the hall. "Not only did I feel betrayed by Luke, but ever since that day, I've told myself that I'm unlovable. Like no one cared or missed me."

"And that's why you didn't come home?"

"Mom and Dad had already moved to Knoxville, and you had recently married. I no longer had a best friend. Why come home?"

"I have something for you." Jill entered her room, opened a dresser drawer, and pulled out a small notebook. When she returned to the hallway, she handed me the book. "This is a journal I kept for you."

On the front cover she'd written, "Lanie's Someday Journal."

"Someday Journal?"

"I believed there'd be a day you'd need to read what's inside." She returned to her room and closed her door.

In my room, I sat on the bed and opened the

journal. Each entry gave the date and the name of a person who inquired about me.

"May 15, John Mason. He asked how you were doing and what kept you in Chattanooga. He said to tell you, hello." I sniffled. My high school principal?

"May 20, Miss Risa, Pastor Johnson, Natalie Simmons, and several others at church. They asked about you and why you didn't return to Pleasant Springs."

"May 23, Mrs. Gibson. She said she misses you. Mr. Gibson too. They hope you'll stop by to see them when you come home for a visit." I ran my finger over their names. A special couple. "They were also concerned about Luke." I tilted my head. Why? I wanted to ask Jill if she remembered any other details, but Luke's name was next.

"June 1. I took my car in for service, and Luke asked about you. Said you hadn't called or texted. He said to tell you he missed you."

I snapped the journal shut. Luke said he missed me? I reopened the notebook, glanced through the pages, and counted the entries with Luke's name. Although they'd slacked off in later years, I counted thirty-six inquiries in the eleven years I was gone. Thirty-six times that Luke asked Jill about me. I climbed off the bed, trudged across the hall, and knocked on Jill's door.

She invited me in and raised her brows. "Are you finished with the journal already?"

"I can't read it all tonight." I showed her the entry from Mrs. Gibson. "Do you remember why they were concerned about Luke?"

She sighed. "He experienced bouts of depression

after graduation. They didn't say whether it had anything to do with you, but they mentioned it when they asked about you. Which makes me think it did."

I sunk onto the edge of Jill's bed. "No. If he experienced depression, it was because of Stephanie not accepting his proposal."

"But you said she accepted."

"At first. But later, she must have turned him down. He told me on the first day I visited him that the woman he loved didn't return his affection."

"But what if that woman was you?"

156

Twenty-one

Friday morning, after my alarm buzzed for the third time, I still couldn't get myself out of bed. My head throbbed, and I wanted to hide under my covers.

"Are you up?" Jill pounded on my door. "Don't you have to take Billy to school?"

"Rats, Billy." I threw off my covers and rolled out of bed. "I'm up."

"May I come in?"

"Sure." I ran my hands through my hair to fluff it.

"That will not help. What happened to you? You look like you had a late night."

"A restless one." I dodged past her, entered the bathroom, and shrieked. "I look terrible and I'm running late. What should I do? I don't have time to shower."

Jill fussed over my hair and darted to her bathroom for concealer. The dark circles under my eyes gave away that I had indeed endured a rough night. After she doctored me up, I threw on jeans and a T-shirt.

"I'll take Billy to school, come home to shower, and grab a bite to eat." I hugged Jill. "Thanks for rescuing me."

"Where's your umbrella? You'll need it today."

"In my car. I'll run." I bolted out the door to my car. Not light rain, but a downpour. When I neared the passenger side, I slipped onto my backside in the wet grass. Not a good start to my day. I pushed myself up. The aches in my body matched the one in my heart.

~

Luke sat at his desk and perused his financials for the month. But he couldn't concentrate on them. He chastised himself for being hateful toward Lanie the night before. How would he make things right with her? He glanced up when he heard Eddie outside his office door.

"How did you sleep?"

"Not well."

"No surprise there. You blew up bigger than a hot air balloon last night."

Luke groaned. "I need to call Lanie and apologize, although I don't look forward to another confrontation."

"What happened to you, bro? You shocked all of us."

"I guess I'd stuffed it all inside for so long that it came flowing out. I couldn't stop it." He shook his head. "I've prayed and asked the Lord to forgive me, but . . ." He bent forward, rested his elbows on his desk, and cupped his cheeks in his hands. "How can I fix this? Mom believes Lanie didn't know Dad died. But how can that be?"

"Ask her."

"I should give her a chance to explain." He leaned back in his chair. "To explain that and why she never contacted me when she came home to visit. So many questions." He rubbed his chin. "I'm sure I didn't do or say anything to hurt her or to deserve her attitude toward me."

"Like I said before. Looks like God is ready to work all things together for good. But you've got to do your part."

~

After I returned home, freshened up, and ate a small container of vanilla yogurt, I spent time at the office updating reports to please Sam and reviewed Kylee's file.

Sam gloated and took a seat across from my desk. "Todd told me that you had a rough visit with our teen from Hamilton County."

"I plan to visit her again this afternoon."

"No need. I'll send Ronni over. I doubt today will go any better than yesterday."

I scooted forward. "She has every reason to be upset with me. But I'd like to try again and work through this with her."

"Todd asked me to remove you." She stood and squinted. "Stay away from the girl."

I plopped back in my chair. Why would Todd want someone else? At first, he wanted a different caseworker, but later he said another visit or two and he thought she'd calm down and be fine. Why did he change his mind and insist someone else visit Kylee?

I left the office and drove home to grab a bite of lunch. Jill pulled in a moment before me. Fridays were her half-day at work.

"How's your morning?"

"Not good."

She wrapped her arm around my shoulder. "Come on inside and tell me about it."

I updated her on Sam pulling me off Kylee's case.

Jill tried to reassure me everything would work out. We made peanut butter and jelly sandwiches and moved out onto the patio to eat. Babs followed us outside.

"Why do you think Luke named his cat after me and planted forget-me-nots?"

"Isn't it obvious?" She sat on her wicker bench. "He missed you and wanted reminders of you."

"But he did those things before his dad died. Right?" I took a seat next to Jill. "Now, he hates me. I know he hates me. He sure *acts* like he hates me."

"Did you read the entries in the journal after the date his dad died? He still asked about you."

"But not as often." I took a bite of my sandwich. "How old is his cat?"

"Ask him."

"You have the records. Did he buy the cat since his dad passed away or before?"

"I can't tell you. And besides, I don't know."

I peeked at a hummingbird slurping from Jill's feeder. "But you could find out tomorrow."

"Don't ask me to do that."

"Please?" I grinned.

"Does it matter?"

"Yes. If he named the cat since his dad's death, it would mean he still held fondness toward me, and perhaps our friendship is restorable, *if* he apologizes for last night."

My phone pinged. "Oh, no. A text from Luke. He wants me to stop by his place this afternoon at 4:30."

Jill nudged my arm. "God restores. Trust Him."

After lunch, I drove to Miss Risa's. The Bible was

what I needed, along with her wise council.

She sat on her front porch. "I hoped you'd stop by."

I climbed her porch steps and peered at her patio furniture. "Where's your Bible?"

"Oh my. Would you like to read to me today?" She padded inside and returned with her Bible. "Have a seat, dear. I have a wonderful chapter for you. One of my favorite books in the Bible." She opened it, handed it to me, and we sat across from one another.

"Ephesians, Chapter Four." I read the first two verses, stopped and reread verse two. "Be completely humble and gentle; be patient, bearing with one another in love." I paused and looked at Miss Risa. "That's hard."

She nodded.

I read to the end of the chapter. Verse thirty-one talked about getting rid of bitterness and anger. And verse thirty-two said to be kind to others and forgive them as Christ forgives us. Seriously, God? Now this?

"But Luke hurt me, and he proved last night he's angry with me too."

"Turn to Proverbs 17:9. What does it say?"

I flipped back to the Old Testament. "Whoever would foster love covers over an offense, but whoever repeats the matter separates close friends." I frowned. "What does that mean?"

"My dear, Lanie. A friendship can't survive when you dwell on the other person's faults. But when you overlook their mistakes, love wins."

"I'm sorry. I don't get it."

"If what you saw years ago was the truth, you've allowed that one thing to come between you and Luke.

You've blamed him for one mistake—not telling you he was dating someone. Your relationship that had lasted for fourteen years ended in a single moment when you saw something you didn't give him a chance to explain."

In an introspective tone, I said, "I dwelt on his fault of not telling me he was dating Stephanie, when I should have overlooked that to keep our friendship intact."

"That's it."

"He named his cat after me and planted forget-me-nots in his yard." I sniffled.

She widened her eyes. "What dear?"

"You and Jill both think Luke planned to propose to me." I looked down and placed my hand on my forehead.

"Let me run inside and grab that box of tissues."

I waved her off. "I'm fine. But please pray for me. I need to meet with a troubled teen at Creekside this afternoon and with Luke at his home." I shared a condensed version of Kylee's story and stood. "Thank you for listening to my troubles, but I need to run."

Miss Risa also stood, squeezed me in a tight hug, and promised to pray.

Time for me to pray too. If God will even listen.

Twenty-two

On my way to Creekside later that afternoon, I whispered a prayer, but would the Lord care? Had He given up on me? He hadn't been my top priority for several years. Besides that, I still needed to forgive Luke.

Inside the children's home, Billy spotted me in the foyer and ran to me.

"Slow down or you'll knock me over."

He wrapped his arms around me. "Can I go see Grizzly now?"

Although he hadn't run into me, my stomach lurched, and my legs weakened. I had to spend time with Luke that afternoon and the following day, too, with Billy. "Tomorrow afternoon."

"Can we go in the morning and spend all day?"

I shook my head. "How's school?"

"Okay." He grabbed my hand. "Come with me. I have a new friend here."

I followed him down the hallway and into the living room where Kylee sat with an opened book.

"Is Kylee your new friend?"

"Do you know her?"

Kylee looked up and frowned. "Are you going to lie to him like you did to me?"

Billy wrinkled his forehead. "She doesn't lie to me."

Kylee stood and eyed me. "Yes, she does. Wait and see." She strutted through the kitchen toward the front of the house.

Billy clung to my arm. "You don't, do you?"

"Let's sit down for a minute and talk."

We sat side-by-side on the sofa.

"I care about you, and I care about Kylee. But sometimes things change. I placed her in a home, told her I'd check on her, and then another agency offered me a new job. I couldn't visit her again."

"You wanted to see her, but you couldn't. Like my mom."

I grinned. "Yes. Your mom wants to see you, but she can't right now."

"After I go to live with Coach Luke, will you come to see me?"

With Sam being disappointed in my work, I had to be careful how I answered him. "If I still work at my same job, yes. If not, I'll visit you if Mr. Luke invites me to his house. Or I might attend your church and see you there."

Billy brought his hands together. "Okay." He slid off the couch and told me it was snack time, and he didn't want to miss it.

I wandered to Todd's office and knocked on his opened door.

He rose from his chair. "Come on in and have a seat."

We sat and I crossed my legs. I wanted to ask about Kylee, but he interrupted me.

"I have a message here for you." He held a sticky note. "Teresa said she and Steve will get Billy to school for the rest of his stay here."

"Oh?" I tilted my head to the right. I'd miss not having that time to spend with Billy. "Is this because I ran a little late this morning?"

"No. Steve thought it would be nice to have some one-on-one time with Billy since Teresa picks him up in the afternoon."

"Okay." I thanked him. "May we discuss Kylee?"

He reached for a paper clip and leaned back in his chair. "I know it didn't seem like you accomplished anything yesterday when you were here to see her, but she's better today. She met with two of her teachers online and completed her assignments. No problems. We were all pleased."

"Does that mean I can talk with her again?"

He furrowed his brow. "I don't know why not." He stood and tossed the paper clip onto his desk. "Let's put you in the visitation room. I'll watch from my office window to make sure everything goes well."

He led me to the visitation room and left to find Kylee while I took a seat at the table.

Todd returned to his office, and Kylee plopped into the chair across the table from me.

"Don't they have someone else who can talk to me?" She slumped back and dangled her arms.

"Is that what you want? Or would it be better for us to work through this?"

She gazed off into space and answered with an attitude. "I don't care."

"If I could go back five years and do this over again, I would. I never meant to hurt you."

"You mean lie to me?"

"Yes, if you want to get technical, I lied to you. But it wasn't intentional. I didn't know a job I'd applied for three months earlier would come through. They called the day after I placed you and offered me the job if I'd start within a week."

"Why didn't you tell me?" She sneered.

"I tried. I called the lady you lived with and asked if I could stop by to see you and tell you goodbye. She said things were going well, and she didn't want to upset you with that news because you'd lived with them for less than a week. She promised to tell you within a few days."

"She told me the day before my first visit with my new caseworker."

"I'm sorry." My chin quivered, and I pressed my hand against my stomach. "I didn't mean to hurt you. I hope one day you'll forgive me."

She jumped up and knocked over her chair. "I don't think so." She darted out the door and called me an ugly name.

I strolled through the kitchen and told Billy I'd see him the next day. On my way out, I stopped by Todd's office and stood in his doorway. "No yelling today."

He smiled. "She'll come around. We talked earlier. She wants to believe you're still that person who cared about her when she entered foster care five years ago."

I thanked him. "Will it be okay for me to check on her tomorrow?"

He arched a brow. "That's always fine. Why do you ask?"

"Sam said you wanted Ronni to visit Kylee." I entered his office and stepped to his desk.

He raised his eyebrows. "She must have misunderstood."

"Or I may have misunderstood her." I thanked him again, left Creekside, and headed south on Main Street toward Luke's.

Had Sam lied to me? Why would she do that? Was my job in jeopardy?

~

Luke had prepared a crock pot filled with roast beef, potatoes, and carrots before he left for the auto shop. The aroma lured him when he rushed into his cabin at 4:30. He lifted the lid, stuck in a fork, and enjoyed a mouthful of goodness.

Relieved he'd arrived home before Lanie got there, he let Grizzly out and met him on the porch a few minutes later for a good brushing. Such a hairy dog. He listened for a car, but only heard birds chirping in the trees. Was Lanie too upset with him to show up? He couldn't blame her.

His phone pinged with a text: Leaving Creekside now. Be there in fifteen.

Luke strode to the far side of his cabin, picked a handful of forget-me-nots, took them inside, and placed them in a small vase on the kitchen table. If nothing else, they would be a conversation starter. While he waited, he paced across his living room and prayed for wisdom. At the sound of spewing gravel, he strode to the door and opened it when she climbed the steps.

"Come on inside." He backed away and allowed her plenty of space to enter, and once she was inside, he followed her into the kitchen.

"Smells good in here." She placed her purse on the table, touched her throat, and turned away.

His posture relaxed. Had she seen the flowers?

"Roast beef with potatoes and carrots. I hope you'll stay for supper."

"I've had a long and exhausting day."

He pointed to the sofa.

"Why did you ask me to come? Do we need to review one of the earlier lessons?"

"I thought it would be good to talk about last night."

She grimaced and placed her hand on her forehead while she focused on the flowers. "Why do you have forget-me-nots on your table and in your yard, and why is your cat named Mims?"

Luke chuckled. "You should see your face all contorted."

"My apologies for an awful face."

"I didn't mean to insult you. You looked cute." That was not a good thing to say. "I mean, you reminded me of a long time ago when you'd get upset with something I said. You'd make that same face."

Her tone softened. "Oh? My face brought back childhood memories?"

He blinked several times and moved to the sofa. After he sat on the end closest to the kitchen, he patted the cushion next to him.

"Ten minutes." She joined him on the sofa but took a seat on the opposite end.

"I need to apologize for my disgusting behavior last night. I allowed a lot of sludge to ooze out. Wasn't fair to you or to my other guests."

"Ooze? More like gush."

He glanced toward the front windows.

"You carried your attack too far. To imply that I might move to Nashville and hurt Billy was one thing, but to say I abandoned you makes no sense at all."

Luke twisted toward her. "I expected you to return to Pleasant Springs."

She folded her hands. "I'm sorry I wasn't here to support you at your dad's funeral." Her chin trembled. "But I didn't know."

"Explain that to me. I sent you an email and a text giving you all the information."

"I never got the messages because I changed my email address twice over the years and my phone number once. You must have sent them to the old ones."

"Jill? She didn't tell you?"

Lanie squirmed. "She tried. I wouldn't listen."

He scooted over onto the middle cushion. "You didn't listen to her when she called you? You didn't read her texts or emails?"

Lanie stood and narrowed her eyes. "We've spent too much time on this conversation. I need to go."

He grasped her hand and tugged until she sat. "We're not finished." He stared at her and waited for her to respond.

She focused on something out the front window. "I deleted all emails, texts, and voicemails from Jill and anyone else who mentioned your name."

"My name?" He pointed to his chest. "Does this have anything to do with the secret you think I kept from you? The secret that kept you away for eleven years?"

She nodded and continued to stare straight ahead.

Luke needed to be gentle with her, but he needed to understand what ended their friendship.

He knew of no secrets.

Twenty-three

A bluebird outside Luke's front window mesmerized me. Beautiful blue head and wings with an orange chest.

Luke whispered, "What secret, Lanie?"

Risa and Jill didn't think he'd kept any secrets from me. They believed Luke wanted to propose to me. How could I tell him if that's what he'd planned to do? That would mean I ruined the last eleven years of our lives.

He jiggled my arm. "Talk to me."

"I believed something to be true that may not have been true at all." I bit my lip. "Were you honest with me when you told me that you'd never dated Stephanie?"

"We're back to Stephanie?"

I wiped my brow. "Please open a few windows. I'm warm."

He did as I asked and returned to my side on the sofa.

My chin quivered. "You proposed to her."

Luke gawked. "Are you crazy?"

I told him what happened the afternoon after

graduation and what secret I thought he'd kept from me. The secret of dating Stephanie.

His face turned red. "Was that when you decided to stay in Chattanooga and not return with me to Pleasant Springs?"

"I knew she'd never let us remain friends. She majored in Jealousy 101."

He jumped up, grabbed a throw pillow from the end of the sofa, and plopped it onto the loveseat. "How could you have been so . . .?"

"What? Stupid?" I squeezed my eyes shut. "You never proposed to her?"

"Of course, I didn't. The ring wasn't for her."

Help me, Lord, to be honest and tell him the rest. I opened my eyes, stood in front of Luke, and touched his upper arm. "It crushed me when I saw the two of you together. Only two weeks earlier, I realized my feelings for you had changed." My pace picked up. "I'd fallen in love with you. When I saw the two of you together, I put a wall around my heart and pushed you away by staying in Chattanooga. I *was* stupid and I'm sorry. Very stupid. Probably the stupidest I've ever been in my entire life."

He took a step backward, pinched his lips together, and pointed at me. "You're sorry? Me too. Eleven years. You threw away. Eleven. Years."

My heart rate increased. "But why didn't you try to stop me? You gave up without hesitation."

He balled and released his fists. "I thought you didn't want to be associated with a mechanic or you assumed I'd planned to propose, and you didn't have the heart to tell me no." He slumped his shoulders.

"I'm not the only one to blame here." I slipped past

him and moved toward the table. "Time for me to go." I picked up my purse. "I'll drop Billy off here around 1:30 tomorrow afternoon, if that still works for you. He's looking forward to seeing you and Grizzly."

His face and tone softened. "Could we take Billy to Fall Creek Falls for a hike after he plays with the dog? Only an hour from here."

"Wouldn't you rather stay closer to home and spend time alone with him to bond?"

"You told me to come up with something, and this is what I'd like to do."

"Okay." We hiked there several times in the past. But why did he want to go back? "We'll see you tomorrow." I placed my purse strap over my shoulder and turned my back to him. I stared at the flowers on the table.

Luke nudged my elbow. "You asked about the forget-me-nots and Mims. Reminders of you."

~

Luke watched Lanie return to her car. She wasn't the only one who'd messed up. He should have tried to find out why she'd stayed in Chattanooga. He gave up too soon. Now what? They still needed to work through this. They would spend time together with Billy the next day and needed to come to an understanding before then. He descended the porch steps and jogged to Lanie's car, where he saw she was on her phone. He tapped on the driver's side window.

Lanie jerked, disconnected her call, and opened her car door. "What?"

"Dinner is ready."

"Dinner?"

"We need to talk before tomorrow afternoon. Billy

doesn't need to sense this tension between us again. He knew something was up when you didn't stay at the fire station. Let's see if we can break through this barrier we've both put up."

She snatched her keys, climbed out of her car, and followed him inside.

~

I hadn't realized how much I missed him over the years. I hadn't allowed myself to dwell on the past, and I'd buried myself in my work and the families I served. But now? Was there any hope that we might become at least friends again?

"That smells good."

"Have a seat. I'll get the plates and scoop us up some grub."

We enjoyed a delicious meal but kept the conversation simple until he asked me about Nashville.

"I applied at two agencies but have heard nothing from either of them."

"Are you still looking?"

"No time. I've been busy with you and Billy." I smiled.

"Does that mean if I keep you busy on weeknights and weekends, you'll stay in Pleasant Springs?"

"How many more foster children are you planning to house?"

Luke stood. "Ready for dessert?"

Did he mean something other than foster children? Did he want to spend more time with me?

"I have chocolate almond ice cream."

"Sounds great, but I ate too much."

He gathered our plates and carried them to the sink. I joined him at the dishwasher and loaded the dirty dishes while he put the leftovers into the refrigerator. After we'd finished, he asked if we could talk.

"Didn't we do that earlier?"

"Let's make sure we agree."

I made my way to the sofa and took a seat at the far end. "Okay."

Luke sat in the middle next to me. "We both messed up eleven years ago. I should have questioned you more about your wanting to stay in Chattanooga."

"And I should have kept my mouth shut about staying and given you a chance to propose."

"That would have been nice."

"I'm sorry. If I hadn't left the spot where you asked me to wait for you, I wouldn't have seen you with Stephanie, and we'd be married with kids of our own."

"And if I hadn't shown her the ring . . ."

"Why did you?"

He rubbed the back of his neck. "She'd suspected I liked you for more than just a friend ever since you were roommates. After I met with my buddy at the University Center, I ran into her and showed her the ring." He grasped my hand and held it. That wasn't something common for us. We'd been great friends, but nothing intimate.

I gazed at our hands. A personal bond. But what did that mean?

Luke yanked his hand away and moved to the loveseat.

Apparently, the handholding meant nothing.

He sighed. "We sat too close." He crossed his ankle over his knee.

"Oh." My heart fell.

He shook his head. "Can we agree to let this go?"

"Let what go?"

"The whole graduation misunderstanding." Tension edged his voice. "Forgive one another. We both messed up."

"I'd like that." I rested my head back on the sofa cushion for a moment.

"Are we ready to call a truce?"

I nodded. "But what does that mean to you?" Did he want what I wanted? A renewed friendship?

He shrugged and sagged back into his seat. "We stop fighting against one another and work together as a team to get Billy placed in my home."

I flinched and widened my eyes. All of this was about Billy? Figures. Everything has always been about him. "Sure." I stood and balled my fist at my side. "And if I get fired, you won't have to worry about fighting against me at all."

He sat forward and uncrossed his legs. "What do you mean, get fired?"

"I'm in danger of losing my job."

"Did my interference with the relative situation cause problems?"

"Sam doesn't know about that. I dropped it because Billy's mom won't approve of a relative."

"Then what?"

"I don't know for sure." I crossed my arms. "But I imagine she has a notebook full of bogus charges against me."

Luke rose from the loveseat and moved in front of me. "If I have nothing to do with that, why do you sound upset with me again?" He placed his hands on my upper arms. "I loved you. I've never experienced that same kind of love with anyone else. But this is hard for me. I want you here, but then I don't. We lost a friendship that's going to take time to regain." He hesitated. "If we want it back."

"I get it. You don't want to be friends."

"That's not what I said."

The skin on the back of my neck tingled. "Well then, what is it? Do you want to work on our friendship or not?"

"Yes."

"Because you want me to approve you to be Billy's foster dad?"

His cheeks glowed. "No, Lanie." He took a step closer. "Because someday I want to do this."

He lifted my chin and kissed me. A sweet, tender kiss.

Twenty-four

A kiss I never thought would happen happened, and I'd blamed God for something that had never happened. Luke hadn't kept a secret from me or betrayed me.

When I'd gone to my car before supper with Luke, I'd called Miss Risa to ask if I could stop by that evening or early the next morning. She said Saturday morning worked best for her. I arrived at her place at 8:10 a.m. With temperatures in the mid-fifties and an eighty percent chance of rain, I thanked her for inviting me inside.

She lived in an older home she kept spotless. Her living room held a sofa, two straight-back chairs, a grandfather clock, and a baby grand piano.

"Do you play?"

"A little. My husband played well." She smiled. "Your sister still plays, doesn't she?"

"Yes, but she doesn't have a piano. I'm not sure if she sneaks over to the church when no one's there to play or not."

"I hope she'll be able to practice at the church when Becca returns to Pleasant Springs."

"Have you heard anything? Did they decide to take

the position?"

She pointed to the sofa, and I took a seat. "Yes, but please say nothing. They want to announce it tomorrow at church. Why not join us?"

"That's what I wanted to talk to you about."

"Yes, dear?" She sat on my left.

I glanced around her living room and peered at her. "I need to confess something."

"To me or to the Lord?"

"The Lord. But I want to share the moment with you because you've helped me rediscover my need for God in my life."

She patted my leg. "Go ahead, dear."

"You and Jill understood what took place on graduation day better than I did." I confirmed with her that Luke had planned to propose to me. "I turned from God when I thought Luke was untrustworthy and then I blamed the Lord."

Miss Risa reached for the box of tissues that rested on her end table. "We all make mistakes. What are you going to do about it?"

"I apologized to Luke, and now I need to pray and ask the Lord for forgiveness. I want to recommit my life to Him. Will you share this moment with me?"

"I'd love to." She took my hand. "God knows your heart. Talk to Him. He loves you more than you can imagine."

I bowed my head and prayed. I confessed my sins and asked God to forgive me and thanked Him for His Son, Jesus, who died for me. When I looked up at Miss Risa, her eyes filled with tears.

She hugged me and held me close. "I had a feeling that today was the day. Thank you for allowing me to be a part of this special moment."

My heart filled with peace, and I thanked Miss Risa for the blessing she'd been to me since my return to Pleasant Springs.

I headed home to relax awhile and eat a quick bite. On my way to my car after lunch, Jill arrived home from her part-time job with Doc Winston.

She pulled into the garage and met me in the driveway. "Where are you off to?"

I told her my plans for the afternoon.

"Luke and Billy? How are things between the two of you?"

"Billy and I get along well most of the time."

She scowled. "You know that's not who I meant."

I giggled. "Luke and I met yesterday afternoon to talk, and today we're taking Billy to Fall Creek Falls."

"Did your talk go well?"

I stared at my car, which I'd parked on the street. "Later. I've got to run."

She walked down the driveway with me. "Pastor Oldham will announce tomorrow that Becca and Ben have accepted the pastorate for our church."

"I'm sure you're thrilled."

"Are you still okay if she stays with us while she looks for a house and while Ben finishes at Hart Fellowship?"

I stopped in front of my car. "Great. That should be fun."

"Are you being nice, or do you mean it?"

"I love the idea." I gave Jill a brief hug and climbed inside.

Before I closed the door, she said, "Are you okay? You seem a little giddy today?"

"Beautiful days do that to me."

She wrinkled her nose and waved while I pulled away from the curb.

Jill would realize something happened. The dark clouds in the sky weren't all that beautiful.

~

Luke putzed around his yard and pulled a few weeds while he waited for Lanie and Billy to arrive. He stopped to watch Grizzly paw at an insect. The dog had been a delightful companion since he joined the family. And Lanie . . . would she become . . . no need to go there. He'd forgiven her for the mess after graduation and for not attending his dad's funeral. And after what she'd shared, he understood why she never came to see him when she returned home.

But could he let go of the fact she had never visited his parents? Her visits would have meant a great deal to his dad. And maybe he would have committed his life to the Lord.

And what about his own relationship with her? He'd moved from the sofa to the loveseat because he wanted to kiss her but knew that was a mistake. Then he kissed her anyway. He asked the Lord to help him slow down and to be sure before his lips met hers again. He still needed to talk to her more regarding his dad and get that out in the open. But what would it accomplish? Besides, he could tell she wasn't where she once was with the Lord. He brooded. He hadn't been such a great Christian either since she came back.

Twenty-five

When I arrived at Creekside, Billy sat on a bench in the foyer near the front door.

He ran toward me. "I get to see Grizzly now."

"And after you play with him, we plan to hike to a waterfall."

"You mean I have to walk a lot?"

I nodded.

"Can't we stay and play with Grizzly?"

"If you don't want to go on a hike, I can bring you back here early, and Mr. Luke and I will hike without you."

He furrowed his brows and took my hand. "I'll stay with you and Coach Luke."

Kylee trudged past us with a frown on her face but appeared less disheveled than when I saw her the past two days. "Smart kid. Anything beats sticking around this deadbeat place." She peered out the front door and turned back to me. "When are you going to take me somewhere?"

I held back a smile. "When and where would you like to go?"

She shuffled her feet and focused on the floor. "A

hike sounds good.”

Billy jumped up and down and clapped his hands. “You can come with us now.”

Kylee glanced at me and raised her eyebrows.

“If Mr. Luke has no objection, and your caseworker from Hamilton County agrees, Billy and I would love to have you join us.”

Her lips twitched upward for a second.

“I’ll shoot Mr. Luke a text and call your caseworker.” I backed away, sent the text, and headed to Todd’s office, where I told him I’d like to take both Billy and Kylee with me for the afternoon.

“That’s a great idea. She needs someone like you to take an interest in her.”

I looked down at Luke’s response: **Yes**.

I called the number for her caseworker but didn’t get an answer. Todd suggested I call Jerome Gower, Hamilton County’s regional director. He was my supervisor when I’d worked for the county, and I knew him well. He was happy to approve our outing.

I met up with the kids in the living room and asked Kylee if she was ready to leave.

“Yes.”

I looked at her feet. “Do you have a pair of tennis shoes? Flip-flops are not the best for hiking.”

“I’ll be fine.” She headed toward the front door.

We followed her into the foyer.

“Billy and I will wait here for you.” I pointed to the bench along the wall, took Billy’s hand, and we sat.

Irritation rose in her voice. “I said these shoes are fine.”

“And we’re waiting for you to change into something more appropriate for walking long distances."

"Do what she says, Kylee. I want you to meet Grizzly."

Kylee stood with her hands clenched. "I'm not going. I'll stay here."

Billy grabbed my elbow. "Make her come with us. I like her."

I rose from the bench, faced Kylee, and peeked at my watch. "We're late. Billy and I are leaving now. Think of something you'd like to do tomorrow to get out of this deadbeat place and let me know. I'll get approval and come by and pick you up after church." I grasped Billy's hand and walked toward the front door.

"Wait. I'll be right back." Kylee zipped through the kitchen and toward her room.

I wasn't sure if she wanted to hike with the three of us or didn't want to spend time with me the following day. But I was glad she agreed to join us.

~

Luke and Grizzly met Lanie, Billy, and Kylee at the bottom of his porch steps when they arrived at 1:45.

Lanie apologized for their late arrival. "Looks like you and Grizzly are enjoying this beautiful day."

He wanted to stare. A glow surrounded her lovely face. "I'm glad the rain stopped this morning to give the ground a little time to dry before our hike." The back of his neck prickled. Did her joy have anything to do with his kiss?

"Me too." She motioned for Kylee to come closer and introduced her to Luke while Billy ran off and laughed, with Grizzly moseying behind him.

Lanie watched Billy and the dog while Luke asked Kylee questions concerning what she liked to do. When he asked about her favorite subject, Lanie turned to face them.

"I can answer that. She loves art and music." Lanie grinned. "How's my memory?"

Kylee grimaced. "Must be in my file."

Lanie took a step closer to her. "No. I didn't see it there. But I remember you drawing a picture of mountains, rivers, and trees for me. I still have it."

Kylee widened her eyes and straightened her shoulders. "And what instrument did I like to play?"

Lanie scanned the blue sky peeking through the clouds before she answered. "Guitar. Do you still have it?"

Kylee shook her head. "It broke." She frowned and traipsed across the gravel driveway to the creek.

Lanie eyed Luke. "Should we leave soon?"

"Yes. But you have time to talk with her."

She thanked him and made her way to Kylee.

Luke didn't feel good about listening in on their conversation, but curiosity got the best of him. He kept his eyes on Billy and the dog but inched closer to Lanie.

"How did your guitar break?"

"I smashed it to pieces after I learned you weren't coming back."

"I'm sorry. Please forgive me. I never meant to hurt you."

When Luke turned toward the ladies, Kylee melted into Lanie's arms and sobbed.

If Lanie hurt her this much, after knowing her for only a short time, how much did Kylee and the other children hurt because of separation from their parents? How did they ever learn to trust again?

Luke turned his head. Lanie held a broken girl in

her arms. A young girl offering forgiveness for Lanie's neglect. He'd forgiven her for not returning to Pleasant Springs eleven years ago, but he struggled to forgive her for her neglect of his family. Even if he'd married Stephanie, Lanie could have visited his parents. *Lord, I need to forgive her too. Completely. Please help me.*

Billy ran to Luke and almost lost his balance as he skidded to a stop on the gravel. "What's wrong with Kylee?"

Luke hunkered in front of him. "She'll be fine. She needed a hug and to work through some things."

Billy smiled. "Miss Lanie gives the best hugs."

Luke didn't think it wise for him to want to know if that was true or not. He had to refrain from both hugs and kisses.

Lanie and Kylee strolled toward Luke and Billy while Kylee wiped her eyes. "Billy, please show Kylee where the bathroom is located."

"Okay. The one inside or outside?"

She stiffened. "Outside?"

Heat rose on Luke's face. "Take her inside, Billy."

Lanie stared at Luke.

"I told him at the fire station if he were busy outside and needed to go, he could step over to the trees."

She placed her hands on her hips. "Mr. Gibson, I'll add that to my report." She winked at him.

He chuckled. He'd missed her teasing, but what if she were flirting? No. He couldn't allow that. "Look, Lanie, there's something I need to tell you."

She gazed into his eyes. "Sure."

"The kiss last night."

She tilted her head. "You mean that sweet little

kiss?"

His heart melted a little. He should let go of the past and grab onto a future with her. "Um. Yes." He pushed his shoulders back. No. He had to put a stop to any kind of friendship at all before he messed up again and kissed her. "Shouldn't have happened." He turned away and watched the kids when they came out the door. "Won't happen again." He strode toward Billy and Kylee. "Ready to go?"

Lanie caught up to him and touched his elbow. "You're right. Won't happen again." She hurried to where they'd parked their vehicles, turned to him, and in a bubbly tone said, "Should we take my car?"

He gave her a thumbs up, and she threw him her keys.

The kids climbed into the back seat, while Lanie and Luke got in the front.

Luke already regretted what he'd said. But Lanie appeared unscathed. He wasn't sure she cared. But if that were true, why did she act flirty earlier?

Twenty-six

If it hadn't been for Kylee and Billy singing and laughing in the back seat, the car would have been silent. I kept a fake smile on my face, but my insides churned. How dare Luke kiss me and tell me it meant nothing to him? What was he uptight about, anyway? He wanted to blame me for eleven years of nothingness between us, but he could have fought for me back then. If he'd cared, why didn't he?

The hour drive seemed like three hours. But at least the two kids in the back seat enjoyed themselves. We parked near the main waterfall, strolled to the viewing area that overlooked the falls, and peered into the gorge where rushing water collided with the creek below.

Kylee's eyes sparkled. "Can we hike down to the bottom?"

Billy clenched his hands under his chin. "Please?"

We made our way to the trailhead where a sign read, "Very Strenuous."

Luke and I agreed to make the trek but reminded the kids we didn't want to hear any complaints about the steep climb back up.

The temperature dropped several degrees as we hiked down 300 feet over rocks and roots into the gorge at the base of the falls. Luke and I took turns holding onto Billy's hand. Mist covered the rocks where we walked, causing us to watch our step as we neared the bottom. I took several photos on my phone of the 256-foot waterfall and snapped a few pictures of the kids with Luke as they attempted to cross over the rocks.

I took a few steps toward a large boulder to my right where they wandered.

Luke called out to me. "Send me your photos, okay?"

"Sure. As soon as we get to the car, if we have cell service." I turned to Kylee and Billy. "Are you ready to head back?"

They loved everything about the experience except for the climb back to the top. I insisted they use the provided handrails, and we stopped to rest a few times where I enjoyed clusters of purple wildflowers. Billy crouched to pick up what he thought was a caterpillar, but I stopped him. He didn't need to make a pet out of a millipede.

When we reached the top, the kids decided they'd had enough hiking for one day. But they wanted another peek at the falls.

Kylee caught my eye and mouthed. "I need to use the bathroom."

"We'll meet you out in front of the building in a few minutes."

She darted toward the restroom and went inside.

I ruffled Billy's hair. "What did you enjoy the most?"

He brought his hands together and opened his eyes wide. "The water crashing at the bottom."

I stared down at the base of the waterfall. "Pretty

cool, isn't it?"

Luke asked him a couple of questions, and we moseyed toward the restrooms to wait for Kylee.

I glanced at my watch. "I'll check inside and make sure she's okay."

The room appeared empty. I took a quick look under the stall doors and didn't see any feet. My heart raced. I zipped outside, ran to Luke, and tried to stay calm for Billy's sake. "She's not inside."

Luke clenched his jaw. "We would have seen her come out."

"Not when we had our backs to the building while we chatted about the waterfall." I squeezed my eyes shut. "How could I be so irresponsible with a child in my care?"

Billy tugged at my shirt. "Maybe she went into the boy's room by accident. I can check."

Luke took Billy's hand. "Check the girl's restroom again. We'll check the boy's and wait for you outside." He leaned closer and whispered. "She's probably hiding in there to scare us or to make us think she ran away."

I dashed inside, although I didn't need to check the restroom again. She wasn't in there. I narrowed my eyes. But I hadn't pushed on the stall doors to make sure. "Kylee? Are you in here?" I tapped one door and it opened. No one was there. I pushed the next door—locked but still no feet. There was a faint sniffle. "Honey, are you okay?"

Shoes clunked onto the cement floor, and I clutched my chest. *Thank You, Lord.*

She unlocked the door, eased it open, and lifted her red eyes. "I'm sorry. I didn't want anyone to see me so emotional. Today felt like I had a real family."

"You gave us a scare, but I'm glad you're okay." I pulled her close and stroked her back. "Why don't you wash your face, and I'll let Luke and Billy know that you'll be out in a few minutes."

I found Luke and Billy outside. "She needed time to deal with her emotions. She wasn't trying to scare us or make us think she split."

Luke crossed his arms. "Are you always a pushover?"

"I believe her." I tucked my hair behind my ears.

When Kylee joined us, we returned to my car and buckled in.

Luke twisted in his seat to see the kids in the back. "Can everyone wait approximately forty-five minutes to eat supper?"

In unison, Billy and Kylee said, "Pizza?" They chuckled and punched each other in the arm.

Hard to believe the two of them got along well after only two days of meeting one another.

"More like Pete's Barbeque in Poplar Ridge." Luke pulled out of the parking lot.

Groans sounded behind us.

Luke cut me a look. "You decide. Pete's or pizza?"

I turned to the back seat. "The driver of my car gets to make the final decision. Usually, that would be me, but because Mr. Luke is at the wheel, looks like Pete's wins."

More groans.

Kylee sweetly said, "Miss Lanie?"

"Yes."

"Could we still do something tomorrow?"

"Do you mean go out for pizza?" I turned again to the back.

She nodded and yawned. "After we all go to church."

I faced Luke. "Would you like to join us?"

He sounded grumpy. "Your church or mine? Or were you only asking about pizza?"

"Both, but does it matter whose church?"

"You haven't been to yours for a while, have you?"

"Not since I've been home."

He sighed. "Let's meet after church." He peeked into the rear-view mirror. "Are they asleep or eavesdropping?"

I twisted to the back seat. The two of them appeared to be sound asleep. "We wore them out."

Luke yawned. "Wore me out too."

"Do you need me to drive?"

He shook his head. "The church thing. Pleasant Springs Community Church is wonderful. Pastor Oldham is a great guy, but there are a lot of gossipers there. I don't want to be a part of Maggie Stone's busybody blog. We attend together or meet there, and she'll have us married in no time."

And I knew how he felt about that. If the kiss was a mistake, a relationship, let alone marriage, was not an option. "I heard what she said regarding Becca's marriage, but I still haven't read her blog."

He huffed. "You didn't read what she said about you and her speculations about why you returned home?"

How could I lighten his mood? "Nope, but I doubt she called me a hot babe." I caught the giggles and covered my mouth to keep from waking Billy and Kylee.

Luke eyed me like I'd lost my mind.

I continued to laugh until tears rolled down my cheeks. I'd experienced wonderful freedom since I came home, learned the truth about Luke and Stephanie, and decided to follow the Lord again. The time had come to enjoy my life along with every blessing God had for me, whether or not those blessings included a relationship with Luke.

Billy sounded sleepy. "What's funny?"

I turned to face him and caught Kylee's eye as well. "Miss Lanie is happy to have spent the day with the two of you. You've brought joy to my heart."

Billy rubbed his eyes. "What about Coach Luke? Does he bring joy to your heart too?"

I gazed at Luke with a silly grin on my face. "Yes. He does."

~

Luke pulled into Pete's parking lot and found a spot close to the door. He turned to the back seat. "Everyone awake?"

Kylee stuck up her nose. "I don't like barbeque."

Billy touched her on her arm. "That's okay. They have mac and cheese on the kid's menu."

She yanked her arm away. In a bratty tone, she said, "I'm not a kid." She sneered and brushed off her arm.

When they all got out of the car, Luke whispered in Lanie's ear. "Did you see that? Kylee's been fine with Billy all afternoon until now. Is she mad because I didn't take them for pizza?"

"That, or she's a little cranky when she wakes from a quick nap."

He opened the door for the three of them to enter Pete's ahead of him.

The host led them to a booth along the windows where Kylee sat next to Billy, and Lanie took a seat next to Luke.

He perused his menu. They'd had a fun time at the waterfall. Felt like a family. Once a dream he'd held close—Lanie and a couple of kids. He saw a change in her, and he'd wanted to laugh with her earlier, but he didn't want to encourage her. They couldn't go back to what they once had.

"They have chicken?" Kylee grinned. "I'll have that."

"Can I have the kid's ribs?" Billy smiled. "I forgot this is the place that makes them good."

Kylee poked Billy in his side. "Does that mean that a poor little kid lost his ribs?"

Billy squirmed and scooted closer to the window. "Stop it. That hurts."

She sounded snotty. "Baby."

Luke smacked his menu on the table. "That's enough. If you don't stop—"

Lanie grabbed his knee and squeezed.

He winced and glared at her. She faced Kylee.

"What Mr. Luke means is that he'd like you to be kind to Billy and treat him how you'd want to be treated." Lanie turned to Luke. "Right, Mr. Luke?"

"That's right." He motioned for Lanie to move over. "I need the restroom."

She slid off the bench and stepped back.

"Order me the pulled pork plate." He bypassed the restrooms and strode outside.

~

"What's with him? Grumpy old man." Kylee slouched in her seat. "Because I stayed in the bathroom so long?"

I reached across the table to touch her hand. "He's not upset with you. He's upset with me."

Billy cocked his head. "Why do you get mad at each other?"

Kylee frowned and wet her lips. "Does this happen often?"

Billy looked at me. "A lot."

"Not a lot." I flapped my hand. "Luke and I have known each other for a long time. Best friends since we were children. And then one day. We weren't."

The server came to our table, and we placed our order. Luke hadn't returned. I scanned the restaurant.

"He's outside in the parking lot." Kylee pointed out the window. "Why aren't you still friends?"

"We're still friends." Anyway, I hoped so. "Just not best friends."

Kylee's eyes grew wide. "Did he hurt you?"

"A story for another day."

Billy fidgeted and pinched his bottom lip.

I reached across the table to him. "Are you okay?"

"I don't feel good."

"What's wrong?"

"My stomach hurts."

I stood and asked Kylee to trade places with me. She complained about having to sit with Mr. Grumpy Pants but moved like I asked. I scooted in next to Billy and felt his forehead. "No fever." I handed him a glass of water. "Drink this."

He took a sip, but a tear formed in his eye. "Is Coach Luke the person you were afraid to see when you moved here? Is he the one who hurt you in there?" He pointed to my chest.

Twenty-seven

Luke decided he'd spent enough time outside sulking and returned to the table. His eyes darted from Kylee to Lanie. "What's going on here?" He focused on Billy and winked. "You okay, buddy?"

Billy didn't make eye contact. He nuzzled his head against Lanie's arm and groaned. She whispered something to Billy, but the only word Luke heard was "later."

Luke took a seat next to Kylee and narrowed his eyes at Lanie. "What happened while I was gone?"

Kylee snickered under her breath. "If you wanted to know, you should have stayed."

"Kylee. That's enough." Lanie nudged Billy and asked him to sit up. "Everything's fine."

Luke wasn't sure if Lanie spoke to him or to Billy.

Lanie gazed across the table at him. "Everyone's tired and hungry from our hike." She tilted her head and lifted her brows. That look she'd given him many times before, as if to ask, "Are you okay?"

Luke placed his elbows on the table and clasped his hands. He turned to Kylee. "I'm sorry I sounded upset with you." He leaned back on the bench. "I'm glad you joined us today and hope you'll join us again. I'll try to be in a better mood next time."

Kylee stared at the table and curled a finger around a strand of hair. "Okay."

The server delivered their food and scurried away.

After a prayer, they ate in silence. Everyone seemed on edge, not just him. He wanted to say something to Lanie, to help the kids relax, but he wasn't too happy with her for shushing him earlier. At least she'd done it with a squeeze that Kylee and Billy couldn't see. And the kiss that never should have happened? What a mess. Did she think there was something more between them? What they'd had in college? He wouldn't let that happen.

He eyed Lanie and in a nasty tone said, "I'm still waiting for those pictures."

Her body jerked and stiffened. She dropped her fork and pulled out her phone.

Luke tapped his fingers on the table. "Whenever. I'm sorry." He pulled out his wallet, stood, and handed Lanie his credit card. "I'll wait for y'all in the car. No hurry."

~

Kylee pressed her fist to her mouth. "Next time. Can we do something without him?"

"He's having a bad day." I forced a smile and rubbed my temples. "Have either of you had a bad day before?"

They both mumbled a yes.

"But he hates me." Kylee whined and stuck out her lower lip. "And I did nothing."

"Didn't you hear him? He's glad you joined us today."

"He acted like everything was my fault when all I did was tease Billy a little."

"As I said earlier. Luke's upset with me." I took another bite of my brisket.

Billy slumped his shoulders and pouted. "He's the person who hurt you, isn't he?"

I looked at my food and sighed. "Yes. But I didn't know the complete story when I told you that someone in Pleasant Springs hurt me. He didn't do what I thought he did."

Billy moaned and crossed his arms. "I don't want to live with him."

"Can't blame you." Kylee chuckled and rolled her eyes. "Can you take us to a different church and not to his tomorrow?"

"I'll decide on that." I wrapped my arm around Billy's shoulder and nudged him to my side. "What you need to realize is Mr. Luke is a wonderful person, and he'll take good care of you. And don't forget, you'll get to see Grizzly every day."

"Can Kylee live with us too?"

"Nope." Kylee raised her palms toward us. "I'd run away again if I lived with him."

I frowned at her and shook my head. "Let's finish our supper. We need to get you both back to Creekside."

The server brought me a box for Luke's leftovers, and I paid for our meal. When I hurried out to the car, Kylee and Billy trudged behind me.

After we buckled in, Luke drove us to Creekside, where I unloaded the kids, took them inside, and chatted with them in the foyer. "I'll call and get approval for Kylee to join us again tomorrow morning.

Be ready by 9:30. We'll go to church and then for pizza."

When they wandered into the living room, Teresa called out my name. "May I have a word with you?" She bit her lip and wrinkled her nose. "I'm not sure what's going on, but Ronni was here this afternoon to meet with Kylee. Ronni said Sam wanted her to visit Kylee and not you. But Todd has said nothing to me about that."

"Was she upset Kylee wasn't here?"

"Not upset. Perplexed."

"Don't worry about it. I'm sure I'll know more when I go into the office on Monday." I said goodbye and headed out the door. Todd told me as far as he was concerned, I could visit Kylee whenever I wanted. He'd never told Sam that he wanted me replaced. What was happening?

I rushed to my car and climbed inside.

Luke drove us to his cabin, but neither of us spoke. When we pulled into his driveway and parked, he faced me. "I need to make sure you understand something."

I nodded and glanced at him.

He averted his eyes and without emotion said, "We are nothing more than business associates. You are conducting my home study so I can become Billy's foster dad."

I bristled and swallowed the lump in my throat. "Your grumpiness today was because you thought I wanted something more?"

"You seemed rather joyful this afternoon when you arrived. I assumed it was because of my kiss."

"You made a poor assumption, Mr. Gibson. I rededicated my life to the Lord this morning. He's the reason for my joy."

I opened the passenger door and plodded to his side. My knees weakened with each step.

Luke waited near the opened driver's door and handed me my keys. "I'm glad to hear that."

"I'll see you Monday afternoon for your next review session." I climbed into the car without looking at him.

Luke clung to the door handle to keep me from pulling the door closed. "Are you planning to bring Billy to church tomorrow?"

I tried to clear my mind. What did Luke ask? Church?

"No. Let's not spend any more time together than what's necessary to conduct our business." I pulled the door closed and backed around while Luke remained in his driveway and watched me. Before I drove away, I rolled down the passenger side window and peered at him. "Do you make a habit, Mr. Gibson, of kissing all of your business associates?" I stomped on the gas pedal and spewed gravel when I sped away.

On my drive home, I contemplated adding a note to Luke's home study. "Applicant is overly affectionate with visitors to his home." But that wasn't true. The old me would add it without hesitation, but Luke would make an excellent foster dad for Billy. I couldn't let his coldness with me interfere with Billy's future.

Luke had made it clear there was no future for us.

~

Luke sat at his kitchen table with his head bowed. *Lord, I'm confused. Why do I still have feelings for Lanie? Please remove her from my life. Bring Victor Clemmons back as my caseworker. Send Lanie to*

Nashville. I'm glad she's following You again, but she's not good for me. She should have been here all along if she wanted more than friendship, like I did. If You want me to have a woman to love and to love me, bring someone else.

Not her, Lord. Please. Not her.

Twenty-eight

Kylee and Billy grumbled on the way to my car after church. "That wasn't fun."

"You seemed to have a lot of fun at everyone else's expense."

Billy tugged on my sweater. "What does that mean?"

"The two of you. You laughed at the choir, snorted when the older gentleman took the offering, and made snide comments during the prayer." I shook my head and suppressed a frown. "You embarrassed my sister and me."

"We were good when the preacher talked." Billy held my hand and pulled me toward my car.

"Did you listen to him? What's one thing he said?"

Kylee stared at the pavement in front of my parking space. "He said God loves you more than anyone else. And He wants us to love Him and others too."

Billy nodded and enunciated each word. "And he said we should forgive other people when they hurt us."

"You both paid attention? I'm proud of you." I helped Billy into the back seat and climbed into the front where Kylee waited.

"But next time, be respectful when others are singing or speaking. Okay?"

Billy said, "We were both nice to that Miss Maggie lady when she gave us candy."

I twisted in my seat and gave Billy a fist bump. I'd visited with Miss Risa for a few minutes and didn't see Maggie or the candy exchange, but Jill said Maggie had a soft spot for kids at the children's home. "I'm glad you thanked her."

"Can we go to a different church next week?" Kylee drew her eyebrows together. "That one was boring."

I pulled out of the parking spot and got behind a line of cars exiting the lot. "And you're, what, an expert on churches?"

"Went to a few I liked in Chattanooga."

"You and I can visit others if you'd like to, but this one will have a new pastor soon. He might make changes you'll like better."

"In two weeks on Mother's Day, right?"

"You paid attention to the announcements?" I smiled, raised my palm, and gave her a high-five. "Pastor Ben Peterson and his wife Becca are moving here from Florida. She's my sister's good friend."

We pulled out onto the road and headed south on Main Street.

"Billy will attend Mr. Luke's church soon with him."

In a bratty tone, Billy said, "I told you already. I don't want to live with Coach Luke." He kicked the back of Kylee's seat.

"Stop you little twerp."

We made it one block before I pulled into Baker's Dozen Bakery's parking lot.

I eyed Kylee and pursed my lips. "I expect you to treat each other with respect and not call one another names."

Kylee gritted her teeth. "Fine. But tell him to stop kicking my seat."

I turned back to Billy.

His bottom lip puffed out, and he sniffled. "I'm sorry."

Kylee peered back at him. "Okay."

My gaze shifted from one to the other. "If you'll agree to treat each other like this for the next two blocks and while at the restaurant, we can get pizza."

They both agreed to show kindness, so I drove to Pizza Shack.

After lunch, I returned the kids to Creekside, where they hurried into the living room while Todd met me in the foyer.

Surprised to see him, I said, "Do you work every Saturday and Sunday?"

"In recent weeks, yes. I lost my codirector and can't seem to catch up."

"Well, I might know someone looking for a job soon." I chuckled under my breath.

Todd invited me to his office, pointed to the chair in front of his desk, and we both sat. "Ronni visited today and informed me that she'll be making courtesy visits to Kylee. She said Sam insisted, and she'd call me tomorrow." He ran his hand through his hair. "What's going on?"

"Like I said, I may need a job soon. Sam and I haven't hit it off."

He flinched and rubbed his forehead. "You were talking about yourself? I don't understand." He picked up a pen and fiddled with it. "You've done an excellent job with both Billy and now Kylee. They were both happy you planned to take them to church today." He tapped his pen a few times on the top of his desk. "The two of them act like siblings and have adjusted well here. Kylee amazes me in the brief time she's been at Creekside."

"Thank you. I'm sure I'll know more tomorrow." My face flushed. "I'll keep you posted."

When I arrived home, I found Jill in the living room watering her plants. All she talked about was how wonderful it would be to have Becca back in Pleasant Springs.

I sighed and rounded my shoulders. "I'm happy for you."

"Is something wrong?"

"You get your best friend back." I slumped onto the sofa. "Mine wants nothing more to do with me."

Jill set her watering can on the floor and took a seat next to me. "What happened?"

"Luke said the kiss meant nothing, and he doesn't want to rekindle our friendship."

"The kiss?" She squealed in my ear and flung her arms in the air.

I jumped up and spun to face her. "Doesn't matter. Meant nothing to him."

Jill lowered her voice. "But it meant everything to you, didn't it?" She stood and embraced me.

"I don't know. But the Lord cares about me. I need to focus on Him, not Luke."

She backed away and touched her lips. "The

Lord?"

"Miss Risa helped me to see that God never left me, though I thought He had." I took Jill's hands in mine. "I'm sorry for cutting you off every time you wanted to share something with me concerning people here in Pleasant Springs. Thanks for not giving up on me and for the Someday Journal you kept updated. That proved many people cared."

She squeezed my hands and pointed to the couch. "Let's talk about the kiss."

"No. I don't want to even think about it." I sat on the sofa.

She took a seat next to me. "Did Luke initiate the kiss?"

I pressed my lips together.

"You said it didn't matter, but a kiss always matters."

"Not this time." I huffed and stood.

"Wait. I need to talk with you about something else."

I plopped down next to her and crossed my arms.

"Becca arrives on Wednesday this week."

"Great." I peeked at a photo on the fireplace mantle of the three of us spending the day together at Ruby Falls in Chattanooga. "When she moves out, would you consider replacing her with another roommate?"

Jill raised her brows and touched her neck. "Who?"

"Kylee."

"Whoa. The girl you had at church today?" She twisted her knees until they touched mine and widened her eyes. "The one who had nothing nice to say? You want me," she pointed to her chest, "to be her foster parent with you?"

"You'd need to go through the training because I live with you in your house."

She faced forward and squirmed.

I patted her leg and tipped my head back. "Never mind. I'm sorry. I shouldn't have asked. Kylee's my responsibility, not yours." Jill never seemed interested in kids.

"Are you having trouble finding a placement for her?"

"Hamilton County's trying to find her another foster home, but she's been difficult in the past." I cringed and glanced away. "I'm concerned about her. Because I'm not her caseworker, I could foster her."

"Let me pray about it."

"No. Forget I said anything. Time for me to find a place of my own."

"Does that mean you plan to stay here in Pleasant Springs?"

I leaned forward and placed my elbows on my knees. "Nashville hasn't come through. I guess I'm stuck here."

Twenty-nine

On my way to the office Monday morning, I stopped by the florist and picked up a small, mixed bouquet for Samantha. I needed to win her over before I lost my job. When I arrived at the office, she sat working on her computer. I strolled to my desk, noticed a manila file folder lying there, and dropped my purse into my lower left desk drawer.

A note on the folder read, "Sign and return to Sam."

I ignored the note, made my way to Sam's desk, and greeted her in a cheery voice. "Here's something to brighten your day." I handed her the flowers. "I'll get a vase from the supply room."

Sam winced and raised her voice. "What are these for? And why do I need my day brightened?"

Her response irked me, but I kept my chipper tone. "I saw them in the florist's window and thought of you."

"And which flower made you think of me?"

I hadn't expected an interrogation. "The white daisies, because I've seen you wear a navy skirt with daisies."

"True. But if anyone needs their day brightened, it's you." She handed me the flowers. Did she smirk too?

"Okay?" I zipped into the supply room for a vase and placed the bouquet on my desk. Not sure about my day, but the flowers brightened my mood. A little.

My hands shook, and I peeked Sam's way. Why was she staring back at me? Was she waiting for me to open the file folder? What would she need me to sign and return to her?

I took my seat and brought my computer screen to life. Instead of opening the manila folder, I read my email. Although I doubted that was what Sam expected or wanted, it allowed me time to calm myself.

While I read, Ronni entered the office. "Good morning. What a beautiful day." She ambled past me, and her face lit up. "Wow. Those flowers are gorgeous. I guess you don't need to hear my news."

"Your news?"

She stopped halfway to her desk. "We have a new doctor in town."

Sam glanced our way and smiled. "The one taking over Doc Brown's practice?"

I snickered and leaned forward. That man was older than Moses. "Doc Brown hasn't retired yet?"

Ronni beamed and chuckled. "He should have years ago. But he waited, and Pleasant Springs is now more pleasant than ever."

Sam hobbled into the restroom at the back of the office.

"Why don't I need to hear about the new doctor? I may get sick and need one too."

"Those flowers say that someone has their eye on

you already. You don't need to meet the handsome, single doctor. He's a hottie."

I stood and blinked several times. "Does your husband know you talk about other men that way?"

"Of course, he does. But he's also aware no other hottie will ever take his place."

Ronni moved closer to my desk. "Here's the new doctor's business card, in case you need to make an appointment to check him out."

I placed the card aside without looking at it and thanked her. "The flowers weren't for me. I brought them for Sam to get on her good side. She didn't want them. She said I needed them more than she did."

When I pointed to the folder, Ronni wrinkled her nose.

"What's in there?"

I peeled back the cover and gasped. "What?" I scanned the dreaded paper. "A disciplinary form for me to sign and return for my file." My stomach turned sour, and my mouth went dry.

"I'm sorry. She's been hard on you, and I can't figure out why."

The restroom door opened, and Ronni bolted to her desk.

My eyes met Sam's, and she motioned me to the back corner of the office. I picked up the folder and plodded to a table used for brief meetings. "I don't understand."

"Read the form."

"Insubordination." I peered at Sam. "That's all it says. What did I do or not do?"

"You took Kylee on an outing when I told you not to have anything more to do with her. She's no longer your responsibility. She's Ronni's."

"But Todd said—"

"Is Todd your supervisor? Do what I say." She pointed to the signature line and shuffled to her desk.

I hesitated to sign the form. Wouldn't that be agreeing I'd done something wrong? Instead, I wrote what Todd had said. Sam must have misunderstood him. "If you talk with him, I'm sure he will explain everything to you, and you'll agree to allow me to visit her."

I placed the unsigned paper in the manila folder and carried it to Sam's desk. "I hope you'll change your mind about this."

She opened the folder and held the form in her hands. "This is not what I asked you to do." She stood, narrowed her eyes, and clenched her jaw. "You are now on a thirty-day disciplinary probation. If further infractions occur, I will terminate your position."

I hurried back to my desk. Her actions didn't make sense, but what could I do? I didn't want to argue with her. But give up on Kylee? I'd hurt her before. That couldn't happen again. I gathered my purse and the bouquet and stopped by Sam's desk on my way out. "I'm leaving to make my visits. This afternoon I'll conduct Luke's third review session. I'll have his home study wrapped up next week."

"Sounds good." She wrote something on a notepad. "And stay away from Kylee."

I dashed out the door. After I dropped the bouquet off at Miss Risa's and had a brief chat and prayer, I made two home visits.

Instead of a regular lunch hour, I dropped by Creekside to talk with Todd in the foyer and filled him in on what had happened. "I need to tell Kylee that she'll see more of Ronni." I rubbed my finger across my lips. "How did this get messed up?"

He shook his head and stared toward his office door. "I'll call Sam and talk with her. Come back later this afternoon. I'll let you visit Kylee, even if I need to stand guard to watch for Ronni or Sam."

"Will you be here later this evening? I'm busy with training until 5:00 and will try to swing by after that."

"Yes. Still catching up on paperwork." He tilted his head from side to side. "What do you plan to do if Sam lets you go?"

I told him about the two agencies I'd applied at in Nashville and how much I'd always wanted to live there.

He nodded and opened the outside door. "I hope everything works out well for you."

I thanked him, drove to Mama Lou's for a to-go sandwich, and pulled into the community park to eat in my car. I opened a Bible app on my phone and read a verse Miss Risa gave me earlier that morning. Jeremiah 29:11: "'For I know the plans I have for you,' declares the LORD, "plans to prosper you and not to harm you, plans to give you hope and a future.'"

My muscles relaxed, and I lifted my chin. Hope and a future. I found comfort in those words.

Later that afternoon, when I arrived at Luke's cabin, Grizzly met me on the front porch. "Hey, boy. You look handsome today."

Luke opened the door and greeted me. "We're halfway through the training. Does everything look good so far?"

I entered the cabin, placed my things on the kitchen

table, and stifled a grin. "Other than my comment on your home study that you greet visitors with a kiss on the lips, I've found nothing that will interfere with your approval."

His voice hardened. "You put that in your report?"

I glared at him and placed my hands on my hips. "Where's your sense of humor? If you're this serious with Billy, you'll continue to carry the nickname of Mr. Grumpy Pants."

He plopped into a kitchen chair and sulked.

I pulled out a chair across from him and sat. "Let's review lesson three, Roadmap to Resilience, which deals with children and attachment."

We finished at 4:55. My hands trembled. Time to discuss the real reason I'd returned to Pleasant Springs.

Thirty

After they finished with the review, Lanie reminded Luke that she'd return on Wednesday for a review of lesson four. He didn't look forward to more time spent with her. He'd remained grumpy throughout the lesson, and she seemed a little too cheery for him.

Lanie closed her notebook and laid her hand on top of it. "Do you have questions before I go?"

"I'm good." He massaged his temples and strode toward the door. Time to get rid of her.

She eyed him but remained seated. "Won't be long now. I'll approve your home study and place Billy in your home." She stood but left her notebook on the table. "There's something I'd like to talk with you about."

"Look. I've got things to do and I'm tired. I need to work on this homework, and I still need to prepare for my Bible study on Thursday. Can whatever it is wait until you come back on Wednesday?"

She huffed and kneaded the back of her neck. "You've been grumpy with me all afternoon. I realize you're still not happy with me being back in Pleasant Springs. But we need to put the past behind us and move on." She clenched her jaw and crossed her arms. "You said you forgave me, but you don't act like you have."

Luke yanked Lanie's notebook from the table and trudged out the front door.

She followed close behind him. "What are you doing?"

"Helping you to your car. I told you. I'm tired. No more today." He descended the stairs but no longer heard her footsteps behind him.

"But we need to talk." She'd stopped at the top of the steps and raised her voice. "My return to Pleasant Springs wasn't a fluke. God brought me here."

He turned back to her. "How do you figure?"

She stepped down onto the gravel and strutted toward him. "I lost my job in Chattanooga. And found one *here* in Pleasant Springs. A place I didn't want to live." She softened her tone and tilted her head. "You applied to become a foster parent and became my first home study in my new job because Victor Clemmons took a leave of absence the weekend before." She moved closer and placed her hand on his arm. "Those are a few too many things to have happened by coincidence. Don't you agree?"

He took a step back and cleared his throat. "And why do you believe God orchestrated all those things?"

"Now is the time to put the past behind us." She pushed her shoulders back. "Not because I'll approve your home study, but we need to move forward and restore at least our friendship."

He shook his head and scowled. "I forgave you for staying in Chattanooga. But I don't see how we can renew our friendship." He turned again, jogged to

Lanie's car, and placed her notebook in the back seat. Nope. Not God. No friendship left to mend. He wasn't to blame for anything.

She stopped in the driveway to answer her phone and turned her back to Luke. "Friday morning works." Lanie thanked the caller and disconnected her call.

When she turned back around, Luke couldn't tell by her facial expression if the call was a good one or not. Lanie climbed into her car without another word, backed out, and drove off.

~

I headed to Creekside to visit Billy and Kylee. If Luke had forgiven me, why his stubbornness? What kept him from renewing our friendship and putting the past behind us? Wasn't that what the Lord would want him to do?

When I arrived at Creekside, I hurried to Todd's office for an update on his conversation with Sam.

He pointed to the chair across from his desk. "I've never known her to be this adamant concerning anything. She's set on Ronni visiting Kylee. She wouldn't budge."

"She hates me and wants me gone."

Todd glanced away and pressed his lips together. Why couldn't he make eye contact?

"That's it, isn't it? She told you she plans to fire me?"

He exhaled a lengthy breath. "She didn't say that, but I got that impression." He grasped a binder clip off the top of his desk and snapped it open and closed. "I can't figure out why."

"Neither can I." I squirmed in my chair. "What did she say?"

"Nothing I can make sense of." He stood and gazed out the front window facing the road. "She mentioned Jerome twice but didn't finish her thoughts." He peered at me and stroked his chin. "Does that make sense to you?"

I joined Todd at the window and reminded him that Jerome had been my supervisor when I worked for Hamilton County. "But why would she mention him?" I clasped my hands in front of me. "He wouldn't badmouth me or my work."

"She sounded paranoid to me." Todd backed away and brushed a wrinkle from his shirt. "Please don't share a word of this with her. She'll be upset with me if you do."

I assured him that I'd keep quiet regarding this information. "On the bright side for me, I received a call from the Meade Agency in Nashville. They want to interview me Friday morning for a position with them. Looks as though one door is closing, but perhaps another is opening."

"If you lose your job, I'm sure you'll find something. I've seen you with these kids. You're one of the best."

"I appreciate your faith in me."

"Kylee's in the living room. I'll stand guard while you talk with her."

I found Kylee and Billy watching a superhero movie.

"He's lightning fast." I opened my eyes wide.

Billy ran to me with his arms open. "That's his superpower. Fastest man in the world."

I chuckled and hugged him before he zoomed back to his chair. "Is your movie almost finished?" I focused on Kylee.

She rose from the couch and sauntered toward me. "It's lame and I'm bored." She yawned and patted her fingers against her lips. "I'm going to my room to read."

"Could you spare a few minutes to talk with me first?"

"I guess." She followed me through the kitchen and into the visitation room, where she sat at the table.

I pulled out a chair across from her and whispered a prayer. *Lord, help her understand this is not my choice. I want to spend time with her.* "Miss Teresa told me that Miss Ronni from my office has been by to see you. Have you met her?"

She glared at me and caressed her arms.

"What did she say that's causing you to give me the evil eye?"

"You want nothing to do with me, and she'll be checking on me now."

A chill ran through me, and I took a shaky breath. "Did she really say that to you?"

Kylee's face turned red, and she leapt from her chair. "She didn't have to. I've been in this situation before, remember? I thought things were different this time. But you haven't changed at all." She rushed toward the door.

I darted in front of her to block her exit. "The decision wasn't mine. My supervisor made it. I must abide by it, or I'll lose my job." I wanted to embrace her but wondered if she would push me away. "This situation disturbs me too. I've enjoyed our time together and wanted to get to know you better." I touched her arm and smiled.

She stepped back and creased her brow. "I don't believe you."

"I'll try harder to regain your trust." I grinned and raised my eyebrows. "Mr. Todd said we'll work out an arrangement where I can still visit you."

Kylee stared at her feet. "Do you promise?"

How could I promise her with the uncertainty of my job? "I will do my best, but I can't promise you anything. My job is still in jeopardy."

She looked up and bit her lower lip. "Why? What did you do?"

"I don't know."

We chatted for several minutes until Teresa called Kylee and Billy to dinner. I stopped by Todd's office on my way out.

"Come on inside. I have good news to share." He offered me a chair across from his. "Kylee's caseworker, Donna Barker, just called. She's found a placement for Kylee in Chattanooga, where she can return to her school."

I crossed my arms over my stomach. "No. That's not good. I want to be her foster mom."

He jerked his head back and widened his eyes. "Have you talked with anyone in Hamilton County?"

"Not yet." I wrinkled my forehead and frowned. With the uncertainty of my job, no house of my own, and Jill not excited about sharing foster care responsibilities, perhaps Ms. Barker had a better option for Kylee. "What did she say about the family?"

"The woman is a single foster mom. She's had a lot of experience with teenaged girls. Many have thrived in her care." He steepled his fingertips on top of his desk. "Ms. Barker thinks this mom will be great for Kylee, and said she'll email me more information."

I squeezed my eyes shut and rubbed my fist over my breastbone to ease the heaviness in my chest.

"Ms. Barker discussed this case with Jerome, and he asked that you be the one to tell Kylee."

My eyes shot open, and I groaned. "Great. My supervisor doesn't want me to talk with her, but our regional director does."

Todd lowered his voice and leaned forward. "Ms. Barker will be here tomorrow evening to take Kylee back to Chattanooga."

"That soon?" I wiped my hands down my pantlegs. "I have another visit to make tonight in Poplar Ridge." I stood on shaky legs. "Send me whatever information you receive about the foster mom. I'll be back tomorrow to spend time with Kylee and give her the news."

I thanked Todd for the information and said goodbye.

Two losses in one day with a strong possibility of a third soon. Losing a renewed friendship with Luke, losing a young girl whom I cared about, and perhaps the loss of my job. *What next, Lord? Is this a test?* Tension climbed from my gut and settled in my chest.

After a visit to one of Victor's foster families, I arrived home and found Jill in the spare bedroom along with four boxes. "Let me help you pack." I entered my room, dropped my purse on the bed, and zipped back to help Jill. "Throw this yarn into a box?" I snatched an orange and yellow multicolored skein of yarn from a pile on the floor and tossed it into a box.

"No. Not like that. I'm boxing them by project." She pushed my hand away. "I'll do it, but will you clean the hall bathroom? I haven't had time."

"Clean the bathroom at 9:00 at night? Can't that wait until tomorrow?"

Jill rose to her feet. "I had the day wrong. Becca will be here early tomorrow evening. She'll pick up a rental car in Chattanooga, stop by the office to say hello to her former coworkers, and we'll be home by 6:30."

"I'll clean the bathroom. But first I need to prop my feet up. I'm exhausted." I plodded to my room, grabbed a book about traumatized children, and read until I couldn't keep my eyes opened. Would the information in the book apply to adults like Luke too? *Lord, help him see You arranged all of this so we could be together. I still love him and want to be with him. Is that possible?*

Thirty-one

When my alarm blared Tuesday morning, I remembered the bathroom. I jumped out of bed, ate a protein bar for breakfast, and grabbed the cleaning supplies. I took a quick shower and scrubbed the bathroom until it sparkled.

Jill stuck her head in while I finished. "I thought I'd have to come home during my lunch hour and do this. Thanks for getting it done." She inspected my work. "The baseboards are grimy too. Will you wipe them off?"

I peeked at my watch. "Sure." I didn't have time, but I needed to do more to help. When I finished, I changed into a pair of navy-blue slacks with a pale blue knit top which reminded me of forget-me-nots and Luke. After daydreaming about love lost, I peeked at my watch again and realized I would be late for my first home visit. I scurried out the door.

I arrived at the office at 9:30, and all the chatter stopped. Gloom hung in the air. Or doom. My heart raced, and I lumbered to my chair. What now? My end here?

Sam met me in front of my desk. "Where have you

been?"

"I had a home visit with one of Victor's families." I peered at Ronni for moral support, but she busied herself at her desk. "My calendar shows—"

"When I schedule a staff meeting, you are to be here. Do you understand?"

I apologized and avoided her stare. "I knew nothing about a staff meeting."

"Ronni did. And Victor called in. He's returning soon." She frowned and shuffled to my side. "Let me see your calendar."

I logged in to my computer and confirmed I hadn't received a meeting request.

Sam said she'd let it go this time but accused me of deleting a meeting request after I'd accepted it. Crazy. Why would I do that?

I opened and updated Luke's home study report. If I had everything filled out to Sam's liking and left no unanswered questions, would that be enough to save my job? At least long enough to ask for Friday morning off so I could go to my interview in Nashville.

I reviewed Luke's information and realized I hadn't completed a final inspection of his cabin to make sure he'd made the updates I'd requested. If I waited any longer to ask for Friday morning off, Sam would be more upset that I asked her late in the week. I rested my elbow on the desk and propped my forehead on my hand. *Lord, please help me.*

Despite it all, I grinned. Good to talk to the Lord again every day. I'd missed Him. But He'd never gone away. That was all me.

I gripped my purse and headed out the door. I needed to complete the home study part of Luke's file, so when he finished his training the following week, his application would be ready for final approval. If I didn't see his car at his automotive shop, I'd drop by his house and pay him a surprise lunch visit.

~

Luke let Grizzly outside and returned to the pot of chili that warmed on the stove. He filled two bowls and placed them on the table. "Can you believe Lanie blames me for the misunderstanding after graduation?" He sat across from Eddie. "Was it my fault she wouldn't tell me what she thought she saw?"

"You could have tried harder to get to the truth." Eddie bowed his head and prayed. When he lifted his head, he said, "You gave up and came home without a fight."

"Don't side with her. She dumped me."

"And you still love her." Eddie glared at him and grunted. "Don't let her get away again. You're an idiot if you do. I'm tired of hearing you whine about it. Go talk to her."

Luke's muscles tightened, and he rolled his neck. "Not happening. I'm not taking the blame for her sending me home alone. She had plenty of time—"

"You know what? You're just making excuses now. Quit blaming her for everything. You have a role in this too."

"But what about Mom and Dad? You know Dad thought of her as his daughter, and she couldn't visit or call?"

Eddie stood and smacked his hands on the table. "As for Dad, he wasn't Lanie's responsibility. Yours and mine. But not hers."

Luke stiffened and narrowed his eyes. "Our

responsibility?"

"How often did we talk with him concerning his relationship with the Lord?"

"You know Dad. He wasn't the easiest to talk to."

"Yet it was Lanie's responsibility to share Christ above ours?" Eddie snagged his car keys off the kitchen counter.

Luke took a bite of soup and met Eddie's gaze. "Victor called and gave me good news. He'll be back soon." Luke smirked and pushed his shoulders back. "After Billy arrives next week, I won't have need for Lanie. But I need to be extra nice to her until then. I want this approval."

"I'm going back to the shop." Eddie gaped at Luke and twirled his keyring around his finger. "I didn't realize until now that you're a nitwit."

"And your boss."

~

Lanie parked her car next to Eddie's and greeted him. "Is Luke getting ready to leave for the shop, or do you think I can have a few minutes of his time?"

"He's in a terrible mood. Enter at your own risk."

"Again? I'd hoped he'd be in a better one today."

"I'll say a prayer for you." He climbed behind the wheel, and I made my way up the steps to Luke's door.

"Why are you here?" Luke opened the door for me to enter.

I spotted an almost full bowl of chili on the table. "To join you for lunch."

"Help yourself. I don't think Eddie took a bite."

"That bad? Did you run out of tomato paste and add ketchup?" I chuckled at the memory.

Underneath his stern face, a tiny smile formed.

"That was a long time ago, and I learned from my mistake." He picked up the bowl of chili and carried it to the counter. "This recipe won the chili cook-off at my church last year."

I stepped closer and congratulated him. "I'm sure it's delicious." I took a spoon from his silverware drawer and dipped it into the pot of chili. "Yum."

"Would you like a bowl?"

I declined. Pretty obvious he didn't want me here. Again. "I thought an impromptu visit was in order. I need to follow up on a few items to make sure you've made the updates I suggested for your cabin."

"You should have noticed the mirror in the bathroom on an earlier visit. What else did I need?"

"A banister in the stairwell to the upstairs bedroom."

"Go look."

I walked to the far corner of the kitchen and glanced upstairs. "Nice job." I climbed the steps to look at Billy's room. A Spider-Man bedspread covered the twin bed, and matching curtains hung from the window. I returned to the kitchen. "He'll love it. You did a fantastic job."

Luke thanked me, and for a moment, I saw a spark in his eye. But before I could blink, it disappeared. "Let me show you the laundry room. I bought a locked cabinet for all potentially harmful cleaning supplies and pesticides."

I checked the laundry room and the refrigerator one more time. Everything was in order. "Do you have a booster seat for your truck?"

He led me outside to his pickup.

The seat passed my inspection too. "After we

review tomorrow's lesson, you'll have the final virtual class Monday with the nurse, along with an in-person wrap-up review session with your trainer Wednesday." The creek behind me gurgled. "I'll update and submit my final report to Sam. If the trainer agrees, we should be ready to place Billy in your home next week." I strolled toward my car and turned back to Luke. "You'll make a wonderful foster dad. One of the best."

Another spark lit his eye and vanished. Why wouldn't he let me in?

I made another foster parent visit and drove to Creekside to meet with Kylee. I prayed a quick prayer in the parking lot before I went inside. Would she hate to say goodbye to me, or was I the only one who would have a tough time with this?

I poked my head into Todd's office. "Did you receive that information we talked about yesterday?"

He handed me an email printout. "Looks like a great opportunity for her."

I skimmed the email and agreed.

"She's in the study room completing her homework."

I trudged my way through the foyer and knocked on the opened door. "Can I tear you away from your homework for a chat?"

We walked to the visitation room and sat across from one another at the table.

"I have something to discuss with you." I clenched my hands, kept them hidden, and tried to steady my fingers from fidgeting.

"Is it good?"

"I think so." I scratched my arm and wrist. "A home has come available for you."

She focused on the table. "Where?"

"A single mom who takes in two teenaged girls at a time. One left yesterday. The lady would like you to live with her." I folded my trembling hands again in my lap. "She has a small farm with horses the girls take care of and a few gardens. Sounds like she gives the girls a lot of attention and teaches them about plant and animal care."

"That sounds cool." She bit her fingernail and in a quieter voice said, "I love the idea of having horses— they're my favorite animal." She gazed out the front window. "Will you visit me there, or could you be my caseworker again?"

"To be your caseworker, I'd have to move back to Chattanooga, and I don't see that happening. But I can try to get permission to visit you at the farm. Sounds like a wonderful place to live." I handed her a business card with my cell phone number. "You can call me anytime you want to talk."

Her damp eyes met mine. "When will I leave Creekside?"

My vision blurred, and my voice hitched. "Ms. Barker will be here later this evening to drive you back to Chattanooga."

She stood, darted to my side of the table, and held me close. "Thank you for being here for me. I like you a lot."

I sniffled and rubbed her arm. "I like you a lot too."

She pulled away and stuck my card in her pocket. "Will you tell Billy for me before you leave? Tell him I'll see him after I pack my things."

After we said our goodbyes, I talked with Billy. He wasn't happy about Kylee leaving, but he understood he wouldn't have seen much of her after he went to live with Mr. Luke.

I stopped by to see Todd before I left to let him know Kylee took the news well.

He touched the corner of his eye. "Looks like she took the news better than you."

"This rarely happens with me. But she and Billy have touched my heart."

He offered me a cookie on a small paper plate. "Here. These always make me feel better."

"Chocolate, chocolate chunk?" I brought the cookie to my nose and breathed in the rich dark chocolate. "My favorite. But I can't take your cookie."

"I snitched three, and I'm happy to share this one with you. Especially now because it almost touched your nose."

I giggled and bit into the soft cookie with melt-in-your-mouth chocolate chunks. "Did Teresa make these?"

"Maggie Stone dropped them off."

I stared at the cookie before taking a second bite.

"She may run a gossip blog, but she's an excellent baker, and she loves baking for the kids here."

"I don't know what to say, except these are the best cookies I've ever eaten."

He agreed and told me he'd stay late to see Kylee off.

I thanked him and hurried into the foyer, but when I got to the front door, I spun and re-entered Todd's office. "If she in any way seems disappointed that I'm not here, please text or call. Although we said our goodbyes, I can be here in five minutes."

He nodded and assured me that I'd done everything

I could to make her stay at Creekside a pleasant one.

I returned to the office to complete Luke's home study. I hoped by submitting the report to Sam in the morning that I'd save my job and have a better chance of getting Friday morning off.

When I arrived home, I prepared chili for supper. Luke's tasted great, and I wanted a bowl full. Jill would appreciate a meal ready when she and Becca arrived.

A few minutes later, dinner was ready, and Jill and Becca came through the door from the garage. We greeted each other with a round of hugs, and they filled me in amidst Becca's giggles.

"Becca thinks she's pregnant. She bought a test kit on her way here." Jill patted Becca on her back. "We get to be the first to know."

Thirty-two

Wednesday morning at breakfast, Becca couldn't keep quiet about her good news. After several minutes of pregnancy talk, I left the table to finish getting ready for work.

When I returned to the kitchen, I placed my purse on the counter and heated a cup of water in the microwave for hot tea. "I learned something strange yesterday."

They both looked at me, and I told them about Maggie baking cookies for the children's home.

Becca put her dirty dishes in the dishwasher. "I'm glad she followed through on that."

"You knew this already?"

Jill put the cereal boxes in the pantry. "She offered to do that last November when we asked for community help to supply gifts for Creekside and the county's foster children."

I leaned against the counter. "With the way people talk about her blog, I wouldn't expect her to do something that nice."

Becca removed my cup of hot water from the microwave and placed it next to me. "We shouldn't be too hard on her. She's a nice person. It's just that people who hurt, hurt other people."

Jill and I stared at Becca and waited for more information.

"If I told you anything more, I'd be guilty of gossiping, too, wouldn't I?" Instead, Becca shared her plans for the day. "I have an appointment with my realtor. She has three houses to show me."

She pulled her phone out of her jeans pocket. "And I need to contact Doc Brown and make an appointment to confirm my pregnancy test before I tell Ben."

I smiled and touched her elbow. "Will he be as excited as you?"

She grimaced and rounded her shoulders. "I'm not sure. We haven't talked about children, except for him to comment he expected his daughter to make us grandparents one day."

Jill wrapped her in a side hug. "He'll be thrilled."

Becca laid her phone on the kitchen counter. "But his daughter's almost twenty. That's a long time to start over with a baby. I don't know how to break this to him." She picked up her phone again. "I have Doc Brown's number here and will call his office later this morning."

"Oh, I forgot. Doc Brown retired. There's a new doctor now." I fumbled through my purse but couldn't find the card Ronni gave me on Monday. I told them about Ronni's take on the good-looking, single doctor. "Jill, go with Becca to her appointment and make eyes at the doctor. Doesn't look like a relationship with Doc Winston will work out."

She'd offered to help Doc on Saturdays with the hope of sparking a romance between them.

Jill sneered and jutted out her chin. "His niece will be here in a couple of weeks. I'm sure he'll ask me out after she arrives."

Becca opened her eyes wide. "You've made progress? Fantastic."

"Not exactly. But I'm staying positive."

While they chatted, I dumped my purse onto the table and sorted through the mess. Wallet, lip balm, keys, nail file. "Here it is. The handsome doctor's name is . . . Nicolas Stewart."

Becca clutched her chest. Jill grabbed hold of the kitchen counter. Both eyed me with their mouths open.

"What? Who is he?"

Becca padded to the table and sat facing us. "My brother is Pleasant Springs's new doctor?"

Jill took both of my hands in hers. "I haven't seen him for a few years, but he's gorgeous, and he'll be perfect."

Becca jerked her head and narrowed her eyes. "Perfect for what?" She shook her head and slapped her palm on the table. "He's my brother, and he's not at all perfect."

"Perfect to make Lanie's Luke jealous when he sees her with Doc Stewart."

I backed away, took a mint tea bag from the cabinet, and added it to my cup of hot water. "No way. According to Luke, we're not even meant to be friends. Unless God performs a miracle, I need to forget Luke Gibson." I poured my tea into an insulated mug and snapped on the lid. Perhaps forget Pleasant Springs too. Nashville was still a possibility.

"Becca can arrange everything with Nick." Jill peered at Becca and nodded. "Right, Becca?"

"Wrong."

I thanked Becca for siding with me and left for the office. If anyone needed to get someone else's attention, it was Jill. Doc Stewart may give Doc Winston a little competition if the light in Jill's eyes meant anything when she heard the name Nicolas Stewart.

The office was quiet when I arrived. Ronni typed away on her computer, and Sam whispered into her desk phone. I reviewed Luke's home study and printed off a full set of documents for Sam.

When she ended her call, I made my way to her desk. "I have Luke Gibson's home study ready for your review. I'm meeting with him today to review the fourth session that he's covering this morning. He'll complete the medication session Monday and meet with the trainer one last time on Wednesday morning in Chattanooga."

She thumbed through the report. "All looks good."

I clasped my hands behind my back. I didn't want her to see them shake. "Would it be possible for me to take Friday morning off? I have an appointment. I hope I won't need to cancel."

She glanced up and raised her eyebrows. "Your turn to meet the cute doctor?"

My chest tightened, and I remained expressionless.

"Sure. What time will you be available?"

"I'll be back in the office at 2:00 p.m."

She rose from her chair and hobbled to the coffeepot. "Your doctor appointment is most of the day?"

"Not here. I need to travel." *Lord, I'm not lying. Am I? I never said a doctor appointment.*

She poured herself a cup of coffee. "I'd like to meet with you at 2:00 when you get back."

I returned to my desk, relieved she didn't question me further. But why did she want to meet with me at 2:00 Friday? Why not meet with me today? After I returned a few phone calls, I left to visit the elementary school. I liked to talk to teachers about students in our care and made appointments with the teachers during their free period. I had two this morning and three this afternoon—all Victor's placements.

~

Luke completed his fourth training session with the trainer in Chattanooga and returned to his cabin. He made a sandwich and took a seat at the kitchen table to work on his homework assignment before Lanie arrived for her review at 3:30. He struggled to concentrate. What if Lanie didn't recommend him? He needed to be nicer to her, but she hadn't made it easy for him. Talk of rekindling their friendship? He didn't need her. Once he got his approval, he'd be fine if he never had to see her again. His heart couldn't take another rejection from his one true love.

He stood and slipped out onto his porch. The creek sloshed against the rocks, and a frog croaked in the distance. Luke pulled out his phone and sent a text to Lanie: **Finished today's training. Working on the homework. All set for this afternoon.** He hit send and decided he needed to personalize his message: **Thanks for all your help.** He sat on the rocker and pinched his lower lip. Nope. He didn't need Lanie.

Luke cringed and rubbed his temples. But was Eddie right about being a nitwit? He should have probed her for a better explanation all those years ago.

He shouldn't have expected her to perform a miracle with his dad. But why didn't she visit his parents?

One thing he knew—he wasn't honest with himself. He wanted to believe that he didn't need her to be a part of his life and future. But he did. What would it take for them to rekindle their friendship and more? Was it too late to fight for her? Was it worth it to try?

Luke needed more time to pray. But, for now, his focus was clearing the last few hurdles so he could foster Billy.

~

I knocked on Luke's screen door, surprised he hadn't greeted me on the front porch as he usually did. "Hello? Are you here? I'm ready to review lesson four, 'Rerouting Trauma Behaviors?'"

His voice sounded muffled and grumpy. "Give me a minute."

Poor Luke must have had his own trauma to deal with. If only I could have understood what he was going through.

He pushed open his screen door to allow me to enter, but he had a distant look in his eye.

"Is everything okay?"

"Grizzly's sick. I had to clean up after him. He's resting on his bed in my room." Luke squinted and pursed his lips. "I'm sure he's okay. Must have eaten something outside that didn't agree with him."

"Poor baby."

Luke asked when he could see Billy again.

"What about Friday afternoon?"

Luke agreed to a visit at 3:00, and we reviewed his lesson. Overall, he seemed quiet. He must have had a lot on his mind. And most likely, it had to do with spending so much time with me.

When I left his cabin, I stopped by Creekside to visit Billy. He'd had a tough day at school that continued into his afternoon at the children's home. We strolled out back to the playground, where I pushed him on the swing. "Do you want to talk about anything?"

He sounded upset. "I'm sad."

"Do you want to tell me why, or should I guess?"

He twisted in the swing. "Guess."

"Do you miss Kylee?"

He wiped his hand over his eyes. "Why did she have to go?"

I moved to the front of his swing. "I'm sad too. We'll both miss her." I patted the top of his head. "Is there anything I can do to make you feel better?"

"Chocolate chip cookie dough ice cream?" He jumped off the swing. "But can I play on the slide first?"

I watched him on the slide from a nearby bench and envied Becca. A husband and now a baby. Not in God's plans for me.

At least not with Luke.

Thirty-three

Friday morning arrived sooner than I'd hoped. I didn't feel confident after I'd tossed and turned all night fretting over my 10:00 interview. If I wanted the Meade Agency to offer me a job, I needed to be at my best. I peeked at the clock on the stove and shrieked—7:58. I grabbed my slice of toast with blackberry jam and rushed to my car. My GPS showed ninety minutes for the trip, but I wanted to allow an extra thirty minutes to be safe.

I drove west to Manchester and took Interstate 24 northwest into Nashville. While I drove, a sense of queasiness erupted in my gut. I should have called upon the Lord before I allowed anxiety to get the best of me. I rolled my neck and shoulders and tried to relax. *Okay, Lord. What do You want me to do? Do I accept the job if they offer me a position? There's nothing for me in Pleasant Springs. Sure, there's Jill, my parents, and Miss Risa. But Kylee's gone and Billy will have Luke, and he's made it clear he wants nothing to do with me.*

Why hadn't I called Miss Risa and asked her to pray for me? I didn't ask Jill or Becca either. What was wrong with me? I turned on a Christian radio station and hoped that would calm me. But I became more nervous the closer I got to downtown Nashville. If Chattanooga traffic was bad, Nashville's was horrible. I couldn't imagine what it had been like an hour or two before during rush hour.

Because I arrived thirty minutes early, I passed the building for the Meade Agency and a couple of parking lots. I focused ahead and slammed my brakes to keep from hitting a pedestrian who'd jay walked. My anxiety rose ten levels. A car honked behind me, and I jumped. I stepped on the gas and almost turned down a one-way street the wrong way.

I continued down several more roads and found a place to park along a curb in front of a few shops. That's when I realized I held my steering wheel in a tight grip. I released my hold and shook out the stiffness in my fingers. I hated Nashville traffic. No way could I drive in this every day.

After I blew out several quick breaths, I reset my GPS. I'd traveled seven minutes away from my destination. I returned to the professional building where the agency was located and parked in a lot across the street. Inside the building, I verified the agency was on the fourth floor, and strolled to the elevator with my head held high.

I arrived at the reception area five minutes early. The receptionist smiled and said all the right things, but I didn't get any warm and fuzzy vibes. Had Nashville grown too much or too fast for my liking? Or had I set my expectations too high? Pleasant Springs didn't seem all that bad.

The receptionist offered me a seat and told me that someone would come for me in a few minutes. I relaxed enough to get my thoughts on the Lord and opened my Bible app to read the verses of the day, Proverbs 3:5-6: "Trust in the LORD with all your heart and lean not on your own understanding; in all your ways submit to him, and he will make your paths straight."

I read the verses three times and mumbled. "Got it." *I trust You, Lord, with this interview and the outcome and believe You will guide me in all things pertaining to my future.*

Soon after, a young woman escorted me into a meeting room for my interview. Over the next hour and twenty minutes, I met with the human resource director, the department manager for the position I'd applied for, and a case manager. We concluded my interview at 11:30. The three interviewers seemed friendly enough. They'd be good to work with, and I was confident the interview went well.

When I left, Nashville sounded better to me, but still not great. Outside, I pulled my key fob from my purse, crossed the street, and scanned the lot for my car. Panic rose in my chest and into my throat.

My car wasn't where I'd parked it.

~

Luke disconnected the call and shook his head.

Eddie stood in front of the desk. "What was that about?"

"Not sure. Lanie planned to bring Billy over for a visit today, but Lanie's supervisor, Samantha, called to say she'd drop Billy off tomorrow morning at 10:00 for a visit. Not today."

"Maybe Lanie called in sick, assumed she wouldn't feel better tomorrow, and they're shorthanded in the office."

"She'd text or call me." He rose from his chair and gazed out into the garage bay. "Something's not right."

~

Someone had stolen my Escape. How could that happen? I looked everywhere but couldn't find it. How would I make it back to Pleasant Springs in time to meet with Sam at 2:00 and take Billy to Luke's at 3:00?

A car door slammed behind me, and I spun. "Miss, are you okay? You look a little lost." The kind-looking man drew his eyebrows together. "May I help you with anything?"

"My car." I brought my hand to my mouth and pulled it away. "It's gone. I parked it right here." I pointed to the spot that held a black sedan.

In a calm tone, he said, "Have you used your fob to find your car?"

I moaned and took several quick, shallow breaths. "What?"

He removed the key fob from my hand. "What kind of car?"

"A Ford Escape."

He hit the fob lock in different directions. After a few clicks, a faint car horn beeped.

"Is your car blue?"

I nodded and stumbled back a step.

"Over there." He pointed across the street to the corner opposite from where we stood.

"How embarrassing." I winced and bopped my forehead. "Please forgive me and thank you for your help."

"Happens all the time. These parking lots all look the same."

I thanked him for not making me feel like an idiot. "Sir, you're a blessing."

He cocked his head and laughed. "Would you call my wife, Allison, and tell her that? She was a little perturbed with me this morning."

"I'd be happy to call her."

He said something about only kidding, wished me a good day, and turned to cross the street.

"Sir. May I have your name? I'd like to ask the Lord to pour out a return blessing upon you."

He twisted back and grinned. "Thank you, miss. Porter. Jim Porter."

By the time I pulled out of the parking lot, it was noon. I had two hours to make a ninety-minute drive and grab a bite to eat before I stopped by the office to meet with Sam. I could do that.

Lord, what do you want me to do? I thought I'd love Nashville, but I don't. Everything that happened before and after the interview makes me question if this is the place for me. I've loved being back home, spending time with Jill, being able to visit my parents, and spending time with Luke. I love him. But he's made it clear there's no future for us. Is Nashville where You want me?

Thirty-four

By the time I got to Manchester, it was 1:00 and dark clouds had formed overhead. I exited the interstate, filled my gas tank, and bought a quick bite to eat. With my ham and cheese sandwich in hand, and a drizzle falling, I traveled east toward Pleasant Springs. The drizzle turned into a downpour before I took a bite of my lunch. My windshield wipers wouldn't work fast enough.

I pulled off the road into a small market to wait it out and gobbled down my lunch with no letup in the rain. After a few more minutes, I grabbed my phone and recited a text to Sam: Caught in a downpour. Pulled off the road. May I stop by the office after I take Billy out to visit Luke? Thanks.

My phone rang. I expected it to be Sam, but instead, it was the HR director from the Meade Agency. She said everyone talked and agreed to offer me the position with more money because of my experience and the wonderful reviews they received from my two former supervisors.

What an amazing offer. But was it right for me? Did I want to move to Nashville or stay in Pleasant Springs? *Where do you want me, Lord?* I thanked the

HR director and asked if I could get back with her. I needed to think and pray.

While the rain continued to pelt my window, my phone pinged with a text from Sam: NO. Saw it on your calendar and handled it. COME TO THE OFFICE.

My elation over a job offer died. A sense of dread, like the downpour outside, flooded over me. She handled it?

This is it, isn't it, Lord? The day I lose my job. Please help me. Should I accept the Meade Agency's offer and move to Nashville? I shook my head and sighed. *I'll trust You to work this all out. Thank you.*

The rain hadn't let up, and I was no longer in a hurry to get back to Pleasant Springs. I typed out a text to Luke: Is Sam bringing Billy out for your visit? Or did she cancel it?

He responded: Tomorrow morning. Where are you? Is everything okay?

Had an interview in Nashville. I think Sam plans to fire me today.

Luke didn't respond, and it didn't matter. He'd made it clear he didn't want to rekindle our friendship. If no friendship, no chance for any kind of relationship with him.

When the rain died down, I drove to the office and arrived at 2:15.

Sam ushered me to the back table with her trusty little manilla file folder in her hands. "This will only take a minute."

I supposed I only deserved a minute of her time.

"I overlooked your missing our meeting this week, but I cannot overlook your insubordination in continuing to visit with Kylee at Creekside. In addition, I understand that you've had several visits with Risa

McDonald during office hours. She has nothing to do with children's services."

"But I have counted none of those visits in my weekly totals. And I've worked plenty of hours in the three weeks I've been here."

"You should have discussed those visits with me beforehand." She opened her folder and handed me an official termination notice. "Goodbye, Ms. Meadows. I wish you well."

She hobbled back to her desk and picked up her phone.

I glanced across the room to Ronni. She shrugged and lifted her palms upward.

I returned to my desk and sat when a wave of lightheadedness washed over me. With my hand pressed against my stomach, I willed the churning there to stop. When I regained some measure of control, I grabbed my purse and a photo of my family from my desk, stood on shaky legs, and headed out to my car.

"Wait." Ronni jogged toward me in the parking lot. "I'm so sorry. I let something slip that I shouldn't have."

"What are you talking about?"

"Risa McDonald." Ronni caught her breath. "She called the office for you one day. Said she'd misplaced your cell number and she enjoyed your morning visits." Ronni turned away and looked down. "I may have implied to Sam that you visited Miss Risa during office hours." She touched my elbow. "I feel terrible."

She should feel terrible. I worked more than enough hours to make up for my time with Miss Risa. "Forget it. She would have found some other reason to fire me." I said goodbye to Ronni and climbed into my car.

Although getting fired didn't come as a surprise, it came with a lot of questions like, what went wrong? Why wouldn't she give me a chance to prove myself? Why did she hate me?

~

At 4:00 p.m., I drove to Creekside to ask Todd if I could visit Billy. He needed reassurance to know how much I cared about him. But he also needed to understand I'd lost my job and didn't know how often I'd get to see him.

When I drove in and parked, Todd stood outside the entrance door and waved to someone who'd pulled away from the curb.

He greeted me and opened the front door. "How did things go in Nashville?"

I told him about the job offer that I no longer wanted. "But when I got back to the office, Sam fired me."

"Why? What reason did she give?"

I shared the reasons with Todd while we stepped into his office.

"Do you think you'll accept the Nashville position?"

I straightened my shoulders and lifted my chin in the hope I could convey confidence. "I don't want to. I feel I belong in Pleasant Springs. But I may not have a choice."

He sat at his desk. "Have you talked with Jerome yet about Sam ending your employment?"

"Do you think I should?" I took a seat across from him.

"I don't see how it could hurt."

I pulled out my cell, clicked on his number, and put it on speakerphone. We greeted one another, and he said, "What can I do for my favorite former case manager?"

Todd raised his eyebrows and smiled.

"Find out why Sam fired me today."

"Samantha ended your employment?" In a skeptical tone, he said, "What reasons did she give?"

I told him her reasons. "I'm guilty of both, but I don't believe either are grounds for termination. I visited the lady on my own time."

Jerome asked me a few questions regarding what I'd already said. "I'll call and talk with her. This makes little sense." He paused and cleared his throat. "We have an opening here in Hamilton County that I'd love to have you fill."

After thanking him, I said, "I'll think about it, but I prefer to stay here in Pleasant Springs."

Jerome chatted for a few more minutes. "Kylee likes her new home and has adjusted well these past three days."

"I'm glad to hear that." I pressed my lips together. "Could you send me her address? I want to send her a gift."

Sounded like Kylee was happy.

But what about me, Lord? Perhaps Pleasant Springs isn't where You want me after all. Would I find happiness in Nashville?

Thirty-five

After my conversation with Jerome, Todd gave me permission to speak to Billy in the living room.

I sat next to him on the sofa, we chatted for a couple of minutes, and I told him my job ended. "You'll have a new caseworker soon."

Billy screamed and kicked his feet against the couch. "No. I only want you."

I wrapped my arms around him and drew him close. "You'll like Miss Ronni. She's sweet." I patted his back while he cried. "Or Mr. Victor might be your caseworker. I'm sure he's nice too." I pulled away. "When you move into Mr. Luke's house, you'll spend a lot of time with him and Grizzly. You won't see your caseworker every day."

"No. I don't want to live with Mr. Grumpy Pants. Why can't I stay here? I like Miss Teresa and Mr. Steve."

"This is a temporary home until a family is available to care for you. And Mr. Luke and Grizzly will soon be available."

He peered at me with big puffy eyes. "But I'll see

you at Coach Luke's because you're friends, right? And he'll invite you."

I tried to sound positive. "Perhaps you can ask him." I placed my hand on his head.

Smiling, Todd entered the living room. "And she'll see a lot of you over the next few days because she plans to volunteer here."

"Yes. Volunteer." I gave Todd a thumbs up when Billy wasn't looking. "We can spend lots of time together." I grinned and ruffled his hair. "What do you think about that?"

He focused on the coffee table with a blank expression. "Okay, I guess."

I snickered and twisted my mouth. "Just, okay?"

His eyes lit up, and he hugged me before he ran down the hallway toward his room.

I thanked Todd for his quick thinking.

"Ulterior motive. I could use another volunteer."

"I'd love that."

When I left Creekside, I went back and forth in my mind juggling the pros and cons of taking the Nashville position. Even though it was a sure thing and a great offer, I didn't feel good about leaving my family or Billy. With or without Luke, Pleasant Springs was where I wanted to live. The Lord would open an opportunity here in my hometown, wouldn't He?

I called the HR director at the agency, thanked her, and turned down the offer. Time to walk in faith.

That evening, Becca and Jill wanted to cheer me up and offered to take me to dinner at Mama Lou's. We sat in a booth with Becca and Jill on one side and me on the other. After we placed our orders and received our drinks, we chatted about Becca's house search, which hadn't turned up any good options yet.

"We need God to answer our prayers. A house for Becca and a job for me."

Becca stroked her throat and nodded. "Although we want you to stay here, Chattanooga isn't that far. You could come home often if you wanted to."

"Perhaps I'm just kidding myself, but I think the Lord wants me here. I don't want to stay away any longer. Pleasant Springs is my home." I glanced across the restaurant and waved at a foster family I'd visited a few days before.

Jill tapped her fingers on the table. "Where have you searched here?"

"I checked the school system and the hospital's websites for anything that might work." I shook my head and folded my hands on my lap. "Zilch."

Jill motioned to someone behind me. When I looked in that direction, Eddie made his way to our booth. Jill asked him to join us, and I slid over to give him room.

"No. A stool at the counter."

I stuck out my bottom lip. "Am I that awful that you can't sit next to me?"

He frowned and scooted in beside me. "No way. But Maggie?"

I inched my glass of sweet tea toward me. "What about her?"

He lowered his head and mumbled. "Her blog."

I moved closer to him and brushed my arm against his. "I don't want her to mention me on her blog either. But we can't hide from her."

Jill chuckled and winked at Eddie. "Think of all the notoriety you'll receive from the ladies if Maggie writes about you sitting at a table with three beautiful women."

"Uh, one's married. Another's taken. And ones . . ." He blushed and stiffened. "Oops."

I wiggled my eyebrows at Jill. "Are you the one who's taken?"

Eddie inched away from me on the bench. "I'll move."

Jill jumped up and blocked his exit. "No." She put her hand on her hip, narrowed her eyes, and looked down at him. "You meant Lanie and Luke when you said another's taken."

I gasped and gaped at Jill. "Stop harassing Eddie. Luke doesn't care a thing about me. What's gotten into you?"

She slid back into her seat. "Sorry, Eddie. We do hope you'll stay."

He relaxed his shoulders and nudged my elbow. "Y'all looked intense."

Becca pointed at me. "We're trying to keep Lanie in Pleasant Springs, so she doesn't move away for a new job."

I filled him in on my termination from the county and my job offer in Nashville. Before I could tell him that I'd turned down the Nashville offer, Lou stopped at the table for Eddie's order. He decided on the daily special—fish and chips with sweet tea.

"When does your coffee equipment arrive?" Eddie unwrapped the napkin from his utensils.

Lou clapped her hands and raised up on her toes. "Tomorrow mornin'. We'll be up and runnin' Sunday."

"Great." Eddie excused himself to the restroom.

Jill's eyes grew large, and she leaned toward Lou.

"What equipment?"

"We're gonna make those fancy big city drinks." Lou's face fell, and she wrinkled her nose. "As long as I can find someone to train the staff and me. The company's trainer is in Georgia and can't make it. I need an experienced barista."

Jill gazed at me and lifted her brows. "You found your job."

Lou peered at me and clutched her chest. "You worked as a barista through college, right?"

I squirmed. "That was a long time ago. I doubt I can remember everything."

"But you know a lot more than I do. Will you train me and the staff?" She opened and closed her mouth. "Did Jill say you're lookin' for a job?"

"I lost mine today."

"You're hired. You'll be my full-time barista. At least until we all get trained."

I smiled and thanked the Lord. "Okay. I'll do my best."

She scurried back to the kitchen with Eddie's order. At least we hoped she wouldn't forget his order in her excitement.

Becca reached across the table and touched my hand. "We just witnessed a blessing from God. You can stay in Pleasant Springs."

My shoulders sagged. "The barista position won't pay much, but it should be enough to keep me afloat."

Our food arrived after Eddie returned to the table, and he offered a prayer of thanksgiving.

Jill placed her napkin in her lap. "What can you tell us, Eddie, about Luke? Does he talk much about Lanie?"

I kicked Jill's leg underneath the table. Hard, but I hoped not enough to leave a bruise.

"Ouch." Becca glared at me and bent forward.

I placed my hand over my mouth and let my hand drop. "I meant to kick Jill."

Eddie tipped back his head and laughed. "You three are a hoot." He quieted and turned toward me. "Luke talks sometimes."

Jill's face glowed, and her eyes twinkled. "Maybe there's still hope."

As much as I wanted to, I couldn't count on that.

~

Luke made sure everything would be ready for Billy's visit the next day. Everything but his aching heart. When he'd hoped he and Lanie might get over their hurtful past, she ran off to Nashville and interviewed for a job.

How could she abandon him again? Him and Billy. Lanie must not have any compassion for anyone except herself.

He placed his hand on his chest and pulled the front of his T-shirt into his fist. Had he never known the truth about her, or had she changed that much in the past eleven years?

And what happened to her job with the county? Did she lose it? But what did that matter? If her dream position came through, she'd take it. What she'd always wanted. The big city life.

He shuddered and rubbed his arms. Nothing she wanted was in Pleasant Springs. Time to let her go.

He grabbed the dog brush, called Grizzly over to him, and moved out onto the front porch. "Time for a good brushing, okay, boy?" He sat on the bench and brushed the dog's fur until he heard a car crunching along his driveway.

Grizzly barked and wagged his tail.

Eddie parked his car along the side of the cabin and climbed the steps. He took a seat in the rocking chair next to Luke and bent forward. "Just came from Mama Lou's." He told Luke that Lanie had lost her job and planned to move to Nashville.

In a defeated tone, Luke said, "No big deal. I'm done with her."

Eddie rested back in his chair and rocked. "You sure about that? When are you going to fight for her? I doubt she has any idea you care about her with the way you act."

Luke stood and pointed the dog brush at Eddie. "If she wants to go to Nashville, I won't stop her. And you need to keep your mouth shut. Not another word."

"Fine." Eddie rose from his chair. "Don't come crying to me when she ends up with someone else." He bounced down the steps, turned, and shook his head.

Luke opened the door to his cabin, stepped inside, and let the screen door slam shut.

Thirty-six

Lou wanted me to be at the restaurant early Saturday morning before the delivery people brought in the new coffee equipment. After an hour of waiting and filling in for a server whose daughter got sick during the night, I wanted to quit. But I needed an income, and this is what the Lord provided. *Thank you, Lord. I'll do my best not to complain.*

I wiped down a table that another server bussed and glanced up when the door opened. "Miss Risa." I hurried to embrace her.

She returned my hug, backed away, and touched her chest. "What are you doing here?"

I explained all that had happened since I last saw her and led her to a booth. "Will you be dining alone this morning?"

"Oh, no, dear. I have a handsome young doctor joining me."

My belly fluttered, and I widened my eyes. "Doctor Stewart?"

"Ah. Yes. Have you met Becca's brother?"

I shook my head and smoothed out a wrinkle on my apron. "Have you known him long?"

"Met him yesterday for my checkup. He enjoyed my stories about our small town and invited me to breakfast to hear more."

"I look forward to meeting him."

The back door opened. Our coffee equipment had arrived.

"I've got to go. Debbie Sue will be your server today." I slipped away to assist Lou with placing her equipment but eyed the front door several times to get a look at the new doctor. I recognized him as soon as he came inside. Gorgeous? Oh my yes, with his short wavy hair, a dark brownish-red, and his rugged square jaw. He strutted to the booth where Miss Risa sat.

Someone nearby snapped their fingers. "Are you listening? I need you to recommend the best layout."

I blinked several times and whirled toward Lou. "Of course. But first I need to take Miss Risa's order. Debbie Sue's too busy." I grasped an order pad from the counter.

Lou snatched the pad from my hands. "I'll get their order." She scurried to their table.

I did what she asked and directed the two men where to place everything. When they finished, I dashed toward Miss Risa's table but slowed a few feet away. "I didn't get to meet him."

"He needed to get to his office to unpack supplies." She grinned and waved her hand. "Besides, you have your hands full with Luke." She slid off the bench.

I rolled my eyes and smirked. Someone that good looking must have a flaw. "Did he chew with his mouth open? Slurp his food? Smack his lips?"

"Not at all." She chuckled, and her eyes shone. "Do you suppose he'll ask me out again?"

I caught the mischief in her eyes. "He'd be a fool not to."

"Oh, my. I don't perceive him to be a nincompoop either. But there's a better match. Let's see if we can get this gentleman together with Jill."

"My sister?"

"A match made in heaven."

"But she likes . . ."

Miss Risa took a step closer. "Who does she like?"

"I have to get back to work so I don't lose this job too." I scooted to the counter, grabbed a cloth, and cleaned the new equipment.

Lou wanted mochas, lattes, and cappuccinos on the menu Monday. When I got everything organized, it was time to get busy with my first drink—a chai latte.

Perhaps I could woo the new doctor with a special blend. Or would this remind Luke of our college days and bring him to his senses regarding our friendship and more?

~

Luke paced on the front porch while he waited for Billy to arrive and hoped Sam wouldn't be difficult to work with. Why had she fired Lanie? At the sound of a car's approach, he peeked at his watch. Right on time— 10:00 a.m.

He descended the steps, closed his eyes, and took a deep breath. Grizzly followed. Excited to see Billy, Luke grinned when he got to the car. But when he peered into the back seat, his smile faded.

Billy's face held a huge pout, and he sat in his car seat with clenched fists.

Luke opened the passenger door next to Billy. "Come on out of there, buddy. Grizzly's been waiting for you."

Billy glared down at the dog behind Luke and continued to pout. "No. I don't need a fake dad."

Sam moved around the back of the car and approached Luke. "Go inside and I'll talk with him. We'll join you in a few minutes."

Luke backed away and called Grizzly to follow. Instead, the dog stepped in front of Sam and laid his head on Billy's lap.

Sam petted Grizzly's head and neck. "The dog wants you inside. He needs you to take care of him."

Billy unhooked his seatbelt, leaned over Grizzly, and rubbed his fur. "I'll take good care of you, Grizz." He climbed out of his chair and traipsed up the steps to the front door.

Sam's gaze followed Billy before she turned to face Luke. "Give him time. This is another big transition for him."

"What did he say in the car? Why didn't he want to come inside?"

"He's upset with me for not allowing Lanie to bring him here. He'll be fine after I leave. If you have any problems, call me." She handed him her business card. "I'll be back to pick him up later this afternoon."

Luke took the card and thanked her. She left him alone with a boy who didn't want to be there. Luke squinted and cocked his head. *Lord, what have I done? Help me.*

~

The lunch crowd thinned out, and Lou hovered over my shoulder. I prepared my first café mocha, poured half of it into a second cup, and offered her my concoction. We each took a sip at the same time.

She licked her lips and bounced from one foot to the other. "Darlin', this is fantastic."

I nodded and giggled at her exuberance.

"What else can you create?"

"This morning I perfected a chai latte and a white chocolate mocha." I gave her a list of other drinks I could make and a list of drinks we could add with the right ingredients and a little practice.

"Try the other recipes you're sure of and give the waitstaff and me samples to try. We'll add the drinks to our specials' board and offer them tomorrow."

My breath hitched, and I tensed. "I thought Monday was the big day. Does that mean I have to work tomorrow?"

"I need you." She looked toward the door that led to the kitchen. "Let me get the servers out here. You can train everyone to make the three drinks you've perfected now, and we'll keep addin' new drinks."

"Don't you think it might be better if we train one or two at a time and offer only a few drinks at first?"

"Good idea. Let's start with six." She snagged a coffee cup. "And the trainin' begins with me."

After Lou created a chai latte worthy to sell, she left me alone to create a few other drinks. By the time 2:00 rolled around, I'd added vanilla lattes to the list.

My cell buzzed, and I pulled it out of my pocket. "Hello. Luke?" I pulled the phone away from my ear. With Billy screaming and Grizzly barking, I couldn't understand anything Luke said.

"I'm on my way. Give me ten minutes." I tugged off my apron and bolted into the kitchen. "Emergency. I've got to go. Be back as soon as I can."

I shot out the front door and darted to my car. Billy

needed me.
Luke needed me too.
I climbed behind the wheel and slammed the door.
When would he realize that?

Thirty-seven

Luke sat across from Billy, who quieted and sniffled when he saw Luke place his phone on the kitchen table.

"Is Miss Sam coming to take me back to Creekside?"

He grunted and stared at Billy. He'd tried to speak calmly to the boy and not call Lanie, but he couldn't take more of Billy's screaming and crying. What had come over this sweet child?

Luke rested his elbow on the table with his palm on his forehead. He peeked at his watch. "I called the person who you most wanted to see."

"My mom?"

Expressionless, Luke said, "Is that what this is about? You want to see your mom?"

Billy nodded and scurried to the living room. He took a seat on the sofa and folded his hands in his lap. "And Miss Lanie. She said she'd only come to see me if you invited her because she's not my caseworker no more."

Luke stood, opened the front door to let Grizzly outside, and knelt in front of Billy. "I can't take you to see your mom, but I called Miss Lanie. She should be here soon."

Billy's nostrils flared, and he stuck out his chin. "Why don't you like her?"

Luke sat back on his heels. "I do like her, buddy. We're just going through a rough spot."

"But you hurt her a long time ago." Billy squeezed his eyes shut. "She told me."

The muscles in Luke's neck tightened, and he rose from the floor. Hard to believe Lanie would share her personal thoughts with an eight-year-old. Especially Billy. She'd known all along Luke hoped to be Billy's foster dad. And she tried to turn Billy against him?

Billy ran to the front door. "Miss Lanie's here." He opened the door and stepped onto the porch.

Luke followed close behind, wearing a scowl. He and Lanie needed to get a few things settled.

~

Billy ran down the steps and greeted me with a hug so tight I had to pull him off. "What's that for?"

"I missed you."

"But we saw each other yesterday."

"But you weren't sure if we'd see each other as much, and I wanted to see you." Billy clung to my left arm.

Luke strutted toward us with narrowed eyes. A vein on his forehead throbbed. "Billy, would you play with Grizzly for a few minutes? He's missed you and needs time with you."

My pulse quickened, and the back of my throat ached. Why was Luke angry with me? Because Billy had a meltdown? I placed my right hand on his shoulder. "Go play. I'll stay awhile."

Billy ran off to find Grizzly, and I followed Luke's stomping to the front porch.

He spun when he reached the top step. "How dare you discuss our past relationship with Billy. Have you been discrediting me all along?"

I grabbed the handrail to steady myself. "What?" I climbed the last step, and we stood face to face. "I've been careful to say little about us to anyone. What are you talking about?"

Luke told me what Billy said about Luke hurting me.

I sighed and explained to Luke how Billy was afraid when I first met him, and how I'd told him that I got scared too. "When he asked why, I told him someone in town hurt me a long time ago and I was afraid to see them again. We agreed that day we'd help one another." I took a chance and touched Luke's arm. "I met with Billy before I knew of your interest in being a foster parent."

Luke took a step back and sounded stern. "Fix it with him."

I kept my voice calm. "We talked about it the day we hiked at Fall Creek Falls, but I'll explain it to him again."

"Good. Today. He's been a handful." Luke rubbed the back of his neck. "Looks as though the honeymoon period is over."

"Might be good for you to review the session on trauma."

Luke huffed and gritted his teeth. "The trauma you've added to his life."

I brought my hand to my chest and raised my voice. "Me? I explained that to you."

He crossed his arms. "And what about your move to Nashville? Don't you think that might affect him?"

Billy bounded up the steps with Grizzly at his heels. "I'm tired and hungry. Can I get something to eat?"

"Sure." Luke softened his tone. "I fixed you a PB&J earlier and stuck it in the fridge when you didn't want it." Luke opened the front door for Billy. "Let me know if you need help."

I moved to the far side of the porch to get away from the screen door. No need for Billy to hear our heated discussion. I faced Luke. "I'm not moving to Nashville."

Luke strode toward me. "What changed your mind? Nashville was a dream come true for you."

I lifted my chin and pushed my shoulders back. "I thought everything I wanted was here in my hometown." I peered into his eyes and whispered, "But it seems I made a mistake."

~

Luke's stomach knotted, and he massaged the back of his neck. "Too much time has passed."

"You may be right." Lanie continued to stare into his eyes. "Until now, my feelings hadn't changed. I still loved you and wanted to spend the rest of my life with you." She took a step back. "But you've made yourself clear. We're done. I won't bother you further." She glanced toward the creek. "There's someone who I'd like to get to know better since there's no chance for us." I was sure the good doctor was beyond my reach, but I didn't want Luke to assume I planned to wait for him. Even though he held my heart.

"He's why you want to stay in Pleasant Springs?"

She tilted her head and gawked at him. "You're an idiot." She pushed him aside and strolled into his cabin.

Luke gazed at the clouds. *What do you want me to do?* He made his way to the door and listened to Lanie's explanation to Billy.

"Mr. Luke never hurt me. He loved me and wanted to marry me, but I never gave him the chance to ask. I was the bad guy in my story. Not Mr. Luke."

"Why is he mad at you?"

"Because I hurt him."

"He should forgive you."

Luke trudged down the steps and plodded to the creek. Birds chirped and sang in the trees nearby. He picked up a stone and tossed it across the water. He should forgive Lanie. He'd held onto his resentment too long. But was he ready to forgive her for everything? *Lord, help me.*

Luke climbed the steps, entered his cabin, and took a seat at the table across from Lanie and next to Billy. "I've forgiven Miss Lanie for hurting me, but there are other things we still need to work through."

Luke eyed Lanie and pressed his hand to his stomach. "I'm sorry. I *have been* an idiot. If you and Billy will give me more time, I'll prove to you both I'm a good guy."

Lanie moved to the other side of the table and patted Billy's shoulder. "I've got to get back to work. Are you planning to give Mr. Luke a tough time again?"

He looked at Luke and touched his arm. "When I need to see Miss Lanie, will you call her for me?"

"Yes. I'm here for you, buddy. I want to take care of you and hope you're happy here with me."

Billy took another bite of his sandwich and grinned at Lanie. "Okay. Bye."

She kissed the top of his head and slipped out the door.

Luke followed her out onto the porch. "I thought you lost your job."

She told him what had happened and how the Lord opened an immediate opportunity.

"You're a barista at Mama Lou's?"

"You never complained when I fixed you free drinks in college."

"You made a mean caramel latte." He stepped toward a hanging basket of pansies and checked the dirt's moisture. He twisted to face Lanie. "I'm glad you want to stay in Pleasant Springs."

She raised her eyebrows and smiled. "Really? To wow you with my coffee creations?"

He forced a chuckle and shook his head. "Billy needs you."

Her expression faded, and she hurried down the steps.

Luke watched her back her car out. He'd hurt her again. What had she said, "Until now, my feelings hadn't changed"? Had he pushed her too far?

He lifted his hand to wave and whispered. "I need you too."

Thirty-eight

Would Luke ever truly forgive me? He said he had, but his anger toward me spoke otherwise. He knew how I felt. I'd leave the next move to him. And it had better include a genuine apology for the accusations he'd made.

When I arrived at the café, I got busy and created more drinks to add to the specials' board. I added two before my cell buzzed again.

Todd called to tell me that two board members had approved my volunteer application, which was protocol. "You may accompany Creekside children to outings and restaurants if the child agrees. And Billy already asked if you could take him to Luke's church in the morning."

"I'd love to. But I have to be at work by noon and will need to leave before the end of service."

"What if I join you? I've wanted to check out Joy Fellowship. Billy and I can meet you there, you can slip out early, and I'll bring Billy back to Creekside."

"A great idea." And sweet of him to offer.

Todd cleared his throat and deepened his voice. "Are you available to stop by here before I leave at

6:00? I'd like to discuss something with you."

I peeked at my watch: 5:33. "No problem. I'll see you in ten minutes."

We disconnected our call. What did he want to discuss that he couldn't tell me over the phone?

I checked in with Lou before I left and told her that I'd added both caramel lattes and caramel macchiatos to our list. "We have six drinks now." I turned to leave. "See you at noon tomorrow."

"What about cappuccinos? Customers have asked if we'll have those too?"

I spun toward her. "No problem. Add them to the list."

I zipped out the door and drove to Creekside to meet with Todd. I found him sitting on the front porch facing the road perusing the contents of a file folder. "You look deep in thought. Everything okay?"

He offered me a seat across from him. "There's something I'd like to ask you."

"Oh?"

"I know you've had a second job offer with Hamilton County, but if you haven't committed yourself to them, would you be interested in working here at Creekside?" He rubbed his stubbled chin. "I would have asked you sooner, but I wanted to make sure you desired to stay here in Pleasant Springs."

I widened my eyes. "Doing what?" And brought my hand to my chest. "Your codirector?"

Todd pulled out a sheet of paper from his folder. "I'd like you to consider it." He handed the paper to me. "This is the job description. The salary quote is at the bottom of the sheet."

I focused first on the salary, which was similar to

what the county paid, and read aloud the responsibilities. "Schedule and oversee the volunteers, manage the clothing closet, create programs and activities for the children during their stay, oversee all government documents and record keeping, supervise family visits." I scanned the full page. "This looks great. But I haven't seen a clothing closet."

"In the garage. We accept new and gently used clothing."

"I'll need to pray about this. May I have twenty-four hours?" I smiled. "This may be God at work."

He rose from his chair, walked to the railing behind me, and gazed across the street. "I won't need to know that soon because there's a possible hiccup."

I twisted to my right and looked at him. "What?"

"We have five board members, two of which approved your application to volunteer and gave me approval to offer you the codirector position. I couldn't reach one member, one I didn't try, and the last member said they wouldn't approve of you until they talked to Samantha."

"My former boss, Samantha?" I stood next to him at the railing.

He slipped his hands into his pockets. "She's the board member I didn't call."

I groaned and in a quiet voice said, "That doesn't sound good."

"But we only need approval from three of the five, and we already have two. When I reach the other member, we can move forward." He frowned and squished his eyebrows together. "But we'll need to start you after the official board meeting, which doesn't meet for another three weeks. The only way around that is if all five members approve of you over the phone."

"You'll never get Sam's approval."

~

Luke ran a comb through his hair. Where would Lanie attend church? Would he see her? He moaned and dropped his chin to his chest. She hadn't deserved his rebuke. He needed to apologize for his behavior.

He arrived at the church ten minutes before service.

Billy ran to him and bounced on his toes. "I'm here with Miss Lanie and Mr. Todd." Billy raised his hand for a high-five and scurried across the foyer back to Lanie and that Todd guy.

Luke steadied his breathing and wiped his sweaty palms on his pants.

"Who's the dude with Lanie?" Eddie stood to Luke's right.

"A guy from Creekside." With his hands shoved in his pockets, he joined Lanie and the group, nodded a greeting, and entered the worship center.

Unbelievable. Lanie wasted no time getting to know another guy better.

~

I stared after Luke when he went inside the worship center without speaking to me. After Todd and I took Billy to the children's wing, we entered the worship center and selected a spot halfway up on the right side. Todd moved into the row before me, and I sat on the end.

"Luke's not much of a talker." Todd placed his Bible and notepad on the wire rack underneath the chair in front of him.

"He's been a little moody lately."

When the song service and a time of greeting those

around us ended, we returned to our chairs for the Bible message. Pastor Avery read Isaiah 55:6-13. The verses flashed onto two screens at the front of the church while he read from his Bible.

He shared background information regarding the people of Israel and their captivity and tied it to people today.

He reread verses 6-7. "Seek the LORD while he may be found; call on him while he is near. Let the wicked forsake their ways and the unrighteous their thoughts. Let them turn to the LORD, and he will have mercy on them, and to our God, for he will freely pardon."

The pastor continued to read two verses at a time and explain them. My mind wandered to Kylee. Was she at church this morning and hearing God's Word? *Touch her heart, Lord.*

The pianist played softly in the background, while Pastor Avery ended the service.

I whispered to Todd. "I must go now." Todd mouthed his goodbye, and I slipped to the back of the church, through the doors, and into the foyer.

"You didn't waste any time, did you?"

I whirled toward Luke and wrinkled my brow. "I don't understand."

He raised his voice and took a step closer. "You made it sound like I was the reason you wanted to stay in Pleasant Springs, but it was him all the time, wasn't it? Your new boyfriend, all because I didn't jump at the chance to rekindle our friendship."

"Lower your voice." I scanned the foyer to see if anyone had heard Luke's outburst. "I can't discuss this now. I have to be at work in fifteen minutes." I touched his arm. "Stop by later, and I'll fix your favorite coffee." I turned and rushed out the door.

Luke followed me to the parking lot. "I need the truth. Now."

I stopped and faced him. "Are you implying I haven't been truthful with you?"

"You tell me."

"Todd offered to attend today so he could get Billy back to Creekside because I had to leave early for work." I winced and backed away. "I didn't want to make Billy leave before the service ended."

Luke softened his tone. "There's nothing between you two?"

I gaped at him and shook my head.

"But you said you wanted to get to know someone better."

"Not him." I smirked, turned, and strutted away. "Although he's kind and likable."

I made my way to my car and drove to work. Was Luke interested in renewing our friendship or not?

Thirty-nine

Lou and two servers did their best to keep up with the flow of customers before I arrived. She opened for lunch on Sundays at 11:30 a.m. but hadn't expected the extra people who stopped by for a specialty coffee on their way home from church. I moved behind the counter to take over.

Lou gave me an enthusiastic hug. "You can have Debbie Sue, but I need the other servers to help on the floor."

Debbie Sue had perfected mochas and vanilla lattes but overdid anything with caramel because that was her favorite flavor. I prepared those. Within fifteen minutes, the line for a specialty coffee thinned out.

I caught Debbie Sue's eye. "Lou seems in high spirits today. She must be excited about all the extra customers coming in for these drinks."

Debbie Sue mumbled and flapped her hand. "Either that or she's seeing her boyfriend again today. She always gets giddy on boyfriend day." Debbie Sue ambled back to the kitchen.

I tidied the coffee prep area with my back to the door. That was the first time I'd heard Lou had a boyfriend.

"Can I have a hot chocolate?"

I turned to see Billy with a huge grin on his face and Todd standing next to him. "I wasn't expecting this surprise. Are you here for lunch?"

"Mr. Todd said I could get a drink, but I need to eat at Creekside."

I slid around the counter and opened my arms. "Debbie Sue will be happy to prepare your order, sir." I caught her attention when she returned to the dining area, and she got to work on Billy's hot chocolate.

Billy laughed. "I'm not a sir."

I grinned, peered at Todd, and touched his arm. "Thank you for bringing him by."

He nodded. "He was excited to see you for a few minutes."

Debbie Sue placed the drink on the counter. "Here's your hot chocolate."

Billy took a sip. "Yum. This is great."

~

Luke stood motionless. He'd caught Lanie in a lie. No feelings for that Todd guy? She couldn't talk her way out of this one. She looked at him like he was the light of her life. And her smile. And his? A man in love?

Lanie hurried to greet him. "I'm glad you came." She motioned to a booth. "Are you staying for lunch or are you here for your special drink only?"

"Neither. I'm leaving." He avoided her eyes.

Lanie tilted sideways until she met his gaze. "You just arrived. What's up?"

"I could ask you the same thing." He touched her elbow and led her farther away from Billy and Todd.

"You tell me there's nothing between you and that guy and then I see you making eyes at each other." He clenched his jaw and narrowed his eyes. "You said I was an idiot, but I'm no one's fool."

She smiled. That sweet, innocent smile of hers. "I can explain."

"I'm sure you can. But I'm done. Go to Nashville. Chattanooga. Anywhere but here."

In a stern but hushed tone, she said, "Listen to yourself. After all we've been through. The reason our friendship disintegrated was because I was unwilling to let you explain. Now, you're walking away without allowing me that same opportunity." She poked her finger in his chest. "I learned from my mistake. Perhaps you'll learn from yours." She stepped back. "And for your information, I'll live here if I want, whether you like it or not."

He glanced over at Billy and waved before stepping out the door.

~

I returned to Todd at the counter, while Debbie Sue showed Billy the coffee equipment.

"Did you hear any of that?" I sighed.

"No. But it didn't look good."

Todd took Billy back to Creekside, and I helped with the lunch crowd.

I needed time to think and pray. Perhaps staying in Pleasant Springs wasn't the best for me. And with Luke wanting me far away, I needed to reconsider. Had I misheard the Lord? Was Jerome's offer in Chattanooga God's plan?

~

Luke stopped by Eddie's house after he ate lunch at

Pete's in Poplar Ridge—a place that reminded him of Lanie, Billy, and Kylee after their hike at Fall Creek Falls.

Eddie's beagle, Hal, barked and tried to jump on Luke. Eddie tried to calm the puppy but had little success. "Outside. We don't need to listen to all your noise and watch you act all crazy." He opened the back door. After Hal ran out, Eddie turned to Luke. "Now we can talk."

Eddie and Luke retreated to the living room and took their seats. Luke told Eddie what had happened with Lanie at the café.

"Bro. You *are* a nitwit." Eddie sat forward in his seat. "What did I tell you?" He arched a brow. "Don't come whining to me." He leaned back. "If you wanna talk about her, you better have a real good reason why you are here."

"But what—"

"Doesn't matter. Let her explain. She may have been as innocent as you were with Stephanie—the reason you're in this mess." Eddie ran his hand through his hair. "If you're interested in rekindling anything with Lanie, you'd better not drag your feet. If this Todd guy doesn't win her over, someone else will."

"And what about Dad?"

"Dad made up his own mind. Lanie couldn't have changed it anyway. She wasn't serving the Lord either when Dad died." He grunted and raised his palms. "Stop blaming her for something she had no control over."

Luke lowered his head. "I don't know if it's worth taking the chance of getting hurt all over again."

"Either swallow your pride or tell her goodbye."

"I told her we were done."

"And do you feel peace and joy that you made the right decision?"

He groaned and spoke just above a whisper. "I feel terrible. I love Lanie, and she'd make a great mom to Billy."

Eddie jumped up and pointed toward the door. "Go find her."

~

When my shift ended at 2:00 Monday afternoon, I drove to Creekside to meet with Todd and to visit Billy after school.

Todd ushered me into his office. "You won't believe what Jerome told me." He pointed to the chair across from his desk, but we continued to stand. "He spoke to Sam this morning. She crumbled during the conversation. She thought you were a mole for him and if she didn't fire you that you'd rat on her, and she'd lose her job."

I stared at Todd and opened my mouth. "Why would she think that?"

"When you applied to work for Clancy County, she called Jerome for a reference. He couldn't say enough good things about you. Told her she'd be foolish not to hire you." Todd and I sat, and I leaned forward. "She thought it all too convenient and had convinced herself that Jerome wanted to get rid of her. She got rid of you first so you wouldn't report anything suspicious to him."

"We didn't get along well, but there wasn't anything suspicious to report."

"Call Jerome. He's expecting you. You can use my office. I've got things to take care of with Teresa." He stood and moved toward his door.

"Before you leave, did you get ahold of another board member who'll approve of me as your codirector?"

"Yes. I have three tentative approvals. Everything looks great, but it won't be official until the board meets two weeks from Wednesday, and one of them could change their mind." He straightened a picture of children playing that hung on the wall. "Talk to Jerome. He has something to tell you."

Todd left me alone in his office, and I dialed Jerome.

After he greeted me, he said, "When will you be joining us in Chattanooga?"

I clutched my rolling stomach. "My heart is here in Pleasant Springs. I appreciate your offer, but I need to stay here."

"Todd said you work at a café there?"

"Yes. I can make that work until I hopefully start a new job with him. He's offered me the position of codirector here at Creekside. If I don't get approval . . ."

"I know all about that." He sighed and muttered something I couldn't make out. "Did he share anything regarding Sam?"

"The reason she fired me."

"There's more."

I scooted my chair closer to Todd's desk.

"I told her that if she wanted to keep her job, she'd apologize to you and offer you your job back."

"No." I contorted my face, thankful Jerome couldn't see me. "I don't want to work with her again."

"We discussed that too. I figured that would be

your response, and I don't blame you. She's agreed to approve your position as codirector of Creekside and contact all members to get immediate authorization for you to begin your job there before the next board meeting."

"That's fantastic."

"But if she doesn't apologize to you, I want to know."

~

The virtual medication administration session went well except for having to sit for four hours. Luke tried not to yawn through the presentation without success. The county should approve his home study after one more session with the trainer in Chattanooga on Wednesday morning. But he missed Lanie.

Had he told her to go anywhere but here? She may never forgive him. Not only was he an idiot, but a stupid fool. Who was the other guy she mentioned she wanted to know better? *Lord, what should I do? I don't want to lose her again.*

~

Billy and I spent a couple of hours together at Creekside after he returned from school. We worked on homework, played a game, and went outside to swing. When it was time for his dinner, I drove home to prepare mine and Jill's.

Jill beat me home and had already grilled chicken for sandwiches. She talked while she set the table. "We saw little of each other all weekend. How are things at the café?"

I told her about the new drinks.

"Becca and I need to stop by." She opened the refrigerator and pulled out the mayonnaise. "Any news on the job search?"

"Todd asked me to be his codirector at Creekside."

"That sounds amazing. What did you tell him?"

I told Jill about the approval process and Jerome's phone call.

"Sounds like you found yourself a new job."

I frowned and closed my eyes. "Except Luke told me that he wants me to leave Pleasant Springs."

Jill embraced me and stroked my arm. "I'm sure he didn't mean it."

"Doesn't matter if he did or not. I told him I'll live here if I want to."

"Good for you. But I think you two are going to work through this."

I shook my head and pursed my lips. "No. I messed up a long time ago. This is my fault. I need to face the truth. Besides, I'm no longer sure I want to rekindle our relationship."

Forty

Luke drove back to Pleasant Springs on Wednesday morning after his 9:30 meeting with the trainer in Chattanooga. She'd told him that she would contact Sam later that afternoon to confirm Luke had completed the required training.

The agency should complete his home study later that day, and either Sam or Victor would bring Billy home the following day after school. Home. Sounded good. But a home without Lanie sounded empty. Very empty.

~

After the Wednesday lunch crowd dwindled, Lou sent me home and asked me to work the following morning. Happy to oblige, I traveled north on Main Street and turned onto East High. I often found comfort at Turtle Creek Park. I passed the playground and parked near the one-mile pond trail.

This place brought back many memories of my high school days. Days with Luke. We'd stroll and talk about our futures, share funny stories, and pray together. He'd often pick a few forget-me-nots, and we'd renew our promise to always remain friends. A promise neither of us kept.

I wandered approximately one hundred feet to the paved trail around the pond. Birds chirped overhead, and turtles sunned themselves on logs that had fallen into the water. A beautiful setting for prayer. When I completed one loop, I sat on a bench that faced the pond. A bench I'd shared many times with Luke. I pulled my legs to my chest and wrapped my arms around them.

"But I'm done. Go to Nashville. Chattanooga. Anywhere but here." *Did he mean that, Lord? Or does the pain run so deep he can't forgive? What do You want me to do? I don't want to leave him or Billy. But our relationship is over. I need to face the facts.* Tears fell when I placed my head on my knees. I'd held them inside for too long.

~

Luke hoped he hadn't missed his chance. He headed north on Main Street and prayed while he drove to Mama Lou's Café. When he got there, Lanie's car wasn't in the parking lot. He pulled back onto Main Street and drove south to Jill's house.

Lanie's car wasn't there either. He tried Creekside with no success. Where could she be?

Would she have gone to the park? He'd often found her there when they were in high school, and she wanted to be alone to think.

Luke headed to Turtle Creek Park at 3:30 p.m. A place filled with fond memories.

He drove past the playground. Joy filled him when he saw Lanie's car. *Help me, Lord. I prayed a stupid prayer and asked You to remove Lanie from my life. I didn't mean that. Help me hear her side of things, to apologize for my actions, and not mess this up. I hope I haven't pushed her too far away. Give me the courage to share what's held me back and ask for her forgiveness.*

He climbed out of his car and surveyed the area near the pond. Lanie sat on a bench—her back to him—they'd shared many times over the years. He snuck past her to her left to an area where blue forget-me-nots grew. He selected a few choice specimens and placed them into his pocket. After he returned to the area of the parking lot, he approached from her right.

Luke's heart stirred. Lanie's head rested on her knees and her shoulders shook.

"May I join you?"

She dropped her feet to the ground and wiped her eyes with the back of her hands. "What are you doing here?"

"I wanted to see you. And apologize for not giving you the opportunity to explain what I saw Sunday."

She slid to the left to allow him room to sit next to her, but she kept her eyes on the pond.

Luke took a seat and peered at Lanie. "Please tell me that your tears are not because of me."

"I'd be telling a lie." She sniffled and pulled a tissue from her pocket.

His throat went dry. In all the years they'd been friends, he'd never seen Lanie sob. Tear up? Yes. Cry a little at a sad movie? Occasionally. But sob? Never. And he'd caused this reaction? "Please talk to me."

She swiped at her eyes again. "You wanted to believe the worst about me. Accused me of lying to you." She looked into his eyes. "I grinned at Todd because of something Billy said. That boy lights up my life. Not Todd." Lanie glanced toward the pond and back at Luke.

"There's nothing between the two of you?" Luke wanted to crawl under the bench.

"I've already answered that question. Why can't you believe me?"

"I want to. But I've questioned so many things since college. About us." Luke clasped his hands together. "I should have listened to you."

She stood and faced him. "True, but I wish I'd given you the opportunity to explain what I saw all those years ago. I'm sorry, Luke, for all the pain I caused you. Caused us." She sniffled again and wiped her nose. "I've decided Pleasant Springs is my home and where I want to live." Her voice hitched, and she bit her lip. "I'll stay away from you and Billy and not interfere in your lives." She made her way to the pond trail.

Luke's heart rate increased, and he followed her. "That's not what I want." He strode to her side, twisted her to face him, and gazed into her eyes.

"I'm not leaving." She placed her hands on her hips. "This is my home too."

Luke shook his head and in a gentle tone said, "No. I want you here. What I don't want is for you to stay away from me or Billy."

Her features softened, and he wanted to take her into his arms and kiss her right there in Turtle Creek Park. When she parted her lips, he did all he could to keep from doing just that.

"I need to apologize for all the times I've treated you unfairly these past few weeks." His chest tightened, and he steepled his fingers in front of his mouth. "I've accused you of dishonesty and spoken spitefully." He squeezed his eyes shut and reopened them. "Will you forgive me?"

She took a step back. "Why has my return been so hard for you?"

"First, let me ask you a question." He fiddled with a button on his shirt. "Why didn't you stop by to see my parents when you returned home to visit?"

"I only came home once."

"Why only one time?"

"Because Jill came to Chattanooga to shop, and we'd spend the day together. And every few weeks she'd meet me at my place, and we'd drive to Knoxville to see our parents." Lanie frowned and rubbed her chin. "I only came home for Randy's memorial service."

"Jill's husband?" Luke swiped his hand down his face. "Our family took a vacation together or I would have attended. Maybe we could have solved this predicament seven years ago." He brushed his foot across the path. "I've blamed you for my dad's nonexistent relationship with the Lord."

She pointed to herself. "Me?"

"He loved you like a daughter. He respected you and your ideas." Luke cringed and shuffled his feet. "I thought if you'd been home before he died, he would have listened to you and surrendered his life to Christ."

"But—"

"I know. You weren't where you needed to be in your own relationship with God. How could you lead Dad into one?" He placed his hand on Lanie's shoulder. "And it wasn't your responsibility to do so." He removed his hand and stared at the ground. "I'm to blame. Not you."

She reached for both of his hands and held them in hers. "I understand your concern for your dad. But how can you be certain he never made that decision?" She released his hands and rubbed his arm. "You lived the life in front of him, you prayed for him, talked to him about God. Between you, your mom, and Eddie, your dad knew the way to the Lord."

Luke's eyes met Lanie's, and she creased her brow.

"What about the discussions we had with him when we returned home during our breaks from college? He asked questions. And he prayed often."

"But I don't think he ever believed in his heart. Dad's belief was all head knowledge."

"His head knowledge may have moved to his heart somewhere along life's path."

"But he wouldn't go to church with the rest of the family."

"Why?"

"Said it was full of hypocrites and he was the worst."

"Sounds like he struggled, like you and me." She sighed and nodded. "We're all sinners."

They returned to the bench and sat.

"Trust that God heard your prayers and answered them. We can't change the past, but we can move forward in faith and hope one day we'll see your dad again."

Luke took her hand in his and thanked her for her encouragement. "Can you forgive me for blaming you regarding my dad and for the way I've treated you?"

"Yes." She smiled and scooted closer. "And I know it's hard to forgive when pain runs deep. Have you fully forgiven me?"

He squeezed her hand and wanted to kiss her. "I have." His heart thumped in his chest. He'd never been more aware of Lanie's beauty. Her short, silky hair blew around her face from the breeze, her deep blue eyes shone with love, and her smile melted his heart.

He angled his knees toward hers, reached into his pocket, and pulled out the tiny, wilted bouquet of blue flowers. "I could never forget you. You belong here with me. I love you, Lanie." He dipped his head and kissed her full on her lips.

Forty-one

Our kisses ended when a flock of geese honked overhead.

Were his kisses for real this time? I needed to be sure. "Will tomorrow bring a confession that today's kisses were a mistake?"

"No way. I want more of those if you'll have me." He wrapped his arms around me and squeezed. His lips found my ear, cheek, chin, and, finally, my lips again.

I pulled away and lifted my brows. "Does this mean we're good?"

His eyes crinkled at the corners, and he nodded.

"How good? Best friends again?"

"More like boyfriend and girlfriend, I hope." He hesitated and lowered his head. "If that's what you want too."

I nuzzled my head into his neck. "Yes."

"I'm so glad you're staying in Pleasant Springs." He rubbed my upper arm.

"Me too. But I've got to be honest with you." I pulled away and gazed into his eyes. "Todd asked me to be his codirector at Creekside."

Luke's face paled. "Todd? You'll see Todd every

day?" He scooted a few inches away from me. "I don't like that." He crossed his arms and faced the pond.

I winced and blinked several times. "There's nothing between Todd and me."

"I'm not so sure. He appeared to be a man in . . ."

"In what?"

"In need of a good woman. I don't want him to go after mine."

"Stop. Jealousy doesn't look good on you." I tugged on his arm. "Look at me."

He peeked at me out of the corner of his eye.

I softened my tone. "I don't care about Todd that way. But I love you."

He faced me, caressed my cheek, and kissed me again. A sweet reminder that we were now a couple.

"Are you planning to ask your girlfriend to dinner?"

"Of course."

We decided on pizza because it was one of our favorites. We arrived at the Pizza Shack and sat next to one another in a booth along the windows. After he grabbed a menu from the holder on the table, Luke ordered a medium pepperoni with sausage and extra cheese.

I bounced my knees up and down. Our first meal as a couple. I wanted to stand and tell everyone.

While we waited and chatted, a woman around my age entered the restaurant with an older woman.

Luke groaned and mumbled into my ear. "Don't look now, but Maggie Stone just pranced in with her mom."

I squinted. "That's Maggie? I can't see her face through all that makeup."

"Her latest look. She sometimes writes about makeup techniques on her blog."

I inched away from Luke but kept my eyes on him. "Should I be concerned you're reading her blog on makeup?"

He laughed and placed his hands on top of the table. "I read it now and then to learn if I'm in it. She covers many topics. Most often, she gets into everyone's business and stretches the truth or only tells part of the story until it's twisted and one-sided." He motioned me back to his side and put his arm around my shoulder.

"I still haven't read it."

Maggie swaggered our way. "And who do we have here?" She tossed her hair back. "The perfect couple?"

"Move along." Luke removed his arm and focused on the menus in the holder. "There's nothing newsworthy here. Having a nice evening out."

"How cute the two of you are. Been a few years, hasn't it?"

Luke inched to his left toward Maggie. "That's enough. We'd like to enjoy our evening."

She narrowed her eyes at Luke and glanced at me. "Please accept my apology. I didn't mean to intrude. I only wanted to welcome you back to Pleasant Springs." She ran her fingers through her long, dark hair. "But may I suggest you catch up on last week's makeup tips? You'll find them beneficial."

Luke slid a few more inches to the left.

I gripped his arm and held on. "Thank you. I'll check them out."

When she left our table, Luke turned to me. "You shouldn't have stopped me. Someone needs to put her in her place."

"Not you." I tugged him closer to my side. "She's right. I could use makeup help."

He touched my cheek and smiled. "You're beautiful, and I love you the way you are."

This was definitely unfamiliar territory for us.

~

Lanie needed to make improvements to her makeup? Luke loved Lanie's wholesome look, although he no longer thought of her as the girl next door. And to think he'd almost allowed his pride and resentment to hinder sharing his true feelings for her. She'd always been the one for him. He looked forward to spending a lifetime with her. If she'd have him.

Would she want a house full of kids like he did? He muttered to himself, "Slow down, Luke. You need to propose first before you plan a future with Lanie." She'd agree. Wouldn't she? He'd thought she'd have said yes years ago, and that didn't work out. But this time, he'd make sure he asked her first and didn't show the ring or mention any plans with anyone else.

~

The following morning, I stared at myself in the bathroom mirror. "Is my makeup dull and unattractive? Should I read Maggie's blog posts?"

Jill scurried down the hallway past my bathroom door. She returned and spoke to my reflection. "As I've told you before. You're beautiful."

My shoulders sagged. "Why did Maggie say I needed help?"

"Maggie Stone?" She scowled. "Don't get me started on that woman. You should have seen her makeup at church on Sunday. A distraction. And I'm being nice."

"I saw her at the Pizza Shack last night. A bit much, but what if she's right, and I need more?" I peered at my face from different angles. "Perhaps I need a fresh look for my new job."

Jill snickered and leaned against the door frame. "If you let Maggie get to you for this, she'll weed her way in to make you find fault regarding other things in your life. Like Luke. I'm sure she'd love to learn more about your new romance with him and come in between you two."

"Why would she do that? She's a member of your church."

"I shouldn't talk about her behind her back. I make my share of mistakes too. Forgive me." She darted into the kitchen and opened and closed the refrigerator door. She called to me down the hallway. "Did she have her dog with her?"

I met Jill in the kitchen. "Her dog? At Pizza Shack?"

"She brought little Snowball, Cottonball, Snowflake, whatever she named her Maltese, to church with her." Jill spoke as if she were talking to a baby. "Come to mommy, my sweet little Snowbunny."

I raised my voice. "To church?"

Jill brought her finger to her lips and shushed me. "Let Becca sleep. This pregnancy has her worn out. And after two miscarriages, she needs lots of rest."

"Did she confirm with Doctor Stewart that she's pregnant?"

Jill shook her head and sighed. "She made an appointment with an obstetrician in Chattanooga and will meet with her next month. In the meantime, she's sure a baby is on its way."

"Has she seen her brother?"

"She plans to see him this week." Jill grabbed her coffee mug and waved. "Got to go, but I want to hear all about how things went with Luke yesterday. Be ready to talk tonight at dinner and don't leave out any pertinent details."

"Talk about Luke? My pleasure." But I didn't plan to share everything about him. Like those luscious lips of his.

Jill dashed out the door and texted me before she backed out of the garage. I invited Mom and Dad to dinner after church on Sunday for Mother's Day. Hope you'll be here too.

I responded with a red heart and pulled out a few minutes later to drive to the café.

From 7:00 a.m. to noon, I worked as the only barista and waited tables because two of the regular servers called out.

Luke stopped by at 1:30 for lunch and his special drink—a caramel latte. I sat with him and slipped off my shoes while he sipped his drink and waited for his burger and fries.

"You haven't lost your touch. This is the best caramel latte I've had in years."

I thanked him and said, "What time does Billy arrive?"

"Sam or Victor will bring him over around 5:00. Do you want to be there?"

"Sam still hasn't called to apologize. Might be fun to see her reaction and have her tell me she's sorry to my face." I rubbed my chin and tapped my finger on the table. "But I think I'll pass. You need to spend time alone with Billy when he arrives.”

Two couples entered the café and made their way to the counter for specialty drinks.

“Break’s over.” I chuckled and hurried to my station.

Within a few minutes, Luke made his way to the counter and winked. “I’ve arranged with Eddie to watch Billy Saturday evening if you can join me for dinner.”

“A romantic dinner for two?”

“Romance?” He wiggled his eyebrows. “I’ll do my best.”

LUANN K. EDWARDS

Forty-two

Thursday afternoon before Billy was due to arrive at Luke's house, he added his last entry for the day into his bookkeeping program. He'd already contacted his Bible study group, canceled their meeting, and asked them to pray for a smooth transition for Billy.

"You look pleased with yourself." Eddie wandered into Luke's office and took a seat across from him. "Is it because Billy arrives today?"

"Yes, I'm glad this day is finally here."

Eddie leaned back and put his feet on top of Luke's desk. "When are you going to pop the question?"

"What question?" Luke bent forward and shoved away Eddie's dirty shoes.

"You know."

He stared at his brother. "We need more time to get reacquainted."

"Wasted time." Eddie stood and placed his palms on Luke's desk. "Don't mess this up, big bro."

Luke rose and looked Eddie in the eye. "This coming from the guy who can't get up the nerve to ask someone out?"

"There's no one worth asking."

"What about Natalie?"

Eddie straightened and frowned.

"Maggie?"

"You must be kidding."

"Jill?"

Eddie hesitated and stuttered. "Um. I don't. I. Um."

"You like Jill?" Luke grinned and eased around to the front of his desk. "That would be great. Two brothers dating two sisters." He patted Eddie on the shoulder. "Go for it, man."

Eddie shook his head. "I. I can't."

"Do you want me to set it up with Lanie?"

Eddie lifted his palm. "No. Leave it alone. Don't need your help."

"But you do, bro. You do." Luke sneered and nudged Eddie's arm. "Don't blow it. If you want her, you've got to go after her." He arched his brow just like Eddie had done. "Don't come whining to me if she ends up with someone else."

~

When I arrived at Creekside after school, I found Billy on the sofa reading a book. "Are you all packed for Mr. Luke's house?"

"I'll go do that now." Billy hugged me and lumbered toward his room.

I met Todd in his office. "Do you know who's taking Billy out to Luke's? Sam or Victor?"

"No. But they should be here soon." He wandered to the front window. "Sam knows you're a volunteer now, so it won't surprise her to see you. Has she called you yet?"

"No." My stomach felt queasy. I didn't want to talk

to her.

"She called me last night and gave me her approval to hire you. I confirmed she'd contacted the other board members too. You've got the job and can begin Monday if you want it."

"She approved me?" I met Todd at the window. "Do you think she'll call me and offer me my job back?"

"Jerome was insistent concerning that when he spoke with me." He returned to his desk and handed me a piece of paper. "Here's Kylee's address."

I thanked him and put her address in my purse. "I'd like to discuss the position with Luke again before I give you my answer. Will tomorrow be okay?"

"Yes, and I hope you'll be able to volunteer the next few days. A sibling group of five arrives tomorrow. Three girls and two boys, all under the age of ten."

"Sounds fun." I chuckled and gave him a thumbs up.

I walked to the back of the house to find Billy. He pulled his clothes from his dresser and placed them into a box. "Do you need help packing?"

"I got it."

When he had everything packed, I prayed with him and told him I'd see him soon.

I passed Sam on my way out of Creekside's parking lot and waved. She didn't wave back.

~

Luke checked Billy's room for the third time in the past hour to verify neither Grizzly nor Mims had made a mess. The downstairs passed his inspection too. He hoped Billy would love it here.

At 5:05, he hurried to the front door at the sound of a car.

This is it, Lord. I'm a dad. Thank You for this amazing opportunity.

Billy seemed in better spirits today than the last time Luke saw him. He wore his backpack and followed Sam up the porch steps with a box of his belongings.

Luke and Sam talked in the kitchen while Billy and Grizzly bounded up the stairs to his new bedroom.

"I offered to bring him out for Victor. You can contact him if you have questions." Sam shuffled toward the door and turned. "One more thing. How would you rate your overall dealings with Ms. Meadows?"

"She's excellent at her job. The best."

Sam opened the door and let it slam shut.

~

At home, it was my turn to cook supper. I prepared meatloaf and garlic mashed potatoes while Jill and Becca talked in the living room.

My phone vibrated in my pocket. I pulled it out and raised my voice. "I've got to take this call from Sam. Can one of you set the table?" I darted down the hallway and into my room to answer her call.

"Seems I made a mistake in terminating your employment. I've spoken to a few people who think I misread my instincts and treated you unfairly." She paused and cleared her throat. "Would you consider returning to your position here in Clancy County?"

"That would be awkward, don't you agree?"

"Yes, it would." She sighed. "But I'm willing to fix this if you are."

Still no apology. Why couldn't she tell me she was sorry? "Let me think it over and get back to you. Will tomorrow work?"

She agreed and hung up before I could say anything more.

I returned to the kitchen, where dinner awaited me on the table.

While we ate, the three of us shared stories of our favorite memories growing up.

Becca shared one about her brother Nick and fiddled with her meatloaf." I love him but don't look forward to having lunch with him tomorrow."

Jill asked her why.

"He was involved with a lady in his church who I'd known from the church we attended in Chattanooga. She'd moved to Nashville a few years after Michael and I came to Pleasant Springs to pastor, and she attended the same church as Nick." Becca shifted in her chair. "She had a questionable past and seemed to stir up trouble in our church when we attended together. I shared my concern with Nick, but he got upset with me and pushed me away. Said she'd changed in recent years. There's been friction between us since."

I swirled my fork to make circles in my potatoes. "Are they still a couple?"

"I don't think so. He kept quiet after that and said little to me or my parents about her."

Jill focused on her empty dinner plate. "I'd be happy to go with you when you see him."

I smirked and gave a slight shake of my head. "Yes, she would. He's a hottie."

Becca and Jill eyed me.

I shrugged. "I saw him at the café on Saturday. He

and another woman ate breakfast together."

Becca widened her eyes. "Who? What did she look like?"

I waved away her comment. "Miss Risa."

Becca and Jill let out lengthy breaths, and Becca accepted Jill's offer to meet with Nick together.

Jill stood, picked up my plate, and added it to hers. "Now. Tell us about you and Luke. What's happening there?"

"He stopped by the café for lunch."

"And?" She glared at me and snapped her fingers.

I pinched my bottom lip. "And he has a romantic date planned for Saturday evening."

Becca pursed her lips. "Then why do you seem a little glum tonight?"

"I have a big decision to make, and I'm not sure what to do." I grabbed the leftover meatloaf plate and carried it to the kitchen counter. "Two job offers again."

"But you already decided on Creekside." Jill picked up Becca's plate and carried the dishes to the sink.

"Yes. But that was Sam on the phone. She asked if I'd return to my position with Clancy County." I pulled out the plastic wrap and covered the leftover meatloaf while I explained to Becca and Jill what had happened.

"I can't believe you'd consider working with her again. You seemed excited about Creekside." Jill placed her palms on the counter and peered at me.

I rolled my eyes and huffed. "But Luke thinks Todd likes me. He doesn't, but I don't want Luke to be unsure about me and what I'm doing."

Becca walked over to me. "Talk to Luke. Tell him

you have another offer, that you prefer the position at Creekside and ask him for his thoughts. Hear him out, pray about it together, and then make your decision."

"Good advice." I took out my phone and called Luke.

~

Luke smiled when he saw Lanie's name light up on his cell. He greeted her, stepped out onto the front porch, and asked about her day. "I wanted to call you after I got back to the shop, but I needed to help in the bay. Now I'm bonding with Billy and his homework."

"How's he doing?"

"He's a different child than the boy who visited five days ago. Thanks to you."

"Thank the Lord." Dishes clinked in the background. "I'd like to discuss something with you. I have a decision to make and would appreciate your input."

"Sounds good. How about tomorrow for lunch?"

"May I stop by tonight?"

Luke remembered the mess in the living room. His mom had stopped by to meet Billy and brought him too many toys. He had to tidy up first. "Wouldn't it be better to discuss whatever it is when Billy's at school tomorrow?"

We agreed to meet for lunch at La Casa.

He disconnected his call and returned to the kitchen where Billy worked at the table. "Are you almost finished?"

"One more math problem." He dropped his pencil on the floor and reached down to pick it up. "Miss Lanie explained these different from my teacher. I understand now."

"I'll tell her when I see her tomorrow."

"Can I see her too?"

"You'll be at school."

Billy stuck out his lower lip.

"I'll invite her over soon." He pointed to the toys scattered around the living room. "I need you to clean this before you go to bed."

Billy put his homework paper inside his math folder. "All done." He tossed the folder and his pencil into his backpack, ran around the living room, and gathered an armload of toys. "Where should I put these?"

"Upstairs in your room."

"Okay." He made his way up the stairs, but a ball rolled down, hit the wall, and bounced onto Grizzly, who rested near the foot of the stairs.

The dog jumped up, whined, and barked.

"Sorry, Grizz. I'll come back for that." Billy bounded down the steps, clutched the ball and a few other items he'd left behind, and scurried up the stairs again. When he returned, he threw himself onto the sofa. "Whew. I'm tired."

Luke laughed and picked up a small toy car Billy had dropped. "After you've rested for a minute, I'd like you to get your bath and get ready for bed."

Billy objected, but Luke didn't back down. He had Billy in bed by 8:00. Luke needed his quiet time to figure out when to ask Lanie an important question.

Forty-three

I looked forward to my lunch with Luke. An hour with him as a couple, not just friends. Friday morning dragged on. I kept my eye on my watch, hoping to hurry the time along.

I arrived at 12:05 p.m. and found Luke seated at a table for four near a small decorative fountain along the left wall of La Casa.

He smiled, stood, and pulled out the chair to his right.

I thanked him and we sat. "Smells wonderful in here—like grilled peppers and onions. Do you know what you'll order?"

"The beef enchilada platter."

"I had a grilled fajita burrito two weeks ago. My new favorite."

The server stopped at our table, took our orders, and whisked himself away to the kitchen.

Luke placed his hand on top of mine on top of the table. "You wanted to discuss something important."

I told him about my new job offer with Clancy County.

He twisted his mouth to one side. "You've turned

down two offers and have two more. You are a lady in demand." He stared at my lips. "And I want you too."

I lifted my hand in front of his face. "Whoa. I need your help here. Will you pray with me concerning this? I need to tell Todd and Sam today what I've decided."

Luke squeezed my hand and bowed his head. *Father, You amaze us with the many opportunities You've placed before, Lanie. She lost her job but found so much more. Thank You for Your provision. Show us which path is Your best for her. For us. I have concerns about Creekside, but I trust her and want what You want for her. Creekside sounds like an exceptional opportunity. In Jesus' name, Amen.*

Luke gazed into my eyes. "What are your thoughts about the county?"

"I'm ready for a change." I glanced away for a moment and bit my lip. "Creekside is my pick."

"And do you feel that's God's best for you?"

"If it won't cause any difficulties between you and me."

"Like I said. I trust you and your judgement."

Our server brought our food, and after a quick prayer, we dove in.

When I lifted my water glass, I saw Jill, Becca, and her brother seated across the restaurant from us. "My sister and her friends." I motioned toward them.

Luke twisted to see them. "Who's the guy?"

"That's the new doctor in town and Becca's brother."

"Good. They're all here as friends?"

"What?"

"I meant Jill and that guy aren't a couple. Eddie has a crush on her, and I hoped you'd drop a hint and have her call him or something."

"Eddie, huh?" I propped my cheek on my fist. "Sounds like he got over me with no problem."

Luke pulled my hand away from my face. "He knew from the start you were off limits."

"He and Jill would make a cute couple." I rubbed my chin and grinned. "I'll see what I can do, but she's got her eye on two other men."

"Two?"

"The handsome doctor over there at her table, and Doc Winston."

"The veterinarian?" Luke paled and a slight growl escaped from deep within his throat. "What did you mean by the handsome doctor? You can't talk like that now that we're a couple."

I patted his hand. "I still have eyes. But they belong to you before anyone else." I rested my elbow on the table with my chin on my fist and lost myself in his handsome face.

"Looks like I need to keep mine on you at all times."

"Please do."

He chuckled and took a bite of Spanish rice.

We finished our meal, paid our tab, and rose from our chairs. Jill and her friends stood to leave too. We congregated outside the restaurant.

Doctor Stewart shook my hand. "The lovely lady with the dazzling smile from the café."

Was Luke taking notes on how to charm me?

Luke stuck out his hand. "And I'm the lovely lady's boyfriend. More than her boyfriend. I'm her . . ."

I eyed Luke and winked. "You're my what?"

Luke dipped his chin and looked at Nick. "Nice to

meet you."

Becca touched my arm. "Nick knows of a house for sale that I haven't seen yet. He said it wasn't right for him, but when I told him what Ben and I wanted, he thought it would be perfect for us. Jill has to finish up a project at work this afternoon, so Nick arranged for us to see the house after she gets off. Please come with us." She peered at Luke. "Both of you. We need as many men's perspectives as possible because Ben won't be here until tomorrow evening. He wants me to put an offer in on anything I think will work, even if he's not here."

"I'm in." I grabbed Luke's hand and nudged his elbow. "Are you?"

"What time?"

Becca said, "We'll meet at the house at 6:00. I'll send Jill the address."

Luke nodded and leaned forward. "I'll ask Eddie to come along. He knows a lot regarding construction and houses. He completed a lot of the work on his home and mine."

I squeezed Luke's hand, and we strolled to the parking lot out of earshot of Jill and her friends.

"Lovely lady?" Luke squinted at me and scowled. "What am I missing here?"

"I was as shocked as you were."

"He's the one, isn't he?"

I wrinkled my nose. "The one?"

"The guy you wanted to get to know better."

Warmth spread up my neck. "You're the only one for me."

"You blushed when he was eyeing you."

"I get nervous when someone pays much attention

to me. And besides, I think he's a flirt."

Luke pressed his lips together and shook his head.

"Luke, I love you. I'm not interested in the doctor. You hold my heart."

"But you were interested at one time, weren't you?"

"I thought he was cute and someone I'd like to know. But I'd *love* to know you better."

"Prove it."

"What?"

"Show me." He smirked and opened his arms.

"Here? In the parking lot?"

His features softened, and his eyes searched my face.

I wrapped my arms around his neck, slid my hands up behind his head, and pulled his face close to mine.

Forty-four

Luke broke Lanie's grasp on his head and lips. "Wow. Okay." He chuckled. "You've made your point."

"Great. Now I need to get back to work. Do you want to grab something to eat before we visit Becca's house or after?"

"Neither. I have a child to care for, remember?"

"And who's going to watch that child while you're at Becca's house?"

"My mom. She stopped by yesterday to meet him and said she'd stop by again tonight."

"You're doing a great job." She cupped his cheeks in her hands. "And I'm still waiting to hear how you're more than my boyfriend."

Luke backed away and strode to his pickup. "Send me the address for the house, and I'll meet you there at 6:00."

Luke climbed into his truck. Lanie could kiss. He couldn't wait to get more of those. Tomorrow after he proposed?

~

I spent most of the afternoon with the sibling group

at Creekside.

Jill sent me a text while I was there with the address of Becca's prospective house.

I texted back: **Are you going there right from work or home first?**

Home to put on jeans.

I'll meet you at the house.

I texted Luke the address, said goodbye to the children, and drove home. Jill pulled in soon after me. I darted into the garage, and we entered the house together.

Jill giggled and walked toward the hallway at the front of the house. "You and Luke seemed rather chummy in the parking lot after lunch today."

I smiled and followed behind. "Who knew that two best friends could become worst enemies and then a couple in love?"

"God and I knew."

I eased up close to her, so Becca, who talked on her phone in the kitchen, wouldn't hear. "Be nice to Eddie." In a bubbly tone, I said, "He has a crush on you."

She jerked her head back and grabbed my arm. "Little Eddie? But he's three years younger than me and two inches shorter."

"But he's adorable, and he likes you. Be gentle when you let him down, okay?"

"Who said I'll let him down at all? He *is* adorable, sweet, kind." She grinned. "And available."

"Really? You two would make a stunning couple."

"Let's see what happens. I doubt more each Saturday that Doc Winston is interested. He's a mystery. I found out last weekend he's almost fifty."

"Ewe. Fifteen years older than you? You don't want to marry an old man."

"Maybe not, because there's an available and younger handsome doctor in town."

"And don't forget Eddie."

"Sweet Eddie." She placed her hand on her chest. "But older has its benefits too."

Smiling, Becca joined us in the living room. "Everyone ready to go?"

Jill glanced down at her slacks. "I want to put on jeans. I'll be a minute." She scurried down the hallway without explaining what she meant. What benefits?

Becca placed her purse strap over her shoulder. "Did Nick embarrass you today?"

"He shocked me. And made Luke jealous."

"He loves to tease and knows women find him attractive."

"Do you mean he lied when he called me a lovely lady?"

She placed her hand on my shoulder. "I didn't mean that. You're beautiful."

I huffed and crossed my arms.

"What are you to Luke if not just his girlfriend?"

"I'm not sure. But I'll get it out of him soon."

Jill returned to the living room. "He didn't know what to say. But he made it clear to all of us that he wants to be more than your boyfriend. It wouldn't surprise me if he proposes to you this weekend."

I raised my left hand and focused on my ring finger. "But I'm not sure how I feel about that. We shouldn't rush into marriage. We just went on our first date two days ago."

Jill snickered and placed her hands on my upper arms. "You've waited eleven years for this. I don't think that's rushing into anything."

"But shouldn't we get reacquainted first? I've only been back home for a few weeks."

She frowned and released me. "What do you think Luke would do if he proposed, and you said, 'I need more time.'?"

I rubbed my bottom lip. "I'm not sure our relationship would survive. With what we've been through these past four weeks, he'd think I didn't love him."

Becca wrapped me in a side hug. "After seeing the two of you together at the restaurant today, and the way he looks at you, I agree with Jill. A proposal is coming soon. Give it to God and trust Him."

"I need to trust Him regarding Luke, marriage, and my job."

My hand flew to my mouth. "I forgot to call Todd and Sam. I told them I'd let them know today."

I zipped down the hallway to my room and hollered to Jill and Becca. "Leave without me. I'll be there as soon as I can." I clicked on Sam's number. She greeted me and said, "What did you decide?"

"Although I'm grateful for your offer to return to my job with Clancy County, I feel led to accept the position with Creekside."

"I think that's an excellent position for you. You have a lot to offer the kids placed there."

I thanked her, but she'd said it because she didn't want me back. No big surprise. I didn't want to go back anyway. I expected her to end the call.

"You were an excellent employee." The line went quiet. "I messed up and I'm sorry." She sighed. "Please accept my apology. If you decide to return to Clancy County in the future, I'll treat you as I should have."

I thanked her again and disconnected our call. It would please Jerome to know I not only received the apology, but Sam sounded sincere.

And Todd sounded relieved when I told him he had a new codirector.

~

Luke and Eddie pulled up to a white country home with wood siding and stonework along the base.

Luke parked in the street and turned off the ignition. "I don't see Lanie's car. She must have come with Jill." He and Eddie made their way to the covered front porch, where Doctor Nick met them.

He stuck out his hand to Luke and greeted him. Luke introduced him to Eddie.

When Lanie pulled up, she parked in the driveway that led to a side entry garage and apologized for being a few minutes late. "Are Jill and Becca inside?"

Doctor Nick presented a wider smile and appeared extra attentive when he spoke to Lanie. "I'm glad you made it. Jill and Becca wanted to wait until everyone arrived. They're around back checking out the yard."

Nick did not impress Luke. Doc needed to keep his smiles for the other ladies. Not his. Luke lunged for Lanie's hand and held it in a tight grip.

Becca rubbed her hands together when she, Jill, and a woman Luke assumed to be the real estate agent rounded the front corner of the house. They all went inside and toured the four-bedroom home.

After the tour, when Becca asked everyone their thoughts, she received three gushing reviews. Eddie only gave a thumbs up.

Jill gazed at Eddie. "Luke said you're the expert. What do you think?"

"Me? Uh. No."

Luke tried to encourage him to speak up. "Did the builder construct the house well?"

Eddie stared at his feet. "Yeah."

Becca asked Eddie if he'd check out the back deck again. "I need to know if we should replace any of the boards."

Eddie followed her outside.

Luke strolled out with them and stood next to Eddie. "Can they get another three to five years without having to replace any?"

"Yeah. New stain. That's all."

Becca thanked him and went back inside.

Luke and Eddie scanned the yard and circled the perimeter of the house. They met the others out front.

"I noticed stonework with a few cracks out back." Jill peered at Eddie. "Would you look at it with me and tell me what you think?"

"Me?" Eddie pointed to himself.

"Please?" Jill grinned and motioned for him to follow her.

Eddie widened his eyes and looked at Luke.

Luke moved closer and whispered. "Now's your chance. Take your own advice. Don't blow it."

Eddie gulped, shuffled his feet, and followed Jill to the back of the house.

Luke turned to Lanie. "Did you tell her?"

"I may have said something." She batted her eyes.

"He talked to Becca like he would to you. Short phrases. But with Jill, he can't put two words together." Luke tightened his hands into fists and released them. "She won't lead him on, will she?"

"Of course not. She said he's adorable."

"That's how a woman describes a baby or puppy." He rubbed the tightness in his neck. "I don't want him to get hurt. Will she go out with him if he asks, or is she waiting for the doctor?"

"I think she'd go out with each of them at least once. But Nick won't get a second date."

Luke raised his eyebrows.

Jill and Eddie returned to the front yard.

"Eddie thought the cracks were minor, but he offered to patch them." Jill winked at Lanie. "He's a sweetheart."

"This place is perfect. I'll make an offer right now." Becca dashed over to where the realtor had waited near her car.

Luke eased Lanie toward his pickup. "Why won't Jill go out with Nick a second time?"

"She's too smart not to see through his fake façade. Guys like him aren't interested in an actual relationship. They know their good looks and sweet talk cause women to swoon."

"Not true. I'm interested in a relationship with you."

Lanie laughed and touched Luke's cheek. "Yes. You make me swoon, but you could improve upon your sweet talk. Until Wednesday, you lacked in that area."

~

Luke went home to relieve his mom from Billy duty, and Jill picked up a large pizza for the three of us girls to share. After dinner, Becca stood in the living room while she spoke to Ben on her phone.

"Yes. Four bedrooms with a bonus room that could be a fifth." She paused. "Yes. You said three, but four makes more sense for us." Her eyes roamed over Jill and me. "One for the master, one for your office, one for your daughter when she visits, and one for her boyfriend if he comes with her." She bit her lip and tugged on her neckline. "The fifth one will make a great place for the grandkids to bunk if Riley and Jeremy get married and have children." She wrinkled her nose. "I realize that. We won't need a fifth one after they're married because they'll share a room. But it can be a playroom for the grandkids." She waved her hands around dramatically.

We giggled at her actions.

"Okay. But it's in the price range you gave me. If you don't like it, we'll give up our earnest money and find something else." She paused and turned away from us. "Love you too." She disconnected her call and faced us. "I need to tell him that I'm pregnant as soon as he arrives, or he may cancel our contract." She plopped onto the sofa next to me. "I love that man, but he can be hard to deal with."

"The news that he's going to have a baby with you will thrill him." I patted her hand. "Please don't fret over this."

"I know. Give it to God and trust Him. Right?"

I nudged her elbow. "A wise friend recently shared those exact words with me."

Forty-five

Saturday morning, Luke sat at his kitchen table with his Bible opened and prepared for his day. *I need Your help, Lord. I need Lanie to say yes. We've waited a long time for this. But she said I need to learn how to sweet-talk her. I have been hard on her since she came back to Pleasant Springs. I know she's forgiven me, but I'd like to make it up to her. Please help me with that, Lord.*

After his Bible reading, he cleaned the cabin until Billy came down for breakfast.

Luke greeted Billy with a high-five and pointed to a bowl and a box of cereal on the table. "I'll grab the milk. Do you need anything else?"

Billy asked for a piece of toast with peanut butter.

Luke popped a piece of bread into the toaster. "Later today, I'll take you to Mr. Eddie's house to race cars and play with Hal. How does that sound?"

"What are you going to do?" Billy pulled out his chair and plopped down.

"I have a date with Miss Lanie."

"Can I come?"

"Not this time. Eddie's counting on you to keep

Hal entertained for a while. He needs your help."

Billy raised the pitch of his voice. "Are you and Miss Lanie going to kiss?"

"Now, what do you know about that?" Luke patted Billy on top of his head.

"My mom and her boyfriends did that." Billy took a mouthful of crunchy cereal.

Luke wanted to end this conversation. "I might give her a little kiss or two." He rubbed his hand across his mouth. "I've got a surprise for her that I hope she'll like."

"What is it?" Billy took another bite.

"I'll show you later. She needs to see it first."

"Don't worry. I can keep a secret." Billy finished his breakfast, scooted off his chair, and carried his bowl to the sink. "Show me now."

~

The lunch crowd at the café thinned out, and Lou gave me the afternoon off. Customers seemed happy with the seven specialty drinks posted on the board. Although I'd trained most of the servers, Lou grumbled about me leaving her, but she understood. I told her that I'd stop by and work on a few more specialty drinks the following week to add to the menu.

I drove to Creekside and spent a few hours with the kids to give Steve and Teresa a break. Todd showed me my new office—the study room. I'd share it with the older kids during homework time, but I wouldn't mind. I'd move in on Monday.

When I arrived home at 4:10 p.m., the luscious smell of brownies brought a smile to my face. Three containers full. "Someone's been busy."

"Ben will be here soon." Becca wiped her hands on

a paper towel and gave a nervous chuckle. "I needed something to do while I waited."

"She made all three boxes of brownies." Jill dried off a nine by thirteen-inch cake pan. "I've added more to our shopping list."

Becca frowned and twirled a strand of her hair around her finger. "Ben left Orlando at 6:00 a.m. and expected an eight and a half-hour drive today plus stops."

"Sit and relax." Jill added a tea bag to a cup of steamy water.

I glanced at my phone and sat at the table. "Just got a text from Luke about our date."

"I hope you have fun tonight." Becca took a seat across from me. "Ben's still upset with me for putting an offer in on such a large house. I'm not sure he'll be any happier after I tell him my news. Please pray."

Jill set a cup of chamomile tea in front of Becca and sat between us. "We'll pray, but he'll be thrilled. If not at first, give him time."

Becca gave a lengthy sigh and thanked Jill for the tea.

Jill grasped Becca's hand and mine. "Father, we thank you—"

Babs barked and howled. A knock sounded at the front door.

"Ben." Becca jumped up and squealed. "But we didn't finish our prayer."

Jill hurried toward the door and turned to Becca. "You'll be okay. Tell him as soon as he steps inside so you can let go of this stress. It's not good for you or the baby." She opened the door and welcomed Ben.

They made their way into the kitchen, where Becca

and I stood. She stared at him with her mouth open.

"Honey, are you okay? You don't look happy to see me. What's wrong?"

Becca swayed to her left.

I grabbed hold of her right arm. "Let's get you on the sofa."

Ben rushed to her left and swooped her into his arms. He placed her on the end of the couch. "You're ill? Why didn't you tell me on the phone?"

"I'm stressed about the house and you not liking it."

"We'll see the house on Monday and decide." He rubbed her back.

Becca glanced at Jill and me and mouthed, "I can't."

Jill snapped her fingers behind her back. When I eyed her, she said, "On the count of three."

We both looked at Ben and counted together. "One. Two."

Ben gawked at us like we were crazy.

"Three."

Becca scrunched her nose. "We need the bigger house because I'm pregnant." She covered her face with her hands.

Ben stopped rubbing her back. "But we. We."

Jill and I held our breath.

A grin grew on Ben's face. "I'm going to be a father again?" He threw his arms around Becca and rocked her back and forth. "That's fantastic." He kissed her as if we weren't in the room.

We tiptoed down the hallway to give them privacy and shared a high-five.

"What happens now?" I squinted and rubbed my

bottom lip. "Will Ben stay here with Becca?"

"Miss Risa offered them a private upstairs bedroom at her house until they can move into their new home."

"That's sweet of her." I peeked at my watch. "Almost 4:30."

"What time is your big date with Luke tonight?" She wiggled her brows.

"His text said he'll pick me up at 5:30, and I'm to wear casual clothes and walking shoes."

"A walk? That doesn't sound romantic."

"It does if you're with the one you love."

Jill grinned and clapped her hands. "And you'll come home with a ring on your finger."

"We'll know soon enough." *Lord, I need wisdom.*

330

Forty-six

Luke dropped Billy off at Eddie's house, made a couple of stops along the way, and hurried back to his cabin. He filled the picnic basket with goodies, snatched the poems he'd written for Lanie, and headed out the door wearing a huge grin.

Had he heard from the Lord? He climbed into his pickup, and his grin faded. He thought he had, but while he drove to Lanie's, he second guessed himself. His heart pounded and his stomach tightened. What if she said no? What would he do?

He pulled into Jill's driveway and turned off the ignition. *Lord, You know all things. If she's going to tell me no, please stop me from asking. I couldn't bear another rejection from the woman I've loved for so long.*

Luke climbed from his truck. A wave of confidence swept over him. He made his way to the front door and threw his shoulders back. Time to do this.

Lanie opened the door before he rang the buzzer and invited him inside. "Am I dressed okay?"

She looked beautiful to him.

"You look stunning." He lifted her hand and brought it to his lips. After a tiny kiss, he released her hand and gazed into her eyes.

Lanie peeked to her left.

Jill stood in the doorway to the kitchen and gaped at Luke. "What about me? How do I look?"

"You look fine, but I only have eyes for your sister." He glanced at Lanie. "Are you ready to go?"

"Do I need to bring anything?"

"I have everything taken care of, my love." He escorted her outside and opened the pickup's passenger side door. When he was sure she was safe inside, he shut her door and climbed into the driver's side. "We'll arrive at our destination in fifteen minutes."

"And where is that?"

"A special place for an extra special lady."

She laughed and slapped his arm. "Is your mom joining us?"

"Ha. Ha." He offered her his hand. "She is special, but I said extra special."

"You sure know how to sweet-talk a gal." She squeezed his hand. "Did you take lessons?"

"No need. I can sweet talk with the best of them." He winked. "Listen in amazement."

~

While we drove to the special place, Luke asked if I'd heard anything regarding Kylee.

I told him what I knew and that I had her address. "I want to send her a gift."

"What do you have in mind?"

"A guitar. She'll love it."

"I feel bad about my terrible attitude the day we went to Fall Creek Falls. Will you allow me to chip in and tell her it's from both of us?"

"Of course. She'll be pleased to know you care about her too."

Luke drove to one of our favorite places as kids and teenagers—Foster Falls in South Cumberland State Park. We'd hiked the park often over the years. His parents took us there when we were young, and when we could drive ourselves, we continued to visit.

"Are we hiking down to the falls?"

He nodded and pulled into a parking space. "Do you want to eat before our hike down or after?"

I turned to the back and touched my chest. A small basket and cooler sat on the back seat near Billy's booster seat. "You brought a picnic dinner?"

"Nothing but the best for you."

"May we eat at the waterfall?"

"Sounds great. I'll carry the cooler and you can take the basket."

When I opened my door, he asked me to wait. He strode to my side and helped me out of his truck. "Thank you, but that's unnecessary."

He lowered his chin. "I want this to be a special evening."

I touched his arm and grinned. "It's already special. We're together as a couple and more than boyfriend and girlfriend."

He handed me the basket, grabbed the cooler, and closed the truck door. We strolled toward the trailhead and onto the boardwalk that led to an overlook at the top of the falls. A beautiful sight, though the large trees blocked part of our view. We continued down the dirt trail into the gorge and over large rocks toward the bottom of the falls. Steep, but not as steep as our recent hike to Fall Creek Falls with Kylee and Billy. When we arrived at the suspension bridge, I stopped and scowled. "I forgot about this half-mile long bridge. You go first, and I'll follow."

"You're not good with distances, are you? Can't be much over thirty feet."

"Doesn't matter. You go first."

"Why?"

"You know why. You'll rock the bridge, and that scares me."

"I'll behave."

"I've heard that before."

He tugged me onto the bridge and moved in behind me.

After several steps, I stopped. "Let me get all the way across first."

He touched my shoulder. "I'll keep you safe, I promise."

I trusted him but hated that feeling of death awaiting me if the bridge collapsed and the stream carried me who knows where.

We took a few more steps together, but the bridge grew more unstable. Again, I stopped. He twisted me toward him and peered into my eyes. "You've got this. You're doing great. I won't let you fall."

I'd forgotten he could be sweet. He encouraged me often through the years. When I lacked self-confidence, he believed in me and cheered me on. He hadn't changed. He'd remained the good friend I'd always known.

To my relief, we made it across the bridge. A group of ten met us on the other side, ready to trek back to the trailhead.

I stared in awe when we arrived at the base of the falls. "Breathtaking."

Luke pulled me close. His eyes were bright. "Not only the waterfall." He caressed my cheek and gave me a soft kiss.

One other couple enjoyed the view. They packed their belongings and headed to the bridge. Only Luke and I remained. We sat on a large, flat boulder and scanned the waterfall and stream. A peaceful place.

"Ready for our picnic?" From the basket, Luke pulled out a small vase, water, and forget me nots and set the vase with the flowers in the middle of a light blue tablecloth that he'd placed over half of the rock.

He spread out chicken salad sandwiches, baked beans, and chips and finished off the meal with sweet tea. "The chicken salad and beans are homemade. I hope you like them."

I took a bite of my sandwich. "This is delicious. I love the added sweetness of the grapes and the crunch of celery." I laid my head on his shoulder. "This has been a lovely evening."

"We're not finished yet. When we're done with our meal, I have a surprise for you."

"Oh?" Was I ready for a marriage proposal? I'd prayed often since my talk with Becca and Jill and believed God answered.

"I wrote you a poem."

"Impossible." I widened my eyes.

"I did a good job too."

"Let's hear it."

"After we eat and pack up."

We finished our sandwiches and put everything back into the cooler and picnic basket.

"I'm ready for your poem." I smiled at Luke and repositioned myself on the boulder.

He pulled an index card from his shirt pocket and stood. His hands trembled when he unfolded the card.

"Lanie, you're a breath of fresh air.
With your gorgeous golden-brown hair.
I can't wait to kiss you under the stars.
And to always be where you are.
To share blessings with the one I adore.
You're my best friend and so much more."

I said nothing. I couldn't. A little corny, but Luke struggled during our sophomore year in high school with the poetry section. For him to write a poem, something he always considered girly, surprised and delighted me. "This is more than I ever imagined you would do for me." I thanked him and wrapped my arms around his neck. "Although it's a little early for stars, I'm eager for that kiss."

He shoved his hands into his pockets. "You won't tell anyone about the poem, will you? It's for your ears only."

"My ears only." I rubbed my finger down his cheek.

He bent forward and kissed me but cut it short. A rowdy bunch of teens ran across the bridge. "I have another poem. But not here. When we get to my house." He grimaced and hunched his shoulders. "We'll pick up Billy first. I need to keep him on a schedule and get him to bed."

"Super. I'd love to see him."

We took our time on the way back to the trailhead. The steep climb up slowed us down. When we arrived at the parking lot, we loaded the pickup and drove to

Eddie's house.

Billy gave me a fist bump when he saw me. After a quick visit with Eddie, we headed South on Main Street.

I gasped and looked at Luke. "If you put Billy to bed, I won't have a way home."

"Already thought of that." He turned in the opposite direction from his house on State Route 481, south of town, and drove to Jill's.

"I'll see you at your place in a few minutes. First, I need to run inside to tell Jill, so she doesn't think someone stole my car."

I climbed out of the truck and threw Billy and Luke a kiss. "Don't put him to bed before I get there. I want to get a big hug from him first." I closed the passenger door and darted toward the house. Maybe this would be the first of many nights to tuck Billy into bed.

Forty-seven

Luke dropped Lanie off at Jill's house. Joy bubbled inside of him. *Thank you, Lord, for showing me that resentment and pride clouded my judgement toward Lanie. I'm blessed to have her a part of my life again. Now's the time to ask her to marry me. I hope she agrees.*

When they arrived at the cabin, Billy unhooked his seatbelt and waited for Luke to open the door. "Can Miss Lanie put me to bed tonight?"

"Sure." Luke took him by the hand and led him up the porch steps and inside. "She should be here soon."

Billy ran to Grizzly and hugged his neck. "I missed you, Grizz. Did you miss me?"

"I'm sure if he could talk, he'd say yes." Luke ruffled Billy's hair. "Would you check in the bathroom and make sure you picked up your clothes before I took you to Eddie's?"

Billy peeked at Luke. "I did, because you asked me to."

"I'd like you to check again."

Billy jumped up and scurried to the bathroom. He came out soon after with the clothes he'd worn earlier.

"I guess I forgot these."

"Run them upstairs and come down and watch for Miss Lanie."

Billy hurried upstairs and returned in a flash.

He opened the door to Lanie when she arrived a few minutes after 8:00 with gifts—six chocolate brownies. "Surprise. Becca made these today." She placed the plate of brownies on the table and hugged Billy. "Is Mr. Luke treating you okay?"

"Yes. And he has a surprise for you too."

Luke's eyes grew large, and he placed his hand on Billy's shoulder. "Time for you to get ready for bed."

"But I want a brownie." Billy whined and looked at Lanie. "Can I have one?"

Lanie crouched in front of him. "You should ask, 'May I have one?' And you need to ask Mr. Luke, not me."

"Not tonight, buddy. Mr. Eddie said you had two cookies after supper." Luke rubbed Billy's shoulder. "I'll save you one for tomorrow."

Billy seemed pleased with that response and grinned at Lanie. "Will you put me to bed?"

She glanced at Luke and raised her eyebrows. "What do you say to that, Mr. Luke?"

"Sure." He focused on Billy. "But can I have a high-five before you go upstairs?"

Billy ran to Luke and raised his hand.

Luke lifted his palm and lowered his voice. "Please keep my surprise a secret like you promised. Okay?"

Billy nodded at Lanie. "But it's really cool." He scurried toward the stairs, and she followed him up to his room.

Luke eyed the brownies, pulled back the plastic

wrap that covered them, and broke off a corner from one. The bite melted in his mouth. He strode to his coffee machine and made a fresh cup. Brownies were good by themselves, but better with a cup of coffee. With his cup in hand, he sat at the table and broke off another corner of the brownie. Would Billy tell Lanie?

"Caught you." Lanie snickered and moved the plate out of Luke's reach. "You could have at least waited for me so we could enjoy them together."

"What? Me? Why do you think I ate a brownie? Didn't you bring six?" He pointed to the plate. "Still six there taunting me."

"Why are there brownie crumbs on your lips?" She returned the plate to the table, bowed close to Luke, and kissed him. "I got them for you. Yum."

He pushed his chair back, stood, and embraced her. "You missed a crumb. Try again." He kissed her and caressed her back.

~

Luke pulled far enough away from me to look me in the eye. "I want to enjoy time with you like this for many years to come."

"Many years?"

His eyes sparkled. He beamed with love. He had a smile like I'd never seen.

My pulse quickened. Neck tingled. Chin quivered. "Is it time for my surprise now?"

"Did Billy say anything about it?"

"Something's outside?"

Luke grasped my hand and pulled me toward the back door. "Follow me out back."

He flipped on the outside light switch, and we made our way outdoors. My stomach knotted and churned.

I raised my hand and gestured across the back of his house. "Why are we here?"

"I want to add on. Two bedrooms and a master bath for my room."

No proposal? Did I really misread all the signals?

I swatted a mosquito off my wrist. "Why?"

He took both of my hands in his. "To make more room for my family." He kissed my nose. "Someone told me that my cabin was a tiny home. My family will need more space."

I pulled my right hand away and waved it in front of my face, hoping the pesky insects would leave me alone. "Your family?"

"Billy for now. More soon."

I stomped my feet hoping the bugs feasting on my ankles would fly away.

Luke grabbed my hand again. "Stop with the mosquitoes and listen to me."

I peered into his eyes. "What?"

"I'm trying to be romantic here. Another poem. Remember?"

"Go ahead." I tried to pay attention, but my ankles itched like crazy. I bent over and rubbed them.

When I lifted my head and straightened, Luke moved underneath the back door light and cleared his throat.

"My heart swells when you cross my path.
My love for you will forever last.
Your kisses make me warm. No, hot.
I'll always love you, please, forget-me-not.
The most beautiful woman by my side.
Will you agree to be my bride?"

I shuddered and slapped my arm. "Can we go back inside?" I brushed off my ankles again and darted to the back door.

Luke followed me inside to the living room. "Did you hear what I said?"

I spun to face him. "Sorry." I wrinkled my nose. "Something about being romantic, and another poem, but there's nothing romantic with mosquitoes." I rubbed my itchy arms. "Do you have anti-itching cream for insect bites?"

Luke huffed. "Sit down on the sofa. I'll be right back." He returned a minute later with a first aid kit, knelt in front of me, and opened a tube of cream. "Looks like he got you here." He dabbed cream onto a welt on top of my right wrist and elbow, checked my other arm, moved to my ankles, and applied cream to five more bites there.

What had he said outside? Something regarding his family and Billy, a poem and bride? I shrieked. "Yes. Oh, yes! I'll marry you." When he raised his head, I hugged his neck.

"Why?" He chuckled and leaned back. "Did you realize I'm a great catch because I'm down on my knees taking care of your wounds?"

I gazed into his eyes. "That's part of it. But I just remembered your poem and the word *bride* while you took care of me. I couldn't focus or respond until now."

"I thought you wanted to avoid the question. But I learned from my mistake eleven years ago. I was ready to ask you again while I knelt here at your feet." He reached into his pocket and pulled out his fisted hand. "I've kept this for you all these years." He opened his hand and took the sparkling diamond ring between his fingers and held it out to me. "As I promised long ago when we exchanged our first forget-me-nots, that I'd never forget you. With this ring, I promise to always love you."

I scooted closer, and he slipped the ring onto my finger. "Perfect." I tilted my head to the right. "I thank the Lord for bringing us back together." My lips met his. I tilted my head to the left. "For our new beginning." I kissed him again, leaned back, and cupped his cheeks in my hands.

"And for our faithful love."

Dear Reader,

Thank you for reading *Our Faithful Love*. If you enjoyed Luke and Lanie's story, please leave a review to help other readers discover it.

Would you like a gift? When you sign up for my newsletter and monthly blog posts, you'll receive a free short story: www.luannkedwards.com.

Where to follow me and connect.
Amazon
BookBub
Goodreads
Facebook

Other books by LuAnn K. Edwards.

Love Comes Again
Only A Glimpse
Let Him Go
Charm And Perfection

An Undeserved Gift (a novella)

Love in Pleasant Springs
An Odd Request
Our Faithful Love

I hope you enjoy the first chapter of Becca and Ben's story from Book One, *An Odd Request*.

One

Early January
Pleasant Springs, Tennessee

My best friend, Jill Drake, entered my home without knocking, laughed, and handed me *most* of my mail. "Your mail carrier gave me this instead of putting it in your box. Must have thought I was you. After all, we're almost twins."

Her long, dark hair and tanned skin looked nothing like my fair skin and strawberry blonde hair. Not to mention my freckles—lots of freckles.

"They think you live here because they see your car here all the time." I chuckled and glanced at the standard-sized envelope she still held. "What's that?"

"Someone was in a hurry or had lousy handwriting. Who do you know in Orlando? Bim Pibersan?"

I took the envelope from her, checked the return address, and squinted. "That's just Ben Peterson, the Missions Pastor from Hart Fellowship. He's raising money for his church's next trip. He's sent me letters before."

"Isn't he the pastor whose wife died in a fire a couple of years ago in Chattanooga?"

I nodded and frowned. "While she visited her mother there. Annie and her mom both died. Tragic." I tossed the envelope into the mail pile on the end table, along with the utility bills and junk mail.

"Aren't you going to open it?"

"Why should I?" I rubbed my chin. "He's only requesting money as usual."

She smirked. "But what if he's not asking for a donation?"

I shrugged. "No big deal. I'll read it later." I smiled and rubbed my palms together. "Ready for hot chocolate?"

Jill and I met most Saturdays at her house or mine to knit and crochet toboggan hats, mittens, and scarves for the kids at Creekside Children's Home. On that early January afternoon, I'd prepared hot chocolate and snickerdoodles and started a fire in the fireplace in the front room of my tiny bungalow.

We didn't need to walk far to enter my kitchen—a few steps to the left of my living room. To the right was the bathroom, bedroom, and my washer and dryer, which stood behind a set of bifold doors in the hallway. That was it. Not a tiny home, but almost.

We stepped into the kitchen and gathered our treats.

"You liked Ben and Annie, didn't you?" Jill took a bite of her cookie.

"I loved them both."

"And you have a lot in common with him?"

"I suppose." I narrowed my eyes. "Why do you ask?"

She took a sip of her hot chocolate. "You should find out if he's dating anyone."

"You realize he lives 600 miles from here." I crossed my arms and sneered. "I can't call him and ask him for a date."

"But you can take a trip to Florida, spend time in Orlando, and ask him to show you around. Discover if there are any sparks."

I shook my head. "Sparks are my middle name according to Michael."

She laughed. "Yep. Fiery and feisty. But you've mellowed out since then."

"Losing the love of your life can do that."

Jill agreed. "If Ben lived here and wanted to date you, would you be interested?"

I stared out the kitchen window. "The opportunity for full-time ministry again?" I grinned at Jill. "Yes."

~

Folks might call Jill and me spinsters. But the term didn't fit either of us. We were both too young to be considered old. Years ago, age thirty-five fit that description, but no longer. And although neither of us were married, we both were at one time. My husband, Michael, died five years before when he fell off a ladder while he cleaned the church's gutters, one of his many jobs as the pastor of a small church. Jill's husband died seven years ago while deployed overseas.

My job as a CAD Technician at an engineering firm in town kept me busy. Jill was a civil engineer at the same company. Our employer may have been small, but we won a good share of major projects—a benefit of being the only firm in the county. Our biggest competition came from the larger firms in Chattanooga located fifty miles southeast of Pleasant Springs.

On Wednesday evening, Ben sent me a message through social media: **Did you receive my letter?**

He must have really needed the money.

I typed out a quick response. **Yes. Will pray and get back to you.**

He responded with a thumbs up.

After I completed chores around the house, I prayed over how much money I should give Ben toward his trip and grabbed my checkbook. I sent him a message: Check ready to mail. Verify your address. Return on envelope hard to read.

The following morning while at work, I received another message from Ben: What check? Did you read my letter?

I cringed. Weren't you requesting money for a mission trip?

No. Read it and get back to me.

Sure thing. I'll read it when I get home.

An hour later, Jill and I went to lunch.

After I told her about my strange messages from Ben, she invited herself to my house after work. She wanted to be there when I opened and read his letter.

~

Jill arrived at 6:00 p.m. "Have you peeked inside yet?"

I frowned and shrugged. "I can't find the envelope."

She scurried to my end table and picked up pieces of mail lying there. "Where did you put it?"

I stomped my foot. "I told you, I don't remember."

"Where have you looked?"

"Everywhere. The kitchen, my dresser drawer where I keep my bills, even the trash can."

"Go check your room again, and I'll check the kitchen."

I darted to my bedroom and checked my drawers, closet, and under my bed. Nothing.

"Found it." Jill hollered from the kitchen. "With some other mail. How did it end up in your junk drawer?"

When I returned to my living room, I joined Jill on the sofa. "I threw everything in there when my parents called to say they were on their way over Sunday afternoon and then forgot about it."

I snatched the envelope from her hand, tore it open, and pulled out the folded letter.

"Read it aloud. I want to hear what he has to say." She wiggled in her seat and clasped her hands under her chin. "He may want to date you."

I placed the letter on the sofa next to me on the opposite side from Jill and wrinkled my nose. "He can't want to date me. We haven't seen each other in years."

"And why is that?"

"After Michael graduated from college in Chattanooga, he attended seminary for three years. By the time we came back to Tennessee, Ben and Annie had moved to Orlando."

Jill sighed. "Why didn't you stay in touch?"

"Annie and I did by email, and Michael and Ben did too. But never Ben and me."

She nudged my elbow and reached across me for the letter. "Hurry and read it. You're not getting any younger."

I shook my head, took it from her hands, and read aloud.

Dear Rebecca,

I hope you are doing well and your new year is off to a good start. Please pray over my request. Annie has been with the Lord now for two years. I'm still at a loss over her death. Her *passing has affected my ministry, professional and personal relationships, my attitude, and caused me difficulty with people in the church. I'd like to remarry, but the thought of dating brings me overwhelming anxiety.*

Jill drew her eyebrows together. "Poor guy. He doesn't want to date."

"No. But it sounds like he's requesting prayer. We were a real foursome all those years ago when he was an associate pastor in Chattanooga, and we prayed for one another often." I glanced at the letter and continued to read aloud.

Will you be willing to become my . . .

"What?" I wadded up the letter and threw it across the room. "I refuse to read any more of this nonsense."

Jill jumped up, retrieved the letter, placed it on my end table, and smoothed out the wrinkles with her fist.

"What's wrong with him?" I stood and tried to snatch the letter from her hands.

She held it over her head, her eyes wide. "Whoa, forget the dating."

I shoved her onto the couch. "Give it to me."

She read, *. . . my wife without doing the dating thing?*

I plopped onto the floor, sat with my back against the sofa, and pouted.

Jill continued to read.

Consider this letter my offer of

marriage. I've prayed over this decision for the past few months and believe we will make a great ministry team.

Sincerely,

Benson E. Peterson

She squealed. "The letter includes his phone number."

I spoke in an annoyed tone. "He's crazy. Annie's death turned him into a lunatic." I twisted toward Jill. "Who in their right mind would send a letter and propose marriage to a woman he hasn't seen in twelve years?"

"A man who thinks you will make the perfect wife for him?" Jill beamed. "Give me your phone. I'll text him for you."

"Oh, no you won't." I jumped up, grabbed the letter from Jill's hands, and paced. "Don't you see? There's nothing personal here except my name. He probably sent it to fifty women hoping one would respond."

"Fifty? But he messaged you too."

I stopped and stared at Jill. "Along with how many others?" I waved the letter in front of her face. "How tacky can you get?"

She rose from my couch. "How are you going to respond?"

"I'm not." I flung the letter across the room and placed my hands on my hips. "He doesn't deserve an answer."

~

After Jill left, I reread the letter from Ben. Marry

him? The man had problems. Mental ones. And because of him, I had a terrible headache.

While getting ready for bed, I received another message from Ben. Are you in?

The nerve of some people.

In what? A harem? Then picking out your bride? A modern-day Esther story? You are out of line, Ben. What's happened to you?

He responded within five minutes: No. A harem? Seriously? You are the only woman I contacted. Pray before you turn me down like I'm crazy.

I plopped onto my bed. He said I was the only woman? Should I give him a chance? But he didn't want to date. How could I give him a chance?

Pray like he asked.

Instead, I found a piece of stationary and carried it to my kitchen table. I wanted to be gentle when I let him down.

Dear Ben,

I understand the pain of losing a beloved spouse, and I'm sorry you have had a challenging time.

Michael and I thought the world of you and Annie. You were instrumental in our coming to know Christ while we were in college and an inspiration to us before we married. We counted you both as dear friends and mentors during our four years together in

Chattanooga.

I'm flattered you considered me as someone with whom you would like to do ministry. But my experience is tiny compared to the megachurch you serve in. I doubt I'm qualified for such a position. For the past five years, since Michael's death, I've done little in serving except to teach a ladies Bible study and pray for those in need.

I've spent time over the past few months asking the Lord to direct me to where He wants me to serve Him, and I sense it's here in Pleasant Springs. Not Orlando. I appreciate your contacting me, but I cannot accept your offer of marriage.

Sincerely,

Becca Hill

I included my phone number and sent Ben this message: I'm responding to your request by snail mail. Blessings.

Thank you for reading, and God bless!

LuAnn

Acknowledgements

First, I'd like to thank the Lord for Luke and Lanie's story and for His guidance in writing it.

To my husband and family who love, support, and encourage me in my writing, thank you.

Special appreciation for Leitte Mull who answered my questions about children's services and read my manuscript. She offered valuable feedback.

To my brother-in-law, Tom, who assisted with my fire station questions—thanks so much.

I appreciate each beta reader who gave of their time and shared their ideas with me. I'd find this difficult to do without your help. You are amazing. A big thank you to Judi, Kim, Leah, and Moss.

Thanks to Larry J. Leech II for your thorough critique and assistance. Your insights and expertise are a blessing.

Finally, I'm grateful to Winged Publications, Forget Me Not Romances for the opportunity to publish this novel and series. Thank you, Cynthia Hickey!

About the Author

LuAnn writes heartwarming Christian contemporary romance filled with faith, hope, and a touch of humor. A 2021 Selah Award finalist for *Let Him Go*, she has lived her own love story and happily ever after since marrying her sweetheart in 1975. She is Mom to three children and Nana to three grandchildren. Besides the Lord and her family, she loves hiking, traveling, pizza, and anything chocolate. When she is not writing, you'll often find her making eyes at her husband, in the kitchen baking bread, or taking photos of birds at their backyard feeders. Visit her at www.luannkedwards.com.

www.ingramcontent.com/pod-product-compliance
Lightning Source LLC
Chambersburg PA
CBHW072043190726

48294CB00005B/1377